MIDLIFE PORTALS

DRUID HEIR BOOK 5

N. Z. NASSER

Midlife Portals: Druid Heir Book 5
Copyright © N. Z. Nasser 2022
Published by Hanora Sky Press

eBook ISBN 978-1-915151-09-4
Paperback ISBN 978-1-915151-10-0

THE PLAYERS

Alisha Verma - Druid Heir
Echo - Alisha's leopard sidekick
Marina Ambrose - Alisha's best friend
Ezra Neuhoff - half-werewolf, half-wizard Minister for Justice
Orpheus Might - Vampire, Minister for History and the Today
Robert Jameson - Detective, Shadow Squad
Fei Yen and Faeza - hu hsien, shapeshifting foxes
Joshi Verma - Alisha's father
Sahil Verma - Alisha's brother
Alma Bluejay - Flour seer and Joshi's love
Rajiv Chawla - Rajika Verma's brother
Gaia - Goddess of the Earth
Flinar - an elf
Maximillian, Dominic, Deirdra, Ruud and Rashida - Ezra's pack
Phinnaeous Shine - Shapeshifter, Prime Sorcerer
Lavinia Drach - Witch, Minister for Defence
Rayna Willowsun - Druid, Minister for Education
Margola Silver - Selkie, Minister for Information
Helio Woodwink - Fairy, Bestiary Minister
Gunnolf Zev - Werewolf, former alpha
Meriel Naehorn - an elf

Mammatas and Rhokon - Wildwoods sphinxes
Mirabel, Briar and Juniper Elmstorm - a fairy family
Armando - a wolf from the SE London pack
Ignacio - rat familiar
The red woman

1

———

A crowd gathered around me as I teetered at the edge of Millennium Bridge, hair whipping around my head.

A policeman, alarm on his pale face, inched closer. "Get down, miss. You don't want to do this."

Behind me, despite the swell of commuters in rush hour London, prowled an Indian leopard. Although, to those without true sight, he seemed to be a Bengal cat.

"She's observing the river, you fool, not jumping in it," Echo purred.

"Listen to this poor fellow's miaows. He doesn't want you to do it either," said the policeman. "Don't give up, miss. Live for your pussy."

A loud whisper reached me. "Poor woman's lost her mind. I wonder what pushed her over the edge?"

"Sir, please," said the panicked policeman. "You're not helping."

I jumped down from the ledge to an audible gasp of relief from the commuters, who'd stumbled across the drama on their way to work. I had somewhere to be, too. My best friend Marina had asked me to swing by, and her unusual caginess on the phone made me think it couldn't wait.

I

This wasn't the first time I'd returned to Millennium Bridge to check for signs of the water goddess I'd battled in the bitterly cold depths of the river Thames. Her tattoo parlour had remained shut, and Kraglek, the octopus I had freed from Wildwoods, might have dragged her out to sea, but I remained vigilant.

Soon, the slain and defeated immortals would return to exact their revenge.

I would be ready to face them. That meant keeping my middle-aged eyes peeled during daylight hours when I could actually see something. Even if it meant run-ins with humdrums, who had no clue about the Otherworld.

Relief bled into the policeman's voice. "How about you come down to the station, love, and we'll get you the help you need?"

Once, a run-in with a police officer would have given me heart palpitations. I'd been the sort of woman who worried about being caught on the train without a ticket, even when I'd bought one. That was in another lifetime before I realised how many truly frightening things went bump in the night.

I made a show of tugging my earlobe for the policeman. It wasn't like I could tell him the truth. "I don't know what all the fuss is about, officer. I dropped my earring down there and couldn't see where it went."

He fiddled with his radio. "What's lost in the Thames is not easily found. They're still dredging up World War Two bombs from down there. You've no hope of finding an earring, miss."

I nodded. "Of course. Silly me."

"Well, I suppose all's well that ends well." He scratched his head. "Where did your cat go?"

"Oh, he's *much* more than a cat. Off on some adventure, no doubt." I gave the officer a cheery wave and jogged off the bridge to where Echo sharpened his claws against the white bark of a Himalayan birch tree.

The leopard retracted his claws and turned his scarred face towards me as I approached. "It's a good thing the policeman didn't pat you down, or he would have found more than a truncheon under your coat. The last thing we need is you being banged up in a humdrum prison or Death's sword being confiscated."

Echo, whose ancestral line had sworn to protect my family, took his duties very seriously unless a poodle was in sight.

I smoothed down my chaotic, windswept hair. "I think finding a sword might have finished him off."

The leopard's unblinking emerald eyes made me squirm. "The Prime Sorcerer has strict rules about peculiars who fall foul of humdrum laws. You'd be on your own. Not even the wolf could teleport you out of Her Majesty's prisons without a ruckus. You have to be more careful."

Echo was right, of course, but I didn't want to tread lightly. Taking a measured approach against the water goddess had almost cost me my life. She had been a formidable adversary, prepared to use my love for my friends and family against me. I'd nearly lost Dad and had been at death's door myself.

There was a clock of dread ticking inside me, and it wasn't my ovaries.

From now on, I'd react to the starting bell like a prize fighter. I'd learned the hard way not to abandon my moral compass, but I wasn't a pushover. I planned to filter the world into two columns: friend or enemy. Then I'd go hell for leather, kicking and punching, gale blowing and sword slashing. I'd animate gargoyles and vampire finches if that's what it took to keep my loved ones safe.

"I know you mean well, Echo," I said, "but I won't apologise for doing what needs to be done. Wait here. I'm just going to nip into the newsagent for a bottle of Fanta. We're already late to see Marina."

A few minutes later, I returned to his side, took a deep swig of fizzy pop, cupped my hands over my mouth and forced out an unladylike burp to the utter disgust of a passing old lady. My cheeks flushed with embarrassment, but sure enough, the Otherworld taxi fleet responded, the one introduced to me by my thieving brother. A black cab, its once sleek body lacerated by claw marks, swerved down the road straight through a red light. The passenger door flew open as it shuddered to a halt beside us. This time, we leapt in without hesitation and issued our destination to the driver behind the darkened dividing screen.

"At least I can thank your brother for saving me the humiliation of being stuffed into a cat carrier on the London bus." Echo stretched out, his purrs blending with the hullabaloo of the engine. "That might be what spares him an encounter with my teeth."

I snorted. "I wouldn't let that stop you. Sahil deserves what's coming to him after stealing the Jericho necklace Mum and Marina worked so hard on. Do you think that's what Marina was worried about on the phone?"

Echo's emerald eyes softened. "Marina Ambrose doesn't usually call for help. However meagre her own powers, she is the first to put herself on the line, without complaints. I fear her insistence she speaks to us in person is about something else entirely."

"Perhaps she's out of wine." Who was I kidding?

My gut was a cauldron of swirling anxiety when we pulled up outside Marina's veterinary surgery. Echo and I left a hair each in payment for the journey. No sooner had we stepped out onto the pavement did the black cab execute a screeching three-point turn in a cloud of diesel fumes, narrowly missing a milk float.

I pressed my hand to the flat buzzer.

"Come on up," said my best friend through the intercom.

Upstairs, she ushered us into her flat, rainbow hair in

space buns, ready for a day's work at the veterinary surgery. Her eye-bags were deep crescents under her baby blues. "Any word on Sahil and the whereabouts of the necklace yet?"

I kicked off my shoes like a good Indian girl—wearing shoes indoors was for brutes—and hugged her hello. "Not yet. We'll find him. Is that why we're here?"

Marina lowered her voice. "No. I've been working on Rob's mental blocks from the night of the dinner party. A little bit of reflexology. A lot of empathy. Some sacral massage which led to all night rumpy-pumpy. A cup or two of midnight rose tea from Shanghai Moon to relax the mind. Anything I could think of, really. Anyway, this morning, he had a breakthrough. He wants to tell you himself."

We followed her into the living room, a veritable boudoir, complete with a gothic chandelier, a dance pole, and an array of sumptuous fabrics, from velvet throws to plush purple sofas, silk cushions and a shag pile rug. In the corner of the room, Detective Robert Jameson, arms folded, stared out of the window.

"Rob?" said Marina. "Look who's here."

Echo gave the dance pole a suspicious look, leapt up, and slid down like a sack of potatoes. "Morning, Detective."

The detective swivelled, his angular jaw tightening at our approach. His slight paunch had disappeared, along with his air of unflappability. This was a broken man. "Thanks for coming. Sorry to be all cloak and danger about it."

An uncertain smile flitted across my lips. "Of course. Whatever you need, Detective."

His movements jittered. "There's no easy way to say this. It's taken weeks, but with Marina's help, I've finally put the pieces together. I know who messed with my mind the night of the coven dinner."

I frowned. "We know what happened. Mami Wata did a number on you while you were carrying out your investigation into the kidnappings. Your connection to Marina brought you back from the brink."

A vein throbbed in Rob's jaw. He swept a hand over his buzz cut. "That's just it, Alisha. It wasn't the goddess."

My heart thudded against the wall of my chest. "Then who?"

He sighed. "People don't last long in the Shadow Squad. I'm more or less a one-man band. But I built up a network of contacts. My go-to in the Otherworld was always the Prime Sorcerer, but he's not my equal. He has a direct line to the Prime Minister. When you came along, Alisha, I suddenly had someone I could share intel with who wasn't a paper pusher or a source. And somehow, I started sharing intel with you first."

"You are as wise as you are bald," said Echo.

Rob continued. "I share intel with you before Phinnaeous Shine. Before my superiors. Hell, you know things even the Prime Minister doesn't."

Marina laid a hand on his shoulder. "It's okay, Rob, just tell her."

The detective drew in a shuddering breath. "I was angry at you when those men died at Mami Wata's hand. I didn't realise Lavinia had given you a single-use spell. So, when I was hatching my plan to save the other captured men, I went to Phinnaeous Shine instead of you. We met on Wimbledon Common before the coven dinner. He brought us coffee. I didn't think anything of it at the time. I took a gulp, and that was it."

Echo emitted a low, rumbling growl. "He turned your mind to soup."

The detective winced. "My memories are back. I don't know yet if he is conspiring with the gods, but I do know he wanted me out of the way. Whatever it took."

I sank down onto the sofa. We had toyed with the idea that the Prime Sorcerer was working against us but ultimately dismissed it. Ezra's words came flooding back to me. *Phinnaeous Shine is an old codger. A dinosaur. A sly fox. But he's not corrupt.* My heartbeat raced.

"Phinnaeous Shine falsely maligned the elves," I said. "He saved his own skin instead of battling Hermes with us at Wildwoods. He advocated for keeping the Pragmatist's Law so we'd turn a blind eye to increasingly dangerous gods."

"And now this. A cabbage detective," hissed Echo.

"It's been in front of our eyes all along." Anger unfurled inside me, hot and blazing. That spiteful old man had been against us from day one. "That's why Rob was the only victim who wasn't branded. How could we have trusted Phinnaeous?"

Marina spread her hands. "We were all in awe of him."

"The shapeshifter is a law unto himself. Your grandmother knew he was a swine," said Echo. "No cat would touch him. We must feed him to the dogs."

Rob paced the room. "Pointing a finger at the most powerful man in the Otherworld is not the act of a sane person. I can't take this to my superiors without watertight evidence. Even if they agree, it is not our place to depose the Prime Sorcerer." He stopped next to me. "That must fall to a peculiar."

Heat roiled in my belly. "Why are you looking at me?"

The detective's mouth twisted in apology. "There are not many who can match Phinnaeous Shine's power, but you can. The man has been in a seat of power for decades. He enjoys unrivalled privileges. He is protected from accusations because his very office gives him a sheen of respectability."

As the prophesied eternal girl, I had a newfound authority, but I was still a newcomer to the hierarchies of the Otherworld. "We can't throw around false accusations. We need to find out what he's done and why. Gather the proof, Rob. Lay it at Ezra and Orpheus's door. If Phinnaeous Shine doesn't deserve his title, it's a matter for the senate, not for me."

Rob gave a bitter laugh. "You think deposing the Prime Sorcerer will be as easy as a simple discussion? He answers to no one. You're not naive, Alisha. You know as well as I do that someone as entrenched as Phinnaeous Shine has built allegiances that won't be dismantled overnight."

Echo's emerald eyes glinted. "Some may say we are in a bleak position, but if Gloria Gaynor's 'I Will Survive' was written for anyone, it is for you. Would you like me to sing it?"

I curled my fingers into his fur to soothe my frayed nerves and shook my head.

"Do not fear, druid. The winds are in our favour," said Echo. "The wolf has wrangled the senate in the right direction. Even the vampire Orpheus seems open to progress. The senate is not as in thrall to Phinnaeous Shine as it once was."

Marina wrapped her arms around the detective's waist. His visible relaxation could have been down to their connection or her empath skills. It was impossible to tell which. "Phinnaeous Shine doesn't know we suspect him. We should keep it that way," she said.

I ignored the grim sense of foreboding that snaked up my spine. Not only could the Prime Sorcerer shapeshift into any two-legged creature, but his wizardry made him a formidable enemy with all the favours and connections he had accrued over the years. "I agree. If it transpires he's up to no good, we'll need all the tools in our arsenal to come out on top. Including the element of surprise."

2

___

That afternoon, a chill wind laced through the bare boughs at Wildwoods, tucked away in the depths of Crystal Palace Park. A cable car glided towards ground level to propel me skywards to the vaulted cabin for a senate meeting about my role as the newly discovered eternal girl.

The absurdity was not lost on me. After centuries of searching for the young girl in the prophecy, I had emerged as the one the magical community waited for: a middle-aged woman with a reluctant womb, grey hair sprouting like weeds and the odd chin hair—less spring chicken than knackered old mare.

"Jameson said what?" Ezra, the werewolf-wizard who'd melted my ice-cold divorcee's heart, flicked his lighter shut. His grey, copper-flecked eyes flashed in alarm. "You've got to be kidding me. I've known Phinnaeous Shine all my life."

Next to him, Orpheus, the vampire, at once cottoned onto the Prime Sorcerer's treachery. His jaw stiffened, but he pushed aside his disquiet and opted for the repartee that had become a source of comfort to us both. *Poor Neuhoff is like a newborn compared to my centuries of experience. He's also at a distinct disadvantage not being able to read that messy mind of yours.*

Stop stirring, Orpheus, or I swear I'll stake you just for fun, I said. Our mental connection riled Ezra, and Orpheus knew it.

You forget, druid, an ordinary stake wouldn't kill me, said Orpheus. *And you need me. Things are about to get rocky around here.*

I turned my attention to Ezra. "Rob's looking for proof of foul play. Let's play it cool until then. No spilling the beans, not even to Lavinia."

"This changes everything." Ezra took a deep drag of his cigarette and then crushed the stub into the ground, where it sizzled and vanished from sight as if Wildwoods wouldn't tolerate any mess. "If Phinnaeous Shine is dirty, mark my words, my aunt already knows about it. I'm surprised your mind trickery didn't alert this to you sooner, Orpheus."

Orpheus raised a well-groomed eyebrow as the cable car jerked to a halt in front of us. "The Prime Sorcerer's mind is like a series of interlocked rooms. His thoughts are more fortressed than the Queen's undergarments at Buckingham Palace."

No sooner had we stepped into the cable car and taken a seat, did it lurch forward, sending me flying into Orpheus's lap, who held onto me for a fraction longer than necessary.

Is that something sticking up, or are you just pleased to see me? said Orpheus.

I extricated myself, my cheeks hot with embarrassment. *You know very well it's my sword.*

Ezra turned a steely gaze on Orpheus and slipped a steadying arm around my waist as we rode up towards the canopies of ancient trees, where Wildwoods School of the Wondrous nestled.

Usually, the school's décor tended towards the vivid and colourful, but this term, the cabins had been dressed like chessboards. The impact was rather gloomier. Squares of black and white encompassed each one, topped with chess pieces carved from obsidian wood. A king crowned the vaulted cabin, a queen adorned the school library, and Phinnaeous' office had a bishop. A knight sat atop Ezra's office while a rook capped Rayna's office. Pawn pieces marked out the bestiary and the teaching cabins. The sense of doom in my belly ratcheted up a notch.

Ezra's low voice sent shivers up my spine. "We're about to enter the lion's den. In that room, there are those who can hear the pace of your heartbeat from across the room. Those who can read your body language as easily as they breathe. Others who will condemn you for the slightest whiff of disloyalty without even considering whether you are in the right."

I braced myself as the cable car docked and stepped out onto the rope bridge. Up amongst the tree canopies, in the bubble of the school grounds, the smog from London buses and heavy traffic seemed a world away. However much darkness lurked in the Otherworld, Wildwoods remained a haven, filled with marvels and a promise of knowledge and community that had awakened my jaded heart.

We just had to keep it that way.

In the vaulted cabin, the afternoon sun streamed in through the stained-glass windows, lending a soft haze to the vast expanse of the room. A distinct buzz in the room reached up to the rafters. Close to a dozen members of the magical community—fairies, fallen angels, werewolves, vampires, plus a witch with a wart the size of Texas on her nose— dispersed from an earlier meeting. Phinnaeous Shine, distinguished with his silver-streaked beard, two-piece suit and flowing Wildwoods gown, shook their hands in goodbye. Behind him, other senate members took their seats at the split stone table for our meeting.

Ezra murmured in my ear, "The Prime Sorcerer handpicked these delegates for a workshop here. Under the umbrella of his Shine Foundation for the Advancement of Peculiars and Humdrums."

"That's quite a mouthful." I stood aside to allow the departing peculiars space to pass. Judging by their stares, they knew exactly who I was, thanks to Margola Silver's constant wittering about me in *The Otherworld News*.

Orpheus inclined his head at a pair of approaching fairies. "Alisha Verma, I'd like to introduce you to Briar and Juniper Elmstorm, Mirabel's parents."

Briar had the same vibrant green eyes as his daughter. "Mirabel has told us so much about you. It's because of you that she knuckled down to focus on her studies."

Juniper's fluttering hands reached out for mine. "Thanks to you, Alisha. Our daughter is usually quite the handful. I blame her fire fairy nature. She'll never step back from a fight. She's been like that since she was a toddler. And once she's interested in someone, the attention can be overwhelming. I'm sorry she turned up at your community centre class last month. Twelve years old and a mind of her own! She's supposed to be home before dark. I gave her an earful about it when she got home. She was thrilled when you started taking classes at Wildwoods."

I clasped Juniper's hands. Her petite frame made me feel like a lumbering giant, even though I was only five-foot-five myself. "Think nothing of it. Mirabel's bright as a button and brave with it. She's always welcome in my classroom."

Juniper beamed. Her auburn hair had been cut in a tousled boy cut, giving her a youthful vibe. "It takes one to know one. You've both been in a tank with Kraglek."

I frowned. "Haven't you?"

"Oh no, I wasn't deemed talented enough."

"Fire fairy powers are notoriously unpredictable, even

within one family like the Elmstorms," said Orpheus. "Mirabel has the most developed magical skills. Juniper is a sculptor. Briar is a well-respected Chief Fire Officer at a local fire station."

Ezra's gravelly voice interjected. "There is more to life than just magical ability. Briar has been decorated for how many people he has personally rescued from seemingly unquenchable fires. Juniper fires up her own work, and it features in art exhibitions across Europe. She has contacts across the art world to match."

She even has trouble lighting a tea light. The most pitiful fire fairy I ever saw, said Orpheus. That is until I witnessed her husband having to light a barbecue the humdrum way. The tittering at the Wildwoods cookout was so loud that I think he rather wished he could go up in flames himself. Except that wasn't in his repertoire either. He is well-suited, however, to extinguishing them. No doubt the result of childhood mishaps.

Juniper's brown eyes filled with gratitude. "That's kind of you, Mr Neuhoff. I've long since come to terms with my limited magical ability. Our daughter outperforms us with a mere blink of the eyes. She can chant spells, too."

"She can certainly hold her own in a rowdy school," said Ezra. "You can be very proud of her."

"I feel nothing but pride that she has surpassed us. Still, it was wonderful to have been called up by the Prime Sorcerer for his latest initiative. He's identified us as having the skills to further equality between humdrums and peculiars. It's very exciting."

Briar cupped his wife's elbow. "We should leave these important people to their work, darling."

"Of course, of course," said Juniper, colouring.

Their feet lifted off the ground as they flew through the arched door, over the rope bridges into the arena.

"It is time." Orpheus stalked to the split stone table.

Ezra brushed his lips against my cheek. "See you on the other side."

They joined the ranks of the senate, leaving me to stand alone, pincered between the open split of the stone table.

Phinnaeous Shine, positioned centrally, spoke first. For the first time, a smidgen of respect filled his sombre voice. "Thank you for appearing before us, Alisha Verma."

He no longer addressed me as the 'granddaughter of Rajika Verma'. Now, I was the eternal girl. The question remained: did he see me as an equal or a threat?

I searched his eyes and found no clues there. "I have no reason to refuse your summons, Prime Sorcerer. After all, we all want to ward off threats to innocent lives."

"Please, sit." Phinnaeous lifted a well-manicured hand and flicked it.

A chair swerved around the stone table and scooped me into a seated position.

Orpheus's eyebrows disappeared into his hairline. *Evidently, you have impressed him—the less worthy stand during senate proceedings.*

"Are we quorate?" The Prime Sorcerer glanced at the eight senators, each with their own quirks and priorities, seated at the table with him.

Lavinia, her hair magnificently coiffed in a purple-grey rinse, displayed her pearly whites. "Indeed we are. Only Calypso remains at her post at the Celestial Library."

A curt nod. Phinnaeous beckoned a pen and block of lined paper with the curl of his finger. It sprang into the air, hovering a few feet above his right shoulder, and minuted the proceedings with a scratching sound. "Then let us begin. One item is on the agenda for this meeting: the future of the eternal girl."

I swallowed my trepidation. Whether Phinnaeous was a traitor or not, my future did not lie in his hands. It was entirely my own.

On the Prime Sorcerer's left side, Margola picked up a sheet of paper and peered at me over the edge of her cat-eye glasses. "As Minister for Information, I can report a surge in interest in Alisha Verma. Readership has exploded in numbers unheard of since the Battle of the Celestial Library." She twisted her flame-coloured hair around her pen. "The Vermas are good for business. Reader polls show an extraordinary amount of goodwill for the eternal girl, even in cases where there is scepticism about interpreting the Chameleon Tale as more than a bedtime story."

I chanted the tale in my head. A mantra that I had told myself over and over during the past weeks.

There will come an eternal girl who blends in even though her talents are brighter than the sun. When Death opens the door, only the eternal girl may stop the coming Dusk, together with a disintegrating tome lost to the world.

All my life, I had fought not to believe the stories other people told about me. Yet here I was, attributing truth to a fairy tale like a child in a princess dress.

Sometimes children recognise the truth better than adults, said Orpheus.

"What say you, Defence Minister?" said Phinnaeous.

Lavinia leaned forward in her pink Spandex yoga kit. At her feet lay her trusty umbrella, an all-in-one broomstick, wand, weapon and weather defence. Ezra's aunt was not to be trifled with. "Just as the dark elf, Meriel Naehorn, once united the Otherworld in disgust, Alisha Verma has inspired everyday peculiars. Hope is powerful. We can harness it. But there is no doubt: there is trouble ahead. The gods will be coming out of the woodwork, and Alisha Verma has put her neck on the chopping block. We must protect her at all costs and assign her bodyguards. Even as a mere emblem, she is too useful to lose."

I gave Ezra's aunt an incredulous stare. A mere emblem? My tone was tart. "I think you'll find that in the past year, I've outperformed every single person in this room when I was pitted against obstacles. I have no rat army at my bidding, no witches' coven, wolf pack or vampire's clan." I tipped up my chin and ignored Ezra's tightened jaw. He obviously agreed with his aunt. "Besides, I already have a bodyguard. His name is Chanakya Gunbir Hredhaan of Maharashtra."

Echo's real name rolled off my tongue. He was out hunting royal deer in Richmond Park, but he would have puffed up with pride if he'd heard me.

Ezra spoke, calm and strong. All eyes snapped in his direction. Despite his discomfort with power, he was good at it. "The New Pragmatist's Law means our hands are no longer tied with regards to engaging the gods, but we must remain vigilant. I have offered the Defence Minister the use of the seekers in my pack to join her rats in gathering intelligence across the city. The gods might be weaker than they once were, but they still pose a threat despite the heroism of Alisha Verma and others who have stood in their paths over the past months."

"The druid is a tool, not a heroine," said Helio, who'd hated me since I'd freed Kraglek from his bestiary. He had no sense of smell, so Echo had taken to sneaking into his house in Wimbledon and rubbing his bits all over Helio's silk pillows. "The octopus may have marked her out as the chosen one, but wouldn't it be far better for her to populate our armies by animating fierce creatures to be commanded by far more experienced warriors?"

No doubt the little weasel was talking about himself. I wouldn't even animate a flying ant for him to control.

I raised my voice and laced it with steel. "The creatures I animate answer only to me. As far as my studies of Otherworld history have revealed, no animator has ever ceded control of their creatures to another person, and that chimes with my own instincts."

"But if you'll consider—" said Helio.

"No." I'd have expected the Bestiary Master to have a love for and a healthy respect for animals. Instead, with the exception of his apparent attachment to the hissing lizard, which darted in and out of his hair, he seemed to view animals as little more than transport and weapons. Whereas I had sent Roger the rooster to live out his days being cock of the manor on an Essex farm, Helio probably would have roasted him on a spit.

Erelim, the Minister for Diplomacy, a fallen angel with matted blond hair and a leather-clad bottom that could crack a nut, flexed his sooty wings. "There are some here who don't believe Death exists in corporeal form. You have read stories of old and mentions of Death as a metaphor, even though our very existence as peculiars teaches us to believe the unseen. The heavens, in their glory, were but a nanosecond ago for me. When they crumbled, the gods and angels fell. Without our Father's light, it was only a matter of time before the darkest gods unleashed hell on earth, and we fell prey to our basest instincts."

My instincts told me that the diplomat was actually playing it straight for once. Still, it was hard to take a man seriously who always had part of his torso on display and who, according to Echo, was addicted to computer games and wasabi crisps. Quite possibly, he had an addiction to socks, too, judging by the mountainous bulge in his pants. Not that I was looking.

Orpheus spluttered until Lavinia offered to do the Heimlich manoeuvre on him. *I've decided it might be in my best interests to stay out of your mind during formal situations. You are as uncouth as a Renaissance wench.*

Erelim dragged a hand through his dirty hair. "There comes a time when diplomacy is no longer an option. We must decipher the meaning of the Chameleon Tale and prepare ourselves. Even if we make fools of ourselves in the process."

Orpheus looked down his Roman nose. "Colleagues, you are jumping ahead of yourselves. Alisha Verma's training is not yet complete. She has yet to complete Wildwoods modules in herbology, healing and ageing. Her knowledge of spells is rudimentary, and while she is beginning to grasp magical history, she has been pulled into battles too often to spend adequate time with books."

I frowned at him. *Charming.*

Fellow druid Rayna pulled her vine-entwined plait over one shoulder. "The vampire is right. Alisha is a quick study, but we have yet to introduce her to wilding. Who knows what the future will bring? She needs all the tools at her disposal if she is to be the central element in our battle against the coming dark."

The leprechaun Cillian shifted in his seat. "Our coffers are full of coin. The Wildwoods vault holds untold treasures. My folk and I have been readying bags of luck, but I am yet to understand what the gods want."

Everyone had an opinion. I acknowledged him with a grateful nod. How rare to find someone willing to listen rather than speak. The senate might think I was the least experienced person in the room, but I had learned fast.

"They want chaos, Finance Minister," I said. "They aren't happy with the world order or the way worshippers prostrate before technology rather than religion. With the Father of the Gods gone, there is no leader amongst them who can control their greed for more power. So how else to create a new world order or, indeed, regress to the old one, without chaos? That is what they desire."

Phinnaeous's eyes came to rest on me, shrewd and cold. The silver-threaded afro around his head bobbed as he spoke. The afternoon sun darted behind a cloud, and I couldn't help wondering if that, too, was in his repertoire as a sorcerer.

"A war approaches," he said. "It whispers to me, just as it does to the rest of you. But wars are like chess. The outcome is determined by a series of moves. What, pray tell, is your move going to be, Alisha Verma? Will you agitate the gods as you have done in the past? Will you act erratically? Or will you join this senate and this sacred school to pool our resources with a frank heart and open mind? Will you share the information given to you by Gaia and by the Shadow Squad? Will you surrender that sword on your back, with its ability to access the spirit realm so others may learn from it, too? After all, the Administrator's Law states that all magical artefacts must be registered with the Sorcerer's Senate within three lunar cycles. That deadline has passed."

Orpheus frowned. *Don't surrender the sword.*

I sucked in my breath. *Of course, I won't.* "Prime Sorcerer, you'll find that the sword is registered."

"Indeed, the paperwork has been filed in the Wildwoods Library. I did it myself," said Ezra, his voice level though his posture had stiffened. "There is no requirement to surrender the artefacts under the Administrator's Law."

"That may be so, Mr Neuhoff," said Phinnaeous. "However, by-law 1005 states that, should the artefact be required by the senate, it should be surrendered as an act of good faith. If it is not, it can be taken forcibly."

Ezra put down his pen, and his grey, copper-flecked eyes narrowed, tracking Phinnaeous's every move.

Transcender quivered in its baldric on my back as if the Prime Sorcerer had exerted force on it. I willed my nervousness not to seep into my voice. "I told you when I agreed to the Kraglek trial that we would be equals. Your opinions are merely advice. You can't compel me to accept bodyguards or animate creatures without warrant or to surrender my sword. Your priorities aren't mine."

My hands tingled with an instinctive reflex to protect myself.

Keep your cool. Orpheus's piano player's hands lay flat against the table. *Now is not the time to lay our cards bare.*

"Her actions don't warrant the stripping of her weapon," said Rayna. "This step is unheard of."

Lavinia murmured in assent. "You cannot possibly expect the druid to surrender her weapon, Phinnaeous. Would you take the shell from a snail?"

"Studying Death's sword may well give us the advantage in overcoming Death herself," said Erelim.

Phinnaeous rose to his feet. Above his head, the pen scribbled with pent-up fury. "In times of strife, the senate has always voted unanimously."

I, too, stood. "We don't have to be enemies."

And yet, that's exactly what he was. Why else had he taken the detective's memories?

We faced each other over the split stone table.

Don't say it, said Orpheus.

I couldn't help it. Fury had a way of loosening my lips. "You were behind the loss of Detective Robert Jameson's memories. Why should I trust you?"

You are incapable of doing what you're told, said Orpheus.

Ezra groaned out loud.

Rayna turned to the Prime Sorcerer. "Phinnaeous?"

Phinnaeous waved his hand dismissively. He cast his eyes around the table. "You dare to question me when Alisha Verma still has not learned to control her impudence? He who holds the sword will determine the future. The question is: do you want it to be this newcomer to our ways? Let us vote. Raise your hands if you think Death's sword would be better off in the senate's hands?"

The pen paused momentarily.

My pulse jerked at the base of my throat. I did a quick count. Calypso wasn't here, so there would be no stalemate. It would be close.

A flurry of hands reached up. Phinnaeous. Margola. Erelim. Helio. Cillian. So much for good luck.

Phinnaeous's lip curled. "And who votes nay?"

Ezra, Orpheus, Rayna and Lavinia raised their hands.

It is over, Alisha. Ready yourself, said Orpheus. *The wolf has opened his mind to me. He will take you from here.*

My heart raced. *I won't run. How can this be fair?*

The vampire's sigh crept into my heart. *What good is the law if it is interpreted by knaves?*

"Let the record show that this senate has voted five to four for the druid to surrender. The lines are drawn, druid." The Prime Sorcerer's midnight skin shone. "Hand me the sword."

Every cell in my body raged against him. The sword had been Gaia's gift to me, not to him. Just like the Jericho necklace had been Mum's gift to me, not Sahil. They were just as bad as my ex-husband helping himself to our savings to fund his gambling habit.

What was it with men taking what was not theirs?

Take it easy, Alisha. Don't make this any more dramatic than it has to be, said Orpheus.

To hell with that. I smiled at the Prime Sorcerer and hoisted my finger like a flag. "Didn't you listen? The sword is mine."

A storm of fury swept into his face. He lifted his hands, and this time, Transcender jostled at my back, pulling towards him with a magnetism I couldn't hold out against.

Unless I retaliated.

The senate sprang to their feet.

So much for the element of surprise.

My hands tingled as I raised them. The single-pane stained-glass windows in the vaulted cabin—decorated with macabre scenes from Hansel and Gretel, the Pied Piper and Rumpelstiltskin—rattled as I called the winds through the crevices and the cracks. Hands outstretched, I built a wall of wind between me and the Prime Sorcerer as Ezra teleported to my side.

The Prime Sorcerer, in his rage, sent projectiles flying our way. Pillar candles, blocks of paper, the very chair that had scooped me into a seating position—all of it became fair game because I had said no.

Are you going to do anything, Orpheus, or just stand there glowering? I said.

I could box his ears, but from where I'm standing, the eternal girl doesn't need my help, replied the vampire.

I scanned the senate, wondering if they would help. Helio and Cillian ran from the room, scuttling like beetles. Who knew if they were running from me or Phinnaeous, whose aim was becoming increasingly erratic. Lavinia and Erelim seemed to have the coolest temperaments. They stayed, along with Orpheus, their faces expressionless. The selkie Margola, her eyes bulging with excitement, took out her mobile phone to film us. Until Orpheus confiscated it. Only Rayna seemed truly troubled. She seemed to be urging Phinnaeous to turn things down a notch.

Hardly likely when he seemed to be channelling a thwarted teenager with anger issues.

Ezra's voice pulsed urgently in my ear. "We won't be able to hold them off for long."

His presence at my side gave me the courage to see this through. I bit down hard on my lip and renewed my efforts. The senate wasn't taking what was mine unless I chose to give it.

Phinnaeous blurred at the other side of the wall of wind, cloak billowing, muttering spells of god knew what power. I didn't know how long I could keep up the resistance. Only that the sword was still on my back, and that was where it was staying. I would cut him down before I would let him take it.

Not because I was Gollum guarding my precious but because Transcender had been gifted to me for a reason by Gaia and because, through it, I could hear my dead mother's voice. And by manipulating laws and using force, Phinnaeous Shine had proved that he was corrupt.

"Christ, could this get any worse?" Ezra touched his thumb and forefinger to his charm necklace, and the light in the room slipped away. Then he grabbed my waist, and the world tipped as we teleported through the monochrome twilight towards a safe haven.

3

I picked up the phone and walked away from prying ears into the chill air outside the cottage I now shared with Ezra. Sleeping with the Minister for Justice meant Phinnaeous hadn't sent enforcers to retrieve Transcender from me, but it was early days. Call it the calm in the eye of the storm.

Transcender, with its shimmering obsidian blade, mammoth-tusk hilt and deep-set blue jewel, hadn't left my side in days. How ridiculous that I had once left it unprotected in my knicker drawer for so long. I knew its worth now. A spirit sword made from a heavenly cloud, blessed by Death, couldn't be anything but extraordinary.

This one had drawn blood from an immortal. No wonder Phinnaeous Shine coveted it.

Lavinia's cajoling voice came down the phone line. She'd called three times in as many days. "Come to the gym, Alisha. You might not like me, but you need me. We need each other. My nephew is a hell of a warrior, but he's only one person now he's shacked up with you and left the pack at the farmhouse."

I'd eat my own granny pants before I upped sticks and moved in with the coven. It was a nest of vipers. Besides, Ezra and I had only just started decorating our place together, and my nesting instinct was out of control. We'd be staying put. Phinnaeous Shine might want my guts for garters, but between my wolf, my leopard and me, we had it covered.

"Not a chance. Sorry, Lavinia. I don't quite understand why you want to help me anyway."

We'd worked together in the past, but Ezra's scheming aunt always had an agenda. The woman had more faces than a town clock.

A tinkling laugh. "Let's just say I like troublesome, talented women."

"Is it Phinnaeous's job you're after?"

Lavinia's tone hardened. "My ambition knows no limits, druid, but think of me as a walnut. I'm hard on the outside but soft on the inside. The bottom line isn't my aspirations. It is the fact that the old codger didn't defend Wildwoods when an enemy desecrated it. He doesn't deserve the honour of being Prime Sorcerer."

I slashed Transcender through the air, needing to blow off steam. It no longer felt heavy in my grip. It belonged there. "I don't think open conflict with him is a good idea."

Lavinia's voice filled with incredulity. "I'd say this conflict is already open, wouldn't you? Neither Rayna, Orpheus, Ezra, nor I are welcome at Wildwoods unless we hand him the sword. Poor Rayna's devastated that Phinnaeous has taken up the role of Headmaster himself. That man is far too used to getting his own way." A pause. "Heed me well, druid. We need a show of force. The best defence is a good offence. George Washington knew that. So did Michael Jordan." She sighed. "If only the witches in Salem had known it, we might be living in a better world."

My brow furrowed. Was she really an altruist? I'd wager not by the hair on my chinny chin chin. "If you want me to trust you as much as Ezra does, then you have to come clean about your motivations."

"If you must know, I've been biding my time for a while. Phinnaeous laying a hand on Robert Jameson was the last straw. It's one thing going after criminals and heathens, but Robert Jameson has gone beyond the call of duty to be a friend to the Otherworld. Technically, Phinnaeous is in the clear. The Jailor's Law only forbids us to interfere with the compos mentis of another peculiar. But where would any of us be without loyalty? I think of Jameson as an honorary peculiar. He should have been off limits."

"You already knew. The rats uncovered the truth." Goosebumps chased up my arms. Ezra had been right. Hiding secrets from Lavinia was next to impossible.

Lavinia gave an impatient huff. "Of course. London rats are tenacious. There is no better creature in this city to form a spy network. Why do you think the coven chose them as our familiars? Do you know the spaces rats can crawl into or the loyalty they will show for a bit of kindness? My rats might not be able to see well, beyond the few I have tampered with, but their hearing is superb. And that shapeshifting wizard can never resist spilling his guts to his favourite succubus house slave." A pause in which I could hear her thoughts whirring. "I was rather impressed you already knew. I will not underestimate you again."

"If Phinnaeous can treat allies like that, just imagine how he would treat enemies." My left eyelid twitched. I needed to book an appointment so six-handed Manfred could knead me into submission. In a strictly professional way, of course.

A harrumph. "Come to Baba Yaga's. We're not London's top protection racket for nothing. We'll keep you safe. He is a formidable foe with an extraordinarily tactical mind. You might think he has decided to back off, Alisha, but you gave his ego a kicking, and he will make you pay."

I sighed. "I'll keep myself safe. Thanks for the offer, though."

I hung up and pocketed my phone. I could have gone

inside to our visitor, but first, I needed to work off some steam. I took a deep breath, put two hands on the hilt of Transcender and commenced a series of drills.

First, a vertical cut, then a horizontal cut, followed by an uppercut and a crosscut. I repeated the sequence, varying my footwork. My breathing came hot and fast, and in my mind's eye, I saw the water goddess's look of terror when I'd cut her. When she'd understood I carried a weapon that could slice the flesh from her bones.

I lunged, spun, thrusting the sword out and up, to the left and right, until my arms burned and my brow swam with sweat.

I'd practised these drills for weeks now, driven by dread of the future. The cottage itself was deserted—the perfect bolthole—but with drones all the rage, I prayed I wouldn't be caught on candid camera.

Consistent training meant not only had I become more comfortable and proficient at using Transcender—and preferred it over bō sticks—but I'd lost the beginnings of my bingo wings. My upper arms had become taut, my belly flatter. Thanks to the lunges, I even had a bit of lift in the bum area. For years, the wrinkles, rounder hips and greys had crept in, softening me into a person who no longer dwelled on my appearance. Now, with a few improvements, I didn't care if I passed some stranger's test for hotness. I was over living up to other people's expectations of me. Maintaining the image of a Bond girl took work, and that wasn't how I rolled. I was too lazy, as demonstrated by the forest of my bikini line.

There were only two reasons to train with my sword: to stay alive and my yearning to hear my dead mother's voice again. But after that night on the Millennium Bridge when I'd fought the water goddess, I'd not heard it again. Even though I had willed it with all my heart. Even though Dad had picked up Transcender and tried the same. Even though our family was in trouble, with my brother in the wind, having taken the necklace I needed to survive. Even though the sound of her voice had dredged up grief and longing I thought I had dealt with.

It turned out that when you truly loved someone, you'd miss them until your last breath, and sometimes—not always—that grief was like a twisting knife in the softest part of you. That was the price of loving someone, and so, when the grief came, I leaned into it.

I spun, sword in hand, and found Ezra lounging against the front door with a rolled-up copy of *The Otherworld News* in his hands. He'd been applying a new lick of paint to the cottage all morning. Autumn had stolen the leaves from the trees as we headed into the winter, and he braved the elements in just his jeans and canvas shoes, with a slick of duck-egg paint smeared across his bicep.

"You're training hard," he said. "Careful not to burn yourself out. Slow and steady, Alisha."

My werewolf-wizard boyfriend had brute strength, sharp teeth, teleportation and a lifetime's experience to get himself out of scraps. Innate talent, luck and loyal friends had helped me keep my scalp, but I had to train hard if I was going to survive the encroaching darkness.

Darkness that swirled all around us and crept into my very bones.

I nodded and let the sword fall to my side. "Are you taking a break from the paint fumes?"

He smiled. "I'm taking a break from Echo grumbling about the paint fumes." He tossed aside the newspaper and sparked up a cigarette, his grey eyes on me. "What did my aunt want?"

"To offer me a place of refuge until Phinnaeous backs off."

His eyes darkened. "She thinks I don't have it in me to look after you."

I approached him and left a lingering kiss on his chapped

lips. "She thinks we stand more of a chance in a group. You'd think that way too if you hadn't always had the ability to teleport yourself out of trouble." I hesitated. "Ezra, I feel guilty that those of you who sided with me at the vote are now out in the cold. Locked out of Wildwoods."

"That's not on you, hellfire. It's on Phinnaeous. He's flexing his muscles, that's all. A tantrum. He'll back down. And if not, we'll take Wildwoods back by force. It's not his. It belongs to all peculiars."

"Except the ones he's never let in. The elves. The ones unwilling to take the blood bond or to adhere to the Magical Constitution."

He raked his hand through his hair. "Every community has rules, Alisha."

I gestured to the newspaper. "So what's the news amongst peculiars then?"

Ezra frowned. "You, of course. That selkie's never going to give it a rest. She couldn't cover what happened at the vote, but she's still spouting shite. You're the prophesied eternal girl, for crying out loud. The first animator in generations. A warrior capable of taking on immortals. What self-respecting journalist would write a feature on the face cream you use?"

I grinned. "It's quite flattering, really. Imagine taking beauty tips from middle-aged me. I'm hardly an oil painting when I get out of bed in the morning."

"I beg to differ." He locked his gaze on mine.

A frisson of pleasure warmed me. After my divorce, I thought I could live without desire. I'd been wrong. "Maybe she should do her next feature on my arm candy. What do you reckon, Neuhoff? Want to be my trophy boyfriend?"

"I'll be whatever you need me to be." His roll-up glowed as he took a deep drag. "I'll have a word with Margola."

I grinned. "My hero."

He stubbed out his cigarette and pulled me against his bare chest. He smelt earthy and safe: of paint, roll-ups and hard work. When he unpeeled my fingers from my sword hilt, I didn't resist.

Ezra laid it against the door frame and scooped me up in his arms. "Consider this an enforced break. I should have done this when you agreed to move in with me."

I squealed as he carried me over the threshold into the warmth of the cottage as if I weighed no more than a feather.

In the compact living room, the Earth goddess Gaia put aside her knitting needles and caressed my grumpy leopard's ears. She smiled with approval, her velvet cheeks falling into folds, and at that moment, I could see the mark of centuries on her skin. "It is nice to see a little bit of foreplay. In my line of work, mating couples are all bang and no sizzle."

Echo's tail swished. "I am glad you are filled with positivity, goddess. I find my own nose is rather out of joint. Why is it that I feel like the unwanted gherkin in a sandwich? Not even my urine can dispel the scent of these paint fumes. You'd think the wolf and druid would be more careful about ambience and having a full fridge when we have a goddess to host. But no, it's all cigarette butts and sword waving. And I don't mean the metal kind."

Ezra placed me on my feet with the air of a man whose grand romantic gesture had been ruined by a petulant child. Without visitors, he would no doubt have carried me straight to bed. He curled his arm around me, reluctant to let go. "No more spraying the walls with urine, cat, or I'll teleport you back to India faster than you can say Lata Mangeshkar."

"Do not take that glorious songbird's name in vain, dog, or you will have me to answer to," Echo hissed.

Gaia tugged Echo's ear. "Shh, Chanakya. You know very well I came here to cheer you up. A change of territory must be disorienting for you, my poor leopard, but you must not give in to gloominess."

"Do you blame me? What hell has Alisha brought me to when the city with its poodle and Labrador hunting grounds await? Here, the only things on my doorstep are dormice, the odd stupid bird and hedgehogs." Echo's sandpaper tongue lolled out of his mouth in disgust.

Gaia's cherubic face became sterner still. "The world always changes. Without change, we wither and die. Consider deciduous trees through the seasons or butterflies in their cocoons. It would be a far less beautiful existence were it stagnant. Let the druid continue her loving and training. The time will come when those things will sustain her."

I stepped out of the circle of Ezra's arms and buried my head in Echo's golden coat. "I haven't sold the Balham flat, Echo, precisely because you've grown attached to it. But I want you here with us. Moving home will take adjustment, that's all."

Echo might have been a pampered puss, but he was my pampered puss and more than earned his keep.

What I didn't say out loud was that, however much I wanted my relationship with Ezra to work, my divorce had taught me to value my independence. Keeping the flat meant I had options if everything went tits up. And by that, I wasn't talking *Kama Sutra* moves, although Ezra was—as befitting his wild wolfish nature—much more adventurous in the bedroom than my ex-husband had ever been.

No wonder Echo felt like the third wheel. I made a mental note to let him invite his harem of cats over to soothe his smarting ego.

Echo rubbed his head against my shoulder. "I accept, druid. It's not like I can stay at the Balham flat alone. Who would bring me prime-cut steaks from the butcher's?"

I felt the ping of the goddess's attention warming me. A teal scarf fell like a waterfall from her knitting needles, intended as a gift for one of the children on her estate this winter. The gentle click-click of her efforts filled the room. For all her claims to be visiting Echo, Gaia's aims were never singular. They were manifold, layered, sprawling, and as abundant as the earth itself.

I bit my lip. "There is something on your mind, goddess."

Ezra, en route to finish the paint job in our bedroom, hovered at the door frame, arms folded, biceps bulging.

Gaia blew out her plump cheeks. "I have heard whispers amongst the gods. The time is nigh when they will kick down doors to reach you. Keep the sword close, Alisha. Keep your allies closer still. I won't always be at your beck and call."

Echo's tail swished. "I won't leave the druid's side. Unless there is a competing offer I must consider."

In Gaia's irises, lava bubbled, and fierce storm winds blew as if she were afraid. "The druid can count on you, Chanakya. When I'm finished with the scarf, I can make this cottage and the Verma house into havens using a mix of clever planting, Alma's flour rituals and koi alarms."

I'd never known the goddess to be afraid. Anxiety swirled in my belly in response. Moments before, I had found the click-click of her knitting needles relaxing. Now, they were akin to nails on a chalkboard. I gritted my teeth.

Her eyes found each of us in turn, and she tucked away her knitting under a pillow. "It's time I let you in on my deepest secret. After all, we all need a little hope to ride out the dark, don't we? And it isn't really a secret. Anyone who's truly looking can't think that He is really gone."

I frowned. "He?"

She mimicked my expression. "Yes, He. Do keep up, Alisha. The gods have been driven to despair and mischief because they believe He is dead. Like little rascals without Daddy to take a slipper to their sorry behinds. But they are wrong."

I blinked hard, wondering if I'd taken a knock to my head when Ezra had hoisted me into his arms. "You told me the Father of the Gods had sent His remaining children to Earth on his last breath when the heavens crumbled."

Gaia's laughter flowed around the room like a river. "Forget all the fire and brimstone malarkey. God is pure love. Pure love doesn't go away. It's always with us. Just like the sun will always rise, there is no keeping light out of the universe. God is the origin of that light, so how can He be gone?"

Echo's emerald eyes gleamed. "If only Rajika Verma could be here to see the day a goddess entrusted the secrets of the universe to her granddaughter."

A vein throbbed in Ezra's jaw. "Are you asking us to believe there is an all-powerful being somewhere just sitting on the sidelines? Just waiting behind a curtain?"

Gaia tutted at him. "This isn't *The Wizard of Oz*, werewolf. He's merely napping. Or sleeping on the job if you're being ungenerous." She sighed. "Actually, it's best not to insult him. As a rule of thumb, we should always mind our words and deeds. Something the other gods have forgotten. He might be able to hear us, and He does have quite a fondness for the fire and brimstone stuff. We wouldn't want to be hit by lightning, would we?"

Ezra and I exchanged horrified glances, and I couldn't help remembering how once he had told me that nothing but trouble came from meddling with the gods. He'd been right, but how could I resist a fate that had been written for centuries?

Gaia fished out a rubber band from her sari blouse and proceeded to plait her loose hair as if she'd suddenly decided she wanted it out of the way. "So you see, the rogue gods are not only morally bankrupt; they are small-minded. What fools to believe God is dead. They failed the test He set us all. It takes constant effort to keep an open heart in the face of disappointments."

"I do miss chomping on poodles. I even miss their stringy fur between my teeth. My desire to go on a rampage to a local park is strong." Echo's face drooped as he hummed Céline Dion's 'All by Myself.'

"Self-pity does not become you, Chanakya." Gaia flexed her knuckles. "We all fall off the wagon. I myself have been destructive through the centuries. Vesuvius might be a high point for geologists, but it was a low point for me."

My eyebrows shot up. "The eruption of Mount Vesuvius at Pompeii was you?"

"Who else? I have mellowed over the years, but I still have it in me to rage like the night. Nowadays, I choose not to take out my anger on the world. That slogan—*be the change you want to see in the world*—it's one of mine." Gaia hoisted her sari up and tucked its train into her waistband. "You might want to collect your sword, Alisha."

Her instruction floated over my head as the enormity of her revelation exploded in my mind like fireworks.

"The Father of the Gods is not dead," I murmured.

Gaia's eyes blazed with pride. "Not permanently. He is infinite. We just need to wake him, that's all." She pursed her lips. "It's a little tricky, but I think we'll be able to do it."

The copper sparks in Ezra's grey eyes flared. "You make it sound easy, goddess, but you forget mortals are fodder in the games of the gods."

"I forget nothing, werewolf. I feel each drop of blood on the soil, every felled tree and falling leaf. I mourn every loss, from crushed beetles to slain human beings, dying rainforests and melting icecaps. But what has been set in motion cannot be undone." She heaved herself up, her upper body parallel to the floor.

I hurried over to help her. "And what is my role in this, goddess?"

She didn't need my help. Gaia might have been the crone, but she was also the warrior. Her arthritic joints couldn't hold her back. She straightened herself with the sheer strength of will, like a car being cranked into the right position. A goddess she might be, but I suspected she was also self-medicating with homegrown cannabis.

"You are the eternal girl," she said. "You must simply be. Like everything in life, when troubles befall us or our enemies attack, we can only do one thing. Put one foot in front of the other and be our best selves. I have made plans that should set us in good stead, but things can always take an unpredictable turn. And where would we be then? At a family dinner without the chapatis, that's where."

You must simply be. When our enemies attack. Bile filled my throat. I loved the power coursing through my veins, but it came with a price. A whooshing sound filled my ears. I grimaced. The old me, the one without true sight, might have become lightheaded at such news, but the new me was a tougher nut to crack.

When the whooshing continued, I realised it wasn't my body playing silly buggers or my, frankly, quite full bladder. It was coming from the door. The hair on the back of my neck rose when I noticed the goddess had already taken a fighter stance.

Her gait had widened, and her palms were outstretched.

Gaia's voice, calm and focussed. "Alisha. Your weapon."

I picked up Death's sword from the open doorway just as a woman dressed in red materialised there.

Blackened, diseased fingers reached for me as I scampered back.

The red woman's smile chilled me to the bone.

4

———

Echo's growl ripped through the cottage as Ezra teleported to my side.

The woman had a plump figure clothed in a knee-length red dress with pockets. She was a head taller than me, statuesque, with luscious cascades of straight, dark hair to her waist. Her nose was small, and her lips full. Shaped eyebrows, thick like the current fashion on Parisian runways, sat above cornflower blue eyes.

I recoiled from her blackened fingers.

I didn't know whether this was one of Phinnaeous' minions, or perhaps a succubi—what did they look like anyway?—or one of the troublesome gods crawling out of the woodwork. It didn't matter. My instincts told me not to offer her refuge and chai, like my Indian father would have, or coffee and macarons like my French mother would have. They told me to shut the door and bolt it tight. To close the curtains and board up the windows if we had to.

Echo's bared teeth told me the same. A rustle of clothes and cracking bones as Ezra changed into his wolf. He and Echo flanked me—the wolf much larger than the leopard.

And still, the woman hadn't spoken.

I gripped my sword, and with my free hand, I summoned the wind to slam the door in her face. The collar of her red dress ruffled, and her hair fluttered in the wind, but the door didn't close. I cursed.

Why wasn't it working? I'd moved far heavier objects before, in training and real tussles. Hell, I'd thrown eighty-kilo wolves to the ground, and here I was, struggling to move a door.

I tried again, narrowing my gaze, envisioning what I needed to happen, my palms raised.

Nothing. The door remained open.

The red woman lifted her foot to step over the threshold.

Gaia's eyes flashed. She was no longer a cherubic granny adept at needlework and making chapatis. She was a combatant, ready to wage war. "You are not welcome here. Turn around before you regret it."

The woman's cornflower blue eyes hardened. "You protect this druid, Gaia?"

A note of sadness in Gaia's voice. These women were kin. Fellow immortals. "We used to be friends. We used to dance in the heavens together."

I raised my sword so the red woman knew I meant business, every nerve-ending tingling with anticipation. But even as I did, I knew I couldn't just hack down a friend of Gaia's. I'd have to follow her lead. After all, if someone known to me acted out of turn, I would want to be given the space to iron things out first.

"That was before," said the red woman. "The world is a big place, and yet you police our actions. As if you were the grand judge. When we know He is long gone. You could have kept your head down and tended to your plants and strays. Instead, you decided to meddle where you weren't wanted. Worse, you gave the druid Death's sword. You have no friends left amongst the immortals."

Waves of melancholy crashed in Gaia's irises. "Has so much changed, Cardea?"

Eyes like chips of sapphire. "You know it has."

I frowned. *Cardea?* The name rang a bell, but the memory was a dusty place, and without wading through my parent's mythology books, I couldn't quite recall any facts about her. One thing was certain—if Gaia didn't trust her, neither did I. The Earth goddess hadn't let me down yet. Even absent, she had looked after me, be it with Death's sword, offering me chai and a heart-to-heart or sending Alma, the—albeit unsuccessful—flour seer, into our lives.

Next to me, the wolf and the leopard's tense stillness belied their heightened awareness and readiness to let their teeth and claws meet soft flesh. When Ezra snarled, I placed my hand on his thick, copper-brown fur to calm him. I didn't want him springing forward, not when we had no idea what the red woman could do.

I balled my fists. "I don't know who you are, but this is my home, and I'd like you to leave."

The red woman examined her cuticles like my desires mattered less than a gnat's. "The druid thinks it matters what she wants." Her eyes flicked from me to Gaia. "All that matters is that you die."

Gaia's voice was a whip. "I will not stand by and watch you murder in cold blood."

My heartbeat ricocheted in my chest like a bat out of hell. Eyes darting to the sideboard, where Dad's newly completed catalogue of creatures lay, I did a mental check of what I could animate quickly to give us an advantage.

The red woman stepped over the threshold and into our cottage.

Too late to animate. I was reluctant to kill a goddess who had once been friends with Gaia, but we would defend ourselves. I raised my sword just as Ezra leapt through the air, a whir of copper brown fur and bared teeth. Hot on his heels was Echo, lunging for the red woman from a different angle, wolf and leopard working in tandem. A pack of our own.

Before they could make contact, a thick vine—with a monstrous mouth—snaked from the lawn. It grabbed the red woman around the waist, yanking her backwards, snapping at her. A feral triffid spat her out a few metres away like a chewed-up lump of unwanted meat.

Only one woman I knew could do that. My eyes snapped to Gaia.

"Stay back," I commanded Ezra and Echo.

A sheen of perspiration broke out on Gaia's forehead as she urged the earth to grow a net of white wisteria and purple clematis. The climbers surged up and around the cottage, blocking the front door and windows and locking the red woman outside. The vines grew ever upwards, winding and coiling up the walls to the roof and up and over until darkness shrouded the cottage.

A cocoon. A prison.

Ezra's howl sent shivers up my spine.

"That will keep her out." Gaia collapsed on the sofa, spent. She patted the pillow. "What a relief that my knitting is safe."

A silhouette of a big cat with mournful emerald eyes approached the Earth goddess. "We will die here. They will find our skeletons centuries after we perish."

"Don't be silly, Chanakya. The teleporting wolf will ensure you can come and go as you please. And I would hardly abandon you to your fate. Not unless my hands are bound, anyway," said the Earth goddess.

For all her support of me, Gaia had skirted the shadows when it came to confronting her fellow immortals. She had rescued me once from the sun god Ra when I had first come into my powers. Since then, she had armed me with knowledge, tools and confidence but had taken care to stay out of the main fray.

Until now. Which could only mean one thing.

We were in the doggy doo-doo.

Behind me, Ezra shifted back into his human form with a groan, his copper-flecked eyes scanning the damage to the cottage his parents had so lovingly nurtured before their deaths. He pulled on his boxers with a sigh. "So much for new beginnings. That woman had murder in her eyes."

I switched on a lamp to counter the pitch black and swallowed the bile in my throat. Then I knelt beside Gaia, my sword still tightly clutched in my grip. "Who the hell was it?"

"That, druid, was Cardea, Goddess of door hinges, thresholds and health. However, you can see by her diseased fingers what has become of that particular talent. Suffering is more profitable to other gods these days than engendering goodwill."

"She looked like she wanted to kill me," I said.

Gaia picked up her knitting. "Unsurprising, really. The gods are used to getting their way. You are like a thorn in their sides. A verruca on their feet. A wart on their noses."

I grimaced. "Thanks. I get the picture."

"I'm afraid things are about to go a little haywire," said Gaia. "Without functioning doors, pandemonium reigns. I fear there are nasty surprises in store for us. If Cardea is here, the other gods are never far behind. Since the heavens crumbled, it has been her duty to fix where the gods meet."

My pulse thundered like horses across an open vista. "We escaped single gods by the skin of our teeth. How are we supposed to survive many together?"

Gaia expelled her breath in a whoosh as if it were a release of stress, worry and even expectations. The wrinkles on her face smoothed, and she yawned. "When you live as long as me, you learn that it does no good to worry, druid. We will need to work faster than I thought, but first, I need to replenish my energy."

She made herself comfortable on the sofa and fell asleep as if she didn't have a care in the world. As if she hadn't just done battle against one of her own. Perhaps the darkness of the cottage made her sleepy, or her exertions against Cardea had simply tired her out. After all, she had told me many times how the powers of the gods weren't what they once were. They were shadows of themselves after the heavens had crumbled and worshipper numbers dwindled. They might be infinite—at least, unable to be felled by mere mortals—but their powers were most definitely finite. A well that could stay empty were it not replenished.

There, in the dark cottage that should have been a new start, I hoped fervently that sleep would replenish her. Without Gaia, there would be no shield between us and the dark desires of her fellow immortals.

I fetched a blanket to cover her and left her snoring lightly in Echo's care.

In the kitchen, Ezra and I sat at our breakfast table with remnants of toast crumbs from the morning and called the detective.

I put him on speaker phone. "Hi, Rob."

His tired voice came down the line. "I've been digging as we agreed, Alisha. I found evidence that it was the Prime Sorcerer masquerading as Ezra who lured you back from the Celestial Library. I've advised the Prime Minister to cease all dealings with Wildwoods until someone more trustworthy takes on the role of Prime Sorcerer."

Ezra grunted. "And the Prime Minister agreed? It seems a harsh step to punish a whole community for one man's indiscretions."

"I don't know what he's going to say, Ezra. The briefing is still in his in-tray. But I'll let you know. Much as it pains me, I didn't have a choice. You've got to see it from my side. You've been turfed out, and Shine has full control. Wildwoods is compromised, and until your house is in order, all liaison stops. Who knows what Shine has in mind or what his motives are."

"Actually, that's not why we were calling." I filled him in on what had just happened as Gaia's snores floated over from the living room.

Rob swore. "This woman came to the cottage? Are you all right?"

"We're fine. But we need intel on her fast," I said.

His voice was muffled, and the sound of typing came down the line. "Cardea, you say?"

Once, we'd shied away from using the gods' names, but there was no hiding now. Not since we were well and truly in their sights.

The detective muttered to himself. "Let me run her through our database. Yes, yes. Here she is. Let me see. Cardea, goddess of door hinges, thresholds and health. I have a picture on file."

Ezra's patience strained. "We know what she looks like, Rob."

"Keep your boxers on, Neuhoff. I'm playing catch-up here. She's one who's been on my radar for a few years, but I've never met her. According to our records, she has close ties with the ancient Roman god Janus, the god of beginnings and endings. She's a protector of children and has, more recently, been known to create portals. She was once a locksmith, then a hotelier and now, a university admissions tutor at Kings College London. Just like her onetime lover Janus, she is depicted as having two faces to see into the past and future. You can't underestimate her."

I frowned. "Any insight into her powers?"

He sighed. "There's some stuff blacked out here. It's above my paygrade, but from what I can tell, there were some disease outbreaks in West London that were linked to her.

When local bobbies apprehended her, she disappeared from jail cells. They just couldn't keep her in. How do you combat someone you can't even capture? So we figured the legends were true. She has power over thresholds, over who comes and who goes." He coughed. "But there's something even more worrying here. Her arrival often leads to a surge in power. Like she is a conduit for the other gods."

"Perfect. Just perfect," I said.

"Look, if I had to place a bet, I'd say she won't harm children," said Jameson. "She is their protector. But no one else is safe…Did she say what she wanted?"

Ezra's jaw clenched. "To kill Alisha."

Determination sparked in the detective's voice. "Then you can't take any chances. This city has been a cesspool for immortal activity recently. I don't know what the hell is going on or whether to believe this bloody prophecy the rest of you swear by, but I know one thing. They're drawn to Alisha like a magnet. Listen, I have to go. Something's kicking off at 10 Downing Street. Protect Alisha with your life, Neuhoff. And don't let anyone get their hands on that sword. It's the only protection she currently has."

The line went dead.

He meant well with the protective bullshit, but he was wrong. I didn't want Ezra's body to be my shield. I didn't want him to put himself on the line for me.

What I needed was what Mum and Marina had worked on. Two women—and Gaia with the sword—who had worked together to protect me. I needed the Jericho necklace. I was going to prise it from my werepigeon brother's hands, and I knew just the way to do it.

Ezra's gravelly voice filled with foreboding. "I know that look, hellfire. What are you up to?"

I met his eyes. "I'm going to ask the foxes for a favour."

5

That afternoon, once Ezra had teleported us out of the now-fortified cottage, I turned up at Dad's house with Gaia and Echo in tow. My jaw—and arse cheeks—clenched tightly as Sahil opened the door. His presence wound me up, but he had as much right to be in our family home as me.

Gaia stormed past him, tutting. "Naughty werepigeon."

Echo hissed, on the heels of the goddess. "Imbecile. I ought to sink my teeth into your behind."

Weeks of pent-up rage broke my restraint. I socked Sahil in the stomach. "You utter wanker."

My thieving brother's face flamed, and then he stood aside to let me pass, winded. "I've heard worse."

We faced each other in sight of Mum's garlanded shrine. My sword hung at my back. Sahil was so untrustworthy that I would have to take the damn thing to the loo with me for fear of him doing the dirty again.

I balled my fists. "Where's the Jericho necklace? Mum left it to me."

Sahil cocked his head, werepigeon-style. "You're not really going to pummel me into submission in front of her photo? If

I wanted to tell you, I'd have answered one of your hundred voicemails or texts."

Little did he know that the foxes had offered to pilfer through his North London penthouse while I kept his attention grounded here. Whatever promises I'd made Dad, I was done playing fair with Sahil.

Dirty tricks called for dirty countermeasures.

"Why are you here then?" I didn't hide my disdain for him and spat the words.

He grimaced. "Turning down a family conference is more than my life is worth."

I sucked in my breath. "You don't want to fall in Dad's eyes. You know, we could have caught you that day, but he begged us to let you go. You don't deserve his love."

Sahil's dark eyes gleamed. "And what about you, sis? Do I deserve your love?"

"I thought we found an understanding when we rescued Dad." A stone of sadness settled high in my chest. "What went wrong?"

He opened his mouth to speak, but Alma came bustling into the hallway.

"There you are." Alma beamed and swept us into awkward hugs. "Nattering away out here. Come on; everyone's waiting."

Sahil nodded. "Best leave something unsaid for the family conference, eh?"

We followed her into the dining room. The table had been folded in two and set aside, replaced by a circle of five chairs, more like an Alcoholics Anonymous meeting than a family home. I recoiled to find Great-Uncle Rajiv between my slumped Dad and a hissing Echo. Alma chose her seat, sitting straight-backed with her hands on her knees, queen of the court.

"This should be good." Sahil sat down, tight-lipped and sullen.

I kissed Dad in greeting. "Hello."

My nose wrinkled. He smelt a little pungent.

"Hello, children." Dad smiled softly, strangely relaxed.

"I didn't expect to see you here, Uncle," I said. For one, he and Dad weren't exactly bosom buddies.

"I invited him along." Alma swept her mouse-brown fringe out of her eyes. "Better to pierce the boil than let it fester. Besides, I did a flour seer reading, and it said Rajiv's presence would be auspicious."

That gave me a lot of confidence.

Rajiv turned his watery, cataract-filled eyes on me. "I am part of this family, am I not?"

There were over twenty years in age between him and Dad, but with his thick thatch of white hair and canal lifestyle, plus his stints as a gravedigger, Rajiv looked the stronger of the pair. For one that embraced solitude, I found it strange for him to have come here.

It would make for an even more fraught meeting than usual. I had dreaded Verma family conferences since I was a child. They tended to end in finger-pointing. It was just a question of who kicked off first.

And who deserved a kicking.

My eyes flicked to Dad, impressed by his calmness. Forty years of experience as his daughter had taught me that emotional low points for Dad usually meant a dip in painting productivity. Today, splotches of primary colours covered his hands, like he'd been doing finger painting with a primary school class. He didn't seem fazed by the coming confrontation. I missed Mum, but I couldn't deny that Alma was really good for him.

"Where's Gaia?" I said, just as the Earth goddess's ghostly face appeared at the window, doused in flour.

Alma grinned. "Isn't she a gem? She's safety proofing the house with a bag of blessed flour, some sprigs of lavender and a generous sprinkling of dill, oregano and parsley, plus some very loud koi alarms."

I'd never heard loud koi, but given how koi had an almost dog-like loyalty, excellent memory and the ability to remember faces, a koi alarm wasn't *that* farfetched.

"I've been forbidden to distract them," said Echo. "This day is on a downward trajectory."

"She did consider the vines technique she used during the attack on your cottage this morning, but your father needs light for his painting, and how would the milkman get to us?" said Alma.

"What would we do without Gaia?" said Dad, serene and mellow. His modus operandi had always been to fly into a panic when we were in danger. Instead, he picked up a bowl from underneath his chair and a glass-blown pipe I hadn't seen before and then proceeded to light the pipe and smoke it.

"What took your nose so long," said Echo. "Your father is puffing the magic dragon."

My mouth fell open. At last, I identified the muffled smell of him. No wonder he was so calm. "Dad, is that weed?"

Sahil reached for the pipe. "Way to go, Dad. Hand it over. Share the love."

Dad swatted him away like a jealous lover and took another puff.

"Gaia grew us a plant. She thought it would take the edge off his nerves," said Alma. "Just until he gets his head around all the happenings around here. Joshi's been struggling to face the chaos our family has been pulled into by magic. Your father may have true sight, but he's been burying his head like an ostrich since your childhood, and he can't exactly go to a humdrum doctor for help."

I sighed. "Can we get on with it?"

Alma nodded. "As I was saying, the point of this family

conference is to air our grievances and find a way forward. Ground rules first. No punching, no kicking, no raised voices or interrupting each other. Everyone gets the chance to participate. We keep it as upbeat as possible and try to see the other person's perspective. We end the meeting with a hug. Agreed?"

"This is going to be a disaster," said Sahil.

"Smells pongy to me," said Echo. "Some of us are choosy about who we hug."

Rajiv folded his arms across his wiry chest. "Why is the leopard more welcome here than me?"

Dad took another puff and started to giggle.

"Joshi," said Alma. "Behave yourself, or I'll confiscate your trouser pipe."

I covered my face with my hands. If there was any time I could have done with an emergency werewolf evacuation, it was now. "Pipe. Pipe. You meant pipe without trouser."

Alma flushed. "I'm sorry, dear. We've been trying filthy talk in the bedroom, and it slipped out."

"My honeysuckle," said Dad.

Sahil and I cringed. I guess we still had some things in common.

Alma took a deep breath. "Rajiv, why don't you start?"

"You ostracised me from our family, Joshi, and I won't ever forgive you." Rajiv pointed at me. "And you. I helped you. You used my paintings and never visited again. You spat me out like chewing gum."

Alma frowned. "Thank you for your honesty, Rajiv."

"Why are you thanking him? That wasn't very upbeat," said Echo.

Dad giggled. "He's never been upbeat. Once a miser, always a miser. Tell them about the time you threw Mum a drawing in the midst of battle, giving her a warthog when she expected a rhinoceros. Just to teach her a lesson."

I silenced Dad with a glare. Being honest while you were stoned wasn't always a good idea. "I'm sorry for hurting your feelings, Uncle. You practice a wilder magic than Dad had advised, but I shouldn't have walked away without explaining myself. I'm glad to see you here."

I bloody well wasn't, but I didn't want to hurt an old man's feelings. For one, the grumpy old codger looked like he could go a few rounds with Mike Tyson and still be swinging. But also, I had learned it was rarely a good idea to hurt someone's feelings. More often than not, it didn't help the situation. A little humility went a long way.

Besides, I didn't know when I'd need him again. With a little distance, I'd realised Rajiv's appeal to a darker side of me had turned up the dial of my talents. I'd never animated multiple creatures in a matter of seconds before. Power had coursed through my veins when I'd sucked the water goddess's breath from her own body and floored her with it.

Rajiv lifted his chin into the air, proud to a fault. "We will make something of you yet, Alisha."

I rolled my eyes. On second thoughts, maybe with arrogant men, it was best to always unleash waspish tongues on them. It wasn't like they'd recognise the truth when it pierced their thick skins anyway.

Echo honked with laughter. "Says the man in harem pants and a string vest. What are you? Svengali?"

Without pausing, Rajiv leapt for Echo, sending the leopard tumbling off his perch. A roar met my ears, but Rajiv remained uncowed. With Echo poised to take a chunk out of his ear, he made to gouge his fingers into Echo's beautiful emerald eyes.

Alma squealed.

Sahil whooped. "Teach that cat some manners."

"Fight, fight, fight," said Dad. "Sink your teeth into that juicy steak, Echo."

I shot Dad a horrified look, called the winds and flung my hands in either direction. "Stop that."

Man and leopard yelped as they hit opposing walls before

returning to their places, grumbling and a little worse for wear.

"What do you have to say for yourselves?" said Alma.

"The leopard can eat my nut sack," said Rajiv.

Echo growled. "With pleasure."

Dad fought to hide his grin, then gurned like a clown. "Speaking of which, has anyone got any peanuts? I really fancy some salted peanuts."

"I think he's got the munchies," I said. "I don't think giving him a pipe was a good idea."

"Alisha's right, Joshi." Alma wrenched it out of his hand.

"Spoilsport." Dad took a deep breath. "The way I see it, we are no different to any other family. My werepigeon son craves attention, so he stole his dead mother's jewellery from the eternal girl. There is one solution."

I leaned forward, hoping that, for once, Dad would step into the patriarch role and lay down the law for my brother.

"What do you say, son?" said Dad. "Give back the necklace, and I'll take you out for a day of pizza and golf."

Unbelievable. Mum would have taken no prisoners at this moment. She would have taken Sahil by the ear and demanded he put things right. In life, her fire had balanced out Dad's softness. Now, we just had marshmallow Papa. Not a backbone in sight; God love him.

I mean, pizza and golf?

The only thing that stopped my fury from erupting was the thought that by now, Fei Yen and Faeza had probably retrieved the Jericho necklace from Sahil's apartment with their fiendish foxy ways.

Sahil grimaced. "It's not as easy as that, Dad. I can't give it back."

I gritted my teeth. "He made a deal with the Ravenmaster, Dad."

Dad hiccupped. "Son, is this true?"

Sahil shrugged. "Is that so bad?"

"We all make mistakes. I know I have," said Dad.

"Yes, you have," said Rajiv.

"What happens if you give the necklace back?" said Dad.

"I lose everything. The ability to fly. My shield. My spider form." Sahil's eyes bulged, and a vein throbbed in his cheek. "Maybe even my life."

What bollocks. I knew that twitchy pigeon look. He was playing Dad like a fiddle. "No," I said, "it's my life that is in jeopardy without the necklace, not yours."

Dad looked from one of us to the other, his mouth slack. Taking sides between us had always been anathema to him.

"Helloooo." Echo waved his paw in the air. "I fear Joshi's brain is hazy from the weed."

I nodded, my mind looping back to Cardea's attack that morning and Gaia's warning. *The gods will come for you.*

Sahil was my brother. He was supposed to be on my side. Hadn't Alma's flour seer powers predicted a good outcome for this meeting?

"If I mean anything to you," I said, "you'll give me back the Jericho necklace."

Sahil gave a sad smile. "Over my dead body. The Ravenmaster is rising, and I still have a job to do."

Anxiety exploded like shrapnel in my belly. I chose words I knew would hurt him. "When Mum spoke to me through the sword, do you know what she said about you?"

He leaned forward. "Tell me."

My voice was cold. "Nothing. She said nothing. Because you're supposed to live up to her memory, and you are utterly failing."

"Hang on a minute, Alisha," said Dad. "Don't put words into your dead mother's mouth."

Sahil shook his head. "Harsh, sis. That was harsh."

Echo growled. "It's hardly a surprise. Once an imbecile, always an imbecile."

Alma clutched her hands together. "Actually, I'm a firm

believer that people can change. Perhaps we all need a little time. Although it would be a shame to make no concrete progress today."

She poked Dad in the ribs.

Dad winced and then spluttered to life. "Rajiv, since you're here, Alma thought you might like to take a look at my studio, and we could throw some paint at a canvas together."

"Or at each other." Rajiv's weathered face softened, whether with malice or appreciation, I could not tell.

I left them to it, turned my back on Sahil and headed out into the garden. There, Gaia continued with her security preparations. The koi chirped at her command as if she were the conductor of nature's orchestra, and the exterior of the house had been doused in so much flour that it looked like it belonged in a bakery.

I found a quiet corner and looked furtively around before dialling the foxes.

Faeza answered on the third ring. "Alisha."

My heart pounded. "Did you get it? Did you find the Jericho necklace?"

A long pause. "We need to speak in person."

6

The bell jangled as Ezra and I entered Fei Yen and Faeza's tea and occult shop, Shanghai Moon, and a wave of musty and cloying scents overcame us. Around the corner, my old flat remained empty and full of light. Unlike the cottage I shared with Ezra, which was now shrouded in darkness. I swallowed the growing disquiet in my belly.

At the counter, Fei Yen looked up in her white pharmacist's coat and smiled a hello. She'd been growing her hair out recently, and it fell in silken, black strands to her shoulders, making her look younger than her fifty years. The shop bustled with half a dozen commuters passing on their way home from Balham tube station. Some shopped for exotic teas, others browsed the crystal display or booked in for a tarot reading, but by far the most popular service offered was Chinese herbal remedies. I spotted the detective in the queue, waiting for Faeza to serve him, just as a familiar set of arms closed around my waist.

Marina squeezed me. "I was going to pop around later. Just to prove to myself that you're in one piece. How dare that cow mess up your love nest."

Ezra growled. "It's enough to wish we were ordinary humdrums."

She gave his arm a playful punch. "You don't mean that. What are you two doing here?"

"Actually, it's us three," I said. "Echo's sulking outside until the crowds clear. What are *you* doing here?"

"Faeza's been concocting an elixir to heal Rob's mind. It's really helping. He's much less foggy, and I think Faeza put in a special something just for me." Her dark, waggling eyebrows contrasted with the pink, purple and blue of her hair. "He has extra pep in the bedroom. Which is quite something, given his workload at the moment. Usually, he'd be flat on his back, snoring on the sofa before I've had time to slip into something more comfortable. Finally, I've been able to shake the dust off my favourite bedroom outfits."

Ezra grinned. "You should take a leaf out of Marina's book, hellfire. Next time I'm asleep on the sofa, I expect a rude wake-up call in a maid's outfit."

I whacked his bottom because touching that peach made any day better. When the shop had quietened, Echo joined us, grumbling at the thousand scents that teased him in Shanghai Moon, from essential oils and incense sticks to meaty mushrooms, Tiger Balm and sweet teas. Fei Yen turned the sign on the front door and locked it to give us some privacy.

Faeza swayed over to the stairwell and called up to their flat. "You can come down now. The coast is clear."

Echo growled low and long, and I raised my hands in alarm as a shadow tumbled into the shop from the stairwell leading up to the foxes' flat. My frown transformed into a whoop for joy as Flinar the elf appeared, dressed in a child's hoodie and tracksuit bottoms, all big grey ears, stocky body and knobbly limbs. Shanghai Moon had been a haven for him since the most recent attempt to purge the elves.

He shook his triangular head and blew out his full lips, his milky eyes wide. "Too many humdrums. I had to hide, but I was worried you would leave without saying hello, Alisha."

I swept him into my arms, trying hard not to baby him. He was a grown man, after all, despite his small frame and childlike ways. A grown man who had become an ambassador for the elven community since they had wrongly been scapegoated for causing tremors in the city.

Scapegoated by Phinnaeous Shine and those who repeatedly ostracised the elves after Meriel Naehorn had waged war during the Battle of the Celestial Library.

I resisted the urge to pat his wispy hair back into place. "I'm so proud of you. You're a leader, Flinar. You've done such good work with the elves. They look up to you. They are thriving because of you. If I had my way, you'd receive a knighthood or a Wildwoods Medal of Honour."

Marina giggled. "You could put it in your loo like Alisha does."

Rob and Ezra shook the elf's hand, pumping hard, as the elf basked in their approval.

Flinar's huge ears billowed like sails as if he tried to soak up every last drop of compliment. Peculiars didn't often praise the elves. Call it history or leadership or a downright inability to unlink what one elf had done and with the potential of her whole community.

"Me?" He hiccupped and then smiled shyly, revealing poor dental work. "I just did what anyone would do."

"From what I'm hearing, crime has been dropping in that community," said Rob.

Ezra nodded. "That's in no small part to your rehabilitation of them, Flinar."

The elf's milky eyes filled with tears as he turned to me. "I am taking an elven class on a trip to Stonehenge with Rayna Willowsun next week. I'd be honoured if you would like to come with us, Alisha. It would be an honour for the eternal girl to show faith in the elven community."

Echo lifted his nose into the air. "The elf wants to parade your friendship for all the world to see, Alisha."

I laughed. "Let him parade me. We *are* friends. I would love to come. I've not been to Stonehenge since I was a teenager."

Flinar's excitement burst out of his little body. He danced a jig, jumping from foot to foot. "Oh, I can't wait to see their faces."

Faeza added some seats around the tarot table for us to gather. "Enough fangirling, Flinar. Sit down, everyone."

We did as we were told, but I couldn't help unleashing my inner teacher. The foxes were still students in my English class, after all. "Fangirls is a great word."

Fei Yen poured jasmine tea into bone china cups for us. "We've been watching a lot of K-pop in bed at night. We are fangirls. It is our guilty pleasure. We might only have eyes for each other, but the catchy tunes and dance moves are so fun to learn. Soon, we will have a K-pop karaoke night, and you are all invited."

Ezra rolled his eyes. "God help us."

"I have yet to learn this K-pop, but I'm in," Echo purred.

"First things first. We have much to tell you," said the foxes in unison, as if they were two halves of the same soul.

My pulse fluttered in my throat. "Don't keep me waiting any longer. Did you manage to find the necklace?"

Fei Yen shook her head. "I wish we could give you the answer you've been waiting for."

My heart sank. "You didn't get it?"

Faeza reached for her wife's hand. "We've let you down. We searched high and low in your brother's penthouse, but it must have been at one of his other properties. We looked everywhere. Even in his cutlery drawer and in the special room he has filled with glass cabinets for his childhood trophies."

Echo gave a honk of laughter. "When he was a boy, he

even celebrated peeing inside the toilet ring. Rosalie and Joshi gave him a sweetie every time because he often hit the wall." A heavy sigh. "When I display my exemplary urination skills in a variety of environments, I don't even get a scrap of fish as a reward."

Marina gave him a sympathetic scratch behind his ears.

In my mind's eye, I sped through the properties I knew of. "We can't break into every single one of Sahil's properties without alerting him to what we are doing."

I wanted to keep this pseudo-war between us under wraps. Not least because poor Dad would be in turmoil if he found out that the mistrust between his children had reached a fever pitch.

"How about I get a warrant?" said Rob. "Technically, he stole the damn thing."

Marina played with the cross at her neck. "I could go to the Celestial Library and try to rework the process using a different jewel. It might work."

"There's no time. That could take weeks. Or forever. You'd have to start again with even less groundwork than Mum had put in place for you." I reached under my jacket for my sword, willing Mum to talk to me. To tell me what to do.

But the sword was silent.

Fei Yen sipped her tea, zen-like, in contrast to my inner turmoil. "We can't help with the gods or with Phinnaeous Shine, but we can help with your brother. Let us poke around a bit. Nobody notices foxes in London. It was one of the reasons we chose to come here when we left China. We are as common as double-decker buses and pigeon splatters."

Faeza stared at her, aghast. "Did you just compare us to pigeon splatters? You're right, of course. As outsiders, we can't help Alisha with her Wildwoods problem, but this city is ours. We know it like we know the lines on our palms. You are more than our teacher, Alisha. You are our friend. Let us help. Just give us a bit more time."

I appreciated their offer, but wasn't Sahil my problem to solve? I flicked my gaze to Ezra and Marina, looking for counsel, but they shrugged. I took a deep breath. "Okay. Find the necklace if you can, but avoid any dangerous situations. My conscience couldn't handle it if anything happened to you. And Echo is tagging along."

Emerald eyes on mine. "I am?" The leopard shuddered. "Fox dens are horrific things compared to the fertile plains and golden sands of India. Still, I promised once to do the bidding of worthy Vermas. And if that means I obey one and spit in the eye of another, then so be it. But perhaps you should bring along some marinated cubes of steak."

Fei Yen and Faeza bowed their heads. "We will not disappoint."

Flinar's leathery, four-fingered hand reached for mine. "Now you can concentrate on the Prime Sorcerer."

I swallowed hard. "I can't shoulder every fight, Flinar. The senate will deal with the Prime Sorcerer. There's a new goddess on the scene. I have to focus on her."

Flinar's nostrils flared. "I know about her. All the elves do. Our black holes are all topsy-turvy. Up is down. Down is up. We make a black hole in front of us, and it ends up behind us or not there at all. Like doors are being closed and opened everywhere to confuse us." He sniffed. "But that's beside the point. Phinnaeous Shine thought the elves were bad eggs, and you stood up against him. You can't walk away now. I've been telling the elves that, one day, we will all be as welcome at Wildwoods as everyone else. All the outsiders will have a chance. Because of you, Alisha. Because the minute you arrived in our lives, it was as if the universe skipped a beat. The old patterns could be changed. As if the possibilities of the universe swirled around you."

Marina frowned. "That's a lot of responsibility for one person to carry, Flinar."

"Rajika Verma carried a heavy load and did it with great aplomb," Echo purred.

I clenched my fists. I knew how much I could handle and was fast approaching my limit. Why couldn't my friends accept a *no* at face value? Sure, it was nice to feel important, but it was better to feel heard. I might be the best person for the job, but I wasn't the only one in a position to face up to Phinnaeous Shine. If the Prime Sorcerer had abused his power and trust had irrevocably broken down, the senate had rules and processes to deal with it. They could leave me out of it.

All I wanted was to keep my bloody sword and focus on the real threat: Cardea.

Rob leaned forward, his dark eyes troubled. "Flinar is right. I have lived and breathed London's Otherworld and Wildwoods for five years. Managing Phinnaeous Shine out of his position as Prime Sorcerer was never going to be easy. Ezra and Orpheus— in some circumstances even Lavinia and Rayna, together with Calypso if she can leave the Celestial Library—are great counterweights to Phinnaeous. But the rest of the senate is quite clearly with him. It's going to take an escalation to oust him. You might not be able to keep your hands clean, Alisha. I have the feeling that all of us will get a little dirty by the end of this."

Fei Yen placed her cup on the saucer, every word imbued with quiet passion. "Doing the right things is never easy. It often takes sacrifice. Sometimes, it's a hungry mother giving her child the last piece of bread. Sometimes, it's a man who stands up to bullies on the tube, even though he knows he will be in the firing line. Sometimes, it's leaving your beloved home and starting over. Where would we all be if good people looked the other way when they saw wrongdoing?"

I bit my lip. "Yeah, well, maybe I'm not willing to make sacrifices anymore."

Mum hadn't been ready but still stepped into the fight.

And she paid with her life. I wasn't prepared to pay with blood for things I had been pulled into.

Rob's Adam's apple bobbed in his throat. "Alisha, the Prime Minister didn't react when I briefed against Phinnaeous. In fact, Phinnaeous was in 10 Downing Street just this morning, having a tête-à-tête with the PM after his protégé became the PM's new private secretary. From what I can piece together, the PM's former private secretary had a dodgy curry at lunch and went to relieve himself inside the Downing Street offices. But he never came out. Could be diarrhoea. Or foul play. Anyway, without a competent private secretary, the PM's office was in such a predicament that, when Phinnaeous called and happened to have a suitable candidate ready, they jumped at the chance."

My brows knitted together. "Who was the candidate, Rob?"

"A peculiar from the Shine Foundation for the Advancement of Peculiars and Humdrums."

Ezra swore under his breath. "You've got to be kidding me. I can't help thinking that Wildwoods being given a chess makeover this term is a sign that Phinnaeous is already ten moves ahead of us, and we are playing catch-up."

"It could be just a coincidence," said Marina.

Rob shook his head. "Something's wrong. There should have been a reaction to my briefing by now."

"It could be your writing is so boring that the PM fell asleep." Echo's emerald eyes twinkled in mirth. "Not everyone has the gift."

Rob grunted. "More like someone found my briefing inconvenient. I can't get close to the PM's office, yet Shine is closer than ever before. What if Shine's guy in the PM's office pulled my briefing from the pipeline?"

Ezra raked his hands through his hair. "The only way to unravel Phinnaeous's secrets is by stealth. We'll need to take him by surprise."

"I can follow him. I might be the most striking creature in London, but in my Bengal cat form, I can blend into any environment," said Echo.

"Your job is to watch over Fei Yen and Faeza," I said. "How about the pack, Ezra? Can't the seekers help?"

"It has to be someone else. Someone he won't suspect." Ezra stood up with a jerk. "And I know who."

I locked eyes with Ezra, expression grim. "I'm coming with you."

Ezra's lips were a thin line as he reached out his hand to me, and I stepped into the circle of his arms.

Flinar's wrinkled grey face softened. "I knew from the moment I met you that you'd stand up for us, Alisha. The elven lives are tied up with yours. Phinnaeous Shine drove us to the edges of the Otherworld. You have to punish him. Otherwise, all your power is for nothing."

"No, Flinar," I said. "I'm on your side, but this is Ezra's fight, not mine."

Flinar's little grey nose twitched. "Then you will fail."

I gave a sad smile as I took in all their faces and adjusted the sword on my back. My beautiful leopard with his scarred face and soft coat. My rainbow-haired best friend and the detective. The foxes, willing to put themselves on the line for our friendship. And small, brave Flinar, who hadn't had an easy life but still hoped for more.

When Ezra pulled me into the folds between the worlds, I wondered if I could ever live up to their expectations of me.

7

———

zra's hard chest crushed against my soft curves as we ricocheted through the universe. He towered over me, strong arms tender around the small of my back, curving me into his pelvis as if nothing else mattered but my safety. I didn't know where he was taking us, but our destination was irrelevant.

I'd follow him to the ends of the Earth if he needed me to.

But whatever Rob and Flinar said, it wasn't my place to challenge Phinnaeous. It was Ezra's. He was the Justice Minister, after all, which made it all the more curious when we emerged in a side street in Green Park, a stone's throw away from The Ritz Hotel. Where the former Justice Minister, Ezra's uncle and former alpha Gunnolf, languished in the dungeons.

I caught my breath—teleporting no longer made me vomit, but it still turned my insides to jelly—and frowned at Ezra. "Now's not exactly a good time to visit Gunnolf."

Ezra's grey eyes darkened. "It's exactly the right time. Rob's right. The senate is divided on this. And Flinar's right, too. I want to tell you to stay out of this, Alisha. But the truth is, I don't think this is a fight we can afford for you to stay out of. Phinnaeous is a vengeful man but also unpredictable. As good in a boardroom as a battlefield. Part of me wants us to stay cocooned in our cottage. But my father taught me the words of the *Pirkei Avot* when I was very young. We should not be daunted by the enormity of the world's grief. We are not obligated to complete it, nor are we free to abandon it. I have an idea that might work. The quickest way to sort this out is to unleash a lone wolf."

My eyes widened. "You want to release Gunnolf? He'll never agree to that. They were friends."

"Once perhaps, but Gunnolf has found himself pretty friendless since his sentence was passed. He's had not one visitor other than me. I think he'll help. He's got nothing to lose. It's not just the mental strain. He's going stir-crazy in there. It's agony for him. He's looking at decades of confinement or the chance to soak up the moonlight or run in the woods again. I know what I'd choose."

I frowned. "But Lavinia cast a binding spell that night at Wildwoods. He couldn't even turn into a werewolf if he wanted to."

Emblazoned in my memory was Lavinia drawing blood from a cowed Gunnolf after his trial with the spike of her umbrella, how she soaked a scrap of his own clothing in the drawn blood and then cast a spell, there and then, in the arena. How the blood-soaked ribbon burst into flames and left clumps of ash. How Gunnolf's body crumpled to think he'd never run free as a wolf again.

Ezra pulled out a small vial from his pocket and held it up to the cool, wintery light. Amber liquid sloshed inside it, thick with clumps of black fur. "My aunt always has contingencies built in. She made an antidote that very night and stored it away at the coven flat. I picked it out of her bedroom the night of the coven dinner while you were with Rayna." He gave a weak smile. "She might think she knows all the secrets in the city, but she forgets the rats see me as one of the family and talk to me too."

I stared at him. "You've considered breaking him out before. Ezra, I knew you missed him, but I didn't think you'd do that."

He slipped the vial into his pocket and reached for me. "I toyed with the idea, maybe. I even manoeuvred it so I'd have the option, but I never considered it until this week." He threaded his fingers through the back of my head and pulled me towards him. His kiss was rough and angry, then deepened, ending on a tender note that made my heart ache. "Phinnaeous came after you, Alisha. He came after our friends. I have to take a risk to bring him down."

"You're bending the rules for me?"

"So what if I am? I've been tossing it over in my head for days, and I keep coming to the same conclusion. Sometimes, justice doesn't take place in a court of law, all tidy and wrapped up in a bow. Sometimes, it's messy and takes place in the shadows."

I swallowed hard. "He might be your surrogate dad, but he deserves all he got. If you let him out, you'll be accused of favouritism. Of breaking the law yourself. What about all the victims that died at his hand? You'd be stealing their justice." My breath hitched in my chest. "Ezra, I don't want you to end up in the same position as Gunnolf."

His body stilled, and I knew then that he had doubts too.

"Ah, hellfire," he started, "I'm not going to lie. This could go horribly wrong. There's no parole board to assess whether Gunnolf should be let out. Otherworld justice is crude. Who even knows if I'll be able to get him back into that dungeon when this is all over? But it's his chance for redemption, you know? I owe him that. He murdered those wolves because he was scared of losing his alpha position. Well, he's well and truly lost it now. There's nothing to kill for. And we need someone to figure out what Shine's up to by stealth."

Fear crept into the corners of my vision, blocking out the bustle of the London street, leaving only Ezra. "What if he tries to kill you? Without you, he'd still be alpha."

Emotion thickened his voice. "He wouldn't do that. He wants to earn back my trust. It's not just because he brought me up or that he loves me. It's because I'm his alpha. When I visit him, I can see he has accepted it. He would die for me."

My chest tightened with nerves. "I hope you're right."

"I should do this alone." Grey eyes darted to my sword. "But after what happened at the cottage…"

"We go together." I hoped we didn't live to regret this.

We had acted spontaneously before and won, but this seemed like a renegade act. Moreover, it seemed to be the work of criminals.

He took my hand and pulled me across the street, stopping to pick up a pasty from a newsagent.

"It's not for me," he said at my quizzical look before leading me through the arched honey-stoned façade of The Ritz and past a po-faced doorman. We crossed the floor of the chandeliered hall, passing sumptuous flower arrangements, and stepped into the panelled lift with its paintings of society ladies.

When a giggling couple in their twenties tried to share our lift, Ezra's gravelly voice brooked no argument, his alpha coming to the fore. "Take the next one."

The couple pranced backwards like skittish deer, and the doors closed.

A nerve throbbed in Ezra's jaw as he pressed an unmarked button on the lift panel. Once, twice, three times.

"Hold on." He urged me back against the wall of the lift, his body covering mine just before the lift plummeted and my stomach with it.

I suppressed a whimper of surprise and held on for dear life, bracing myself against the falling box, my nails digging into Ezra's forearms. The Otherworld wasn't like the humdrum reality. It wasn't calendars, bank accounts, supermarket shops, teacher meetings, dinner dates and bedsheets that smelt of fabric conditioner. It was grittier than that. It was hidden foes in basements, shapeshifting wizards with shadowy objectives, witches who could strip you to your essence with makeshift ingredients, a spell and a cackle, and buttons in plain sight that could drop you a hundred feet. Werewolves who sometimes gave in to their animal nature.

The lift jerked to a halt, and the doors shuddered open.

Ezra bent his lips to my ear, his murmur sending vibrations through me. "He'll try to rile you. Don't give him the satisfaction."

Our footsteps tapped against the stone floor of the basement as we made our way across the vast expanse of the basement, which appeared to split into quadrants. Flickering bulbs emitted low light, and a generator hummed. This world —dark, damp and colourless—was entirely different to the luxury of the hotel. We hurried past rows of blue iron doors without prisoner names or windows, deadbolted at the top, bottom and middle.

"How many prisoners are on the books?" I asked.

"A hundred and thirty, perhaps. Maybe more. It's not the sort of place where you have a census."

I leapt in fright as a projectile clanged against a cell door.

He cupped my elbow. "Just keep moving. Once the throwing starts, everyone joins in."

Right on cue, a great thumping broke out all around us. The eruption of shouts and missiles could surely be heard in the hotel upstairs.

I winced. "Where are the guards?"

"A magical prison doesn't need guards. All it needs is a willing coven, a handful of spells, and the odd life-or-death check. The practices here are archaic. A little torture, scraps of food—just enough so the body doesn't shut down—and no rehabilitation." He grimaced. "Come on. The high-value prisoners are just down here."

We came to the final two doors, both red.

Ezra lifted the deadbolts. "Ready?"

I nodded and followed him into the cell, my eyes taking a moment to adjust to the dim light and shifting shadows within. A man sat on a sparse bed, his body curved like a question mark. My nose wrinkled. The cell stank of squalor. A toilet stood in the corner next to a sink. The bristly toothbrush, more suited to clean the toilet than teeth, had seen better days. The tap dripped, audible in the silence of the cell.

It would have driven me crazy.

The man spoke. "Nephew." His eyes spat fire at me. "You brought the druid."

"I did." Ezra handed him the pasty and laid a gentle hand on his bony shoulder.

The man tore open the wrapper and ate without manners or dignity until he had consumed every crumb. Once, Gunnolf had been a grizzled bear of a man, tall and heavy set, with a fiery temper and a penchant for denim. Now, he sat in greying cotton, his body halved in size, reeking of piss and sweat. His hair had greyed, and his once groomed beard had become tufty against his black skin. His wolf had been stolen, but his human body had withered too. He wiped his forearm, with its slack skin, across his mouth. Then he dragged himself across the cell to the dripping tap and lowered his mouth to suck its meagre supply, all pride stripped away.

Despite all he had done—his murderous ways, his manipulation of the pack, his imprisonment of me—I couldn't help but feel sorry for him.

Gunnolf returned to the bed and looked longingly at the empty pasty wrapper before turning empty eyes on us.

"Once, I wanted to tear your skin from your bones, druid," His voice, once a commanding boom, was as dry as sandpaper. "But months in this hell have left me speaking to my own shadow. I find myself strangely grateful to see your face. Maybe I would have acted differently with you had I known you were the eternal girl." He sounded contrite, but true change came from making amends, not just pretty words.

"Ezra told you," I said.

There were untold depths in those black eyes. "He is a good nephew. Despite the sins of his uncle." His mouth twisted in self-pity. "How the tides turn. I longed for power, and now all I crave is the moonlight."

"Much as it pains me, this is not a family reunion," said Ezra. "We have an offer for you."

Interest sparked in that crafty old wolf's eyes. "I would tell you I don't have all day. But that would be a lie. Tell me, is it my adopted son who makes the offer, the pack alpha or the Justice Minister?"

Power pulsed from Ezra. The copper flecks in his eyes glimmered, and the cell seemed even smaller with his sheer power. "You won't get this chance again."

Gunnolf shrank back. A little crack appeared in his voice of both self-pity and acceptance. "So the alpha then. What do you need?"

"Phinnaeous Shine is acting in a way not befitting his office. First, he falsely maligned the elves. Then, the night of your sentencing, he fled Wildwoods, though it was under attack. He disrupted the mind of a humdrum ally, the detective from Shadow Squad. Now, he has turfed half the senate out of Wildwoods for voting against his attempt to take possession of Alisha's sword. He is becoming increasingly dangerous—"

A bark of laughter, much like the old Gunnolf. The one who had told me to clean the farmhouse and shifted into his burly black wolf to intimidate me. The one who had killed younger, stronger wolves without a whisper of warning. Was that a gleam of satisfaction I saw in his eyes?

"Who has that shapeshifting wizard cast out?" Gunnolf asked.

"Lavinia. Rayna. Orpheus. Me," said Ezra quietly.

Gunnolf chuckled. "It's not easy being ostracised, is it, nephew? But then that's a lesson you know well." A pause. "Why don't you take back your rightful place by force and storm Wildwoods?"

"Because we haven't reached that point yet. You know as well as I do that aggression is not always the answer," said Ezra.

A smirk. "Or maybe you just down have the balls for it, boy. You want me to kill that old goat, don't you? You wager I've already got blood on my hands, and you want to keep yours clean. That's the difference between us. I know how to see things through. Even if I pay dearly for it."

"No, that's not what we are asking. We aren't condoning murder." I had a right mind to call a whirlwind and leave his sorry behind spinning in it.

Gunnolf smiled. "Aren't you? How quaint you are, Alisha Verma, like those parasoled ladies on the lift that brought me down into this hell. The Otherworld is a murderous place. If you're not willing to get your hands dirty, you won't last long."

Ezra growled, his wolf close to the surface. "You will not murder him, however he provokes you. You will stick to the shadows, follow him, light of foot, uncover the secrets we are missing. That is all. Your actions have shown how underhanded you are. And your imprisonment means he won't suspect you. Will you do this for me?"

"You don't call me uncle anymore," said Gunnolf.

Ezra folded his arms across his chest, silent.

Deep down, I knew he loved Gunnolf, but the men were

at an impasse. There could be no coming back from what Gunnolf had done.

A nod of understanding. "Message received, loud and clear. What's in it for me, nephew? Why should I help you?"

Ezra sank his hand into the pocket for the vial. "Do you want a chance to run in the moonlight or not?"

A swift intake of breath. "That concoction would return my ability to shift?"

"Yes. Yes, it would," said Ezra.

Gunnolf lunged for it. "Give it to me."

Ezra barged him with his shoulder, sending the older, now weaker man flying back onto the bed. "Why must you take when I am willing to give?"

A sigh. "Old habits die hard. How will you get me out of here?"

"We came in the old-fashioned way," said Ezra. "But we'll be teleporting out. At least, you will be. I'll take you outside and then return for Alisha so that we can pass the CCTV cameras. Call it a precaution, just in case your cell is discovered empty. We were here visiting you, that's all."

"You were always our best seeker and the brightest spark in the pack." A flash of admiration in Gunnolf's dark eyes, quickly replaced by wariness. "I can't come back here."

"I'm giving you a week, Gunnolf. Then I'll come to find you to bring you back." Steel laced Ezra's voice. "But you have my word. If the intelligence you provide results in Phinnaeous's downfall, I will lobby the senate for your release. You won't be able to return to the pack or the farmhouse, but you can start a new life in another city on the proviso of a blood bond to never take another's life again."

A raised eyebrow. "My nephew wants me never even to take a rat or rabbit's life again. Hardly seems a fair deal."

I shot him a scathing look. "I advised Ezra against this deal altogether, so I'd count your lucky stars."

"What's your decision?" Ezra held the vial between his

thumb and forefinger, tipping the golden liquid back and forth, tantalising Gunnolf, but we both knew he'd take the bait. What other choice did he have?

Gunnolf grimaced. "Give me a light."

Ezra lit a roll-up, took a drag and then passed it to his uncle.

"What if I get caught?" Gunnolf put the cigarette to his lips, inhaled deeply and puffed the smoke back into the cell.

Ezra's voice reverberated with sadness. "Then I can't protect you. The truth is, you deserve whatever comes your way."

A scowl. "There speaks the Justice Minister. Maybe you are as cold as me after all, Ezra."

"You know as well as I do that justice doesn't always have to be public. Sometimes it is quick and dirty and hidden from sight," said Ezra.

A shiver ran up my spine, twisted thorns of foreboding. I wasn't sure this was the right thing to do, but didn't a relationship mean trusting each other, even if we didn't agree? Gunnolf's fate wasn't my call to make.

Gunnolf's face hardened as he cast his eyes around the windowless cell. His eyes found me—curiosity where there had once been malice—and finally came to rest on Ezra. His expression softened before he dropped the cigarette on the stone floor and ground it out. "What the hell, I'll do it. But can you live with the consequences, Ezra? You're making me a fugitive and yourself a criminal."

Ezra's body grew still. There was no doubt we stood at a precipice. "It's temporary."

He thrust the vial at Gunnolf quickly, almost so he wouldn't change his mind.

The vial seemed smaller still in Gunnolf's hands. He regarded the amber liquid with its tufts of black fur. "The witch Lavinia concocted this." A bitter laugh. "I'd know her handiwork anywhere."

Ezra nodded.

"I've missed my wolf." Gunnolf's voice bristled with emotion.

"Drink up, and you'll be whole again," said Ezra.

Gunnolf lifted a sardonic eyebrow as he uncorked the potion. "The things you do for love." When he drank the potion, his mouth contorted in disgust. He tossed the empty vial aside. "How do I know it's worked?"

"I'll set you loose in Hyde Park so you can give that black beast of yours a trial run." Ezra held out a hand. "Let's get out of here."

"I've not held your hand since you were a boy." A pause. "You've never offered to teleport me before, nephew. Why now?"

Ezra's mouth was a grim line. "What can I say? It's a day for firsts."

"Hopefully not lasts." Gunnolf turned shrewd, tired eyes on me. "Goodbye, druid. This can't have been easy for you. As a peace offering, I have a piece of information for you. The other high-value prisoner in here, two doors down, is none other than Meriel Naehorn, once Queen of the Dark Elves. Of course, there's nothing queenly about her nowadays, but she's still fearsome."

Goosebumps ran up my arms. "How do you know this?"

A wry twist of his mouth. He dropped Ezra's hand. "You forget, I was Justice Minister once, before my beloved nephew overthrew me. Meriel was there the night darkness last swept through the Otherworld during the Battle of the Celestial Library. The night your grandmother died protecting the book in the prophecy."

I frowned. "A disintegrating tome lost to the world…"

His eyes gleamed. "Precisely. Your place in the prophecy is more than fate. It's more than an entanglement of Verma women. I can sense it."

"Where's the book, Gunnolf?" I asked. "What kind of book is it?"

He splayed his hands. "You think I haven't tried to prise it from the prisoner? We know Meriel didn't leave the library with it. Rajika Verma did her job. It's the reason she's most celebrated of all the Custodians of the Celestial Library. She faced down the enemy with barely an ally to aid her. The defences tell us the book remains within those great halls. Yet, somehow, it has remained hidden from all subsequent Custodians, even Calypso."

My brow knotted together. If the book was key to the prophecy, why hadn't Gaia told me about its whereabouts? Why, too, had Calypso kept stumm? "The Celestial Library is a tricky place. It's very trusting and prone to secrets. There is a reason why it has kept the book safe. I'm sure of it."

"I came to that conclusion too, druid," said Gunnolf. "Your grandmother can no longer speak to us, but Meriel shields secrets of her own. We kept her alive in case she could one day be persuaded to tell the truth. But torture only made her more determined to keep her lips sealed."

"Funny that," said Ezra.

Gunnolf scoffed. "You're hardly a paragon of virtue, nephew."

"My role models were a little wanting," snapped Ezra.

"I've had a lot of thinking time in here. It makes me wonder what would have happened to Meriel Naehorn's secrets if we hadn't made the elves the enemy. Perhaps the Otherworld would be a different place." He launched a gloop of spittle on the floor. Then he unzipped his trousers, took out his schlong and sprayed the cell liberally as if his penis were a fireman's hose.

Revolted, I turned my eyes away, but there was no blocking the splashes out. "For a minute, I thought you were advocating making the Otherworld a better place, Gunnolf."

His laugh reverberated around the cell, rejuvenated by the thought of freedom. "Oh, it's too late for me."

Ezra cupped his elbow. "Enough of this child's play. We must go. Time waits for no man."

"Never a truer word spoken," said Gunnolf.

"Good luck, Gunnolf," I said.

"And you, eternal girl."

They disappeared between the worlds, leaving me alone in the stinky cell, mere metres away from the woman who had killed my grandmother.

8

______

While Ezra was gone, I gingerly stepped through the pungent puddles to retrieve the discarded vial and cork. It wouldn't do to leave any evidence of our presence there. With any luck, if anyone did check on the prisoner and found him missing, it would seem he had evaporated in a cloud of piss.

I was sure stranger things had happened in the Otherworld.

The air shifted behind me as Ezra returned, mountain air and earthiness filling my nostrils. I swivelled, welcoming his familiar presence in such a wretched place. "That must have been hard. Are you okay?"

His handsome face was pale and strained. "I hope it gives us the upper hand."

I hugged him. "Did you see him shift?"

"It makes me wonder if we have to strip people of their dignity to serve justice." He murmured into my hair, "Let's get out of here." He drew away, plucked the vial from my hands and dropped it into his pocket.

I bit my lip. "Ezra…"

He scanned my face. "No, hellfire. Absolutely not. It's not

a good idea for us to swan into another prisoner's cell. We've already taken one too many risks today. We'll be found out."

"You're still Justice Minister, Ezra." I arched an eyebrow. "Phinnaeous Shine might have banned you from Wildwoods, but as far as I know, Rayna's the only one he's stripped of her position and even that is questionable without a majority senate agreement. Besides, no one will take her word for it, even if she says she saw us."

He clenched his fists. "Alisha, she's dangerous."

I shrugged. "We deal with danger all the time. We'll be fine. I take it her magic has been stripped?"

"Her black hole magic, yes. But you can't strip someone's cunning or their warrior instincts. And Naehorn was the best warrior the elves had. She proved herself against their fiercest men." He paused. "You must hate her for your grandmother's murder. How do you know you'll be able to hold yourself in check?"

I suppressed the shiver of fear that ran through my body. For all I'd been compared to Rajika Verma, I had no real memory of her. "I was so young when my grandmother died. Mum and Dad avoided speaking about her, so in many ways, I know her through Otherworld legends. That is all. She didn't bake cookies with me or braid my hair. She didn't have me for sleepovers or walk me to school. The thing that connects us is Echo. And I can never really see her through his eyes because, to him, she was a saint, not a real person who was capable of flaws. And Dad… he's too fragile still for me to poke around in the past. So you see, what I feel about the whole thing is more like an emotional emptiness. Hatred is a living, breathing thing. What I feel for Meriel Naehorn is nothing."

He sighed. "My answer is still no."

"I'm not asking permission. I'm asking for backup. Your love and worry don't override our need to find out Meriel's secret. Not after what Gunnolf said."

"My father used to say that love overrode everything." His jaw tightened. "If there's no dissuading you, I guess we better get it over with."

I squeezed his calloused hand. "Thank you."

Momentary relief swelled in me as we left Gunnolf's cell, only for it to be punctured as we faced another red door.

"It's this one." Ezra unlocked the deadbolt. "Are you ready?"

Of course, as Justice Minister, he knew she'd been here all along. I couldn't help thinking that Orpheus wouldn't have kept this from me. For all his vampire stoicism with everyone else, he was an open book with me.

I gave Ezra a weak smile. "As I'll ever be."

I had heard Naehorn's name whispered a thousand times since my druid awakening. The whispers varied in tone. There was awe, fear and even a frisson of excitement. It was a name that lingered on the lips of Otherworld mothers schooling their misbehaving young. *Choose wisely, dear child, lest you grow up to be like dark queen Meriel Naehorn, imprisoned for her crimes against the Otherworld. Wouldn't you rather be Rajika Verma, true of heart and courageous until the end?*

Maybe if Naehorn had been executed, her legend would have been cut short. Instead, it grew, a thorny, nightmarish tale twisting in the minds of all those born into magic, Naehorn's imprisonment making her story more monstrous still. Had she grown claws to match her whip-smart tongue? Who did she blame for her downfall? Did she seek revenge all these years later?

As I pushed open the door with Ezra on my heels, none of those questions mattered.

Only one thing did. The book my grandmother had died protecting.

I blinked as we walked into a blinding light, my heart ricocheting. Ezra closed the door behind us as I got my bearings. This wasn't the dimly lit, mucky dungeon Gunnolf had dwelled in. The space, though small and equally windowless, had a hundred bulbs hanging from the ceiling, each emitting an angry buzz. No putrid smells. The bed was sparse but tidy, and a small stack of letters lay in the middle of it. But it was the walls that caught my attention. The prisoner had carved her first name into the walls. Spots of dull red sullied the grooves as if, without tools at her disposal, she had used her own nails to make painstaking progress. An attempt to make a permanent mark on something when the world had all but erased you.

The once elf-queen lay curled in a ball on the stone floor.

She looked up with bloodshot blue eyes. Whereas Flinar's skin was a dull grey, hers had a translucent silver quality. As if, regardless of circumstances, she had a fire in her veins. A mettle few others could match. Shorter and slighter than Flinar, with matted, grey curls wild about her bony shoulders, she wore a coarsely cut beige dress that might as well have been a potato sack. She rose in jerky movements, adopting a serene smile with a touch of crazy that I didn't trust one bit.

"There's no one there. Not a single soul." She had a paper-thin voice no longer capable of a battle cry. "I won't fall for your tricks."

Her nose twitched, and she looked through us.

All logic flew out of my mind. I suddenly grew fearful that she could sniff out my secrets or had other powers I hadn't accounted for. Ones even Ezra hadn't known about. What did we really know about her other than rumours and intrigue? Even Orpheus's history lessons provided mere glimpses of Meriel Naehorn. Like she was a mythical beast that had been locked in a cave and only grew stronger and more virulent. A pathogen. A toxin. A poison.

I pictured my grandmother's lifeless body in the Celestial Library. I heard Echo's howls of pain, envisaged Dad crumpled in grief and Rajiv being robbed of the chance to reconcile with his sister.

Ezra poked my back, bringing me out of my head and back into my body. "Have you got this?"

I nodded and focussed my attention on my grandmother's murderer.

She was flesh and bone. A captive animal with neither magic nor weapons here in the basement of The Ritz.

"We have some questions for you." My voice jittered, and I cursed myself for it.

Naehorn's vacant eyes roamed over me. "Questions. They all have questions. Never kindness, though. Only questions."

I frowned, stepping forward. "We won't take much of your time."

The elf shrank back. "You're *her*. You're Rajika. How have you not aged? I killed you once. I killed you a thousand times in my nightmares." Her face hardened. "I can do it again. I mean it. Stay away."

"She's not in her right mind. We should go." Ezra turned to go.

I touched his arm. "No. Wait. I need to try."

Naehorn rocked on her bare heels. "You are not there. You're a wicked figment of my imagination."

She inched backwards without taking her eyes off us, balled up the sheet on her bed and chucked it at us. I sent it into the corner of the cell with the slightest flick of my hand.

Naehorn mouth slackened. "Hell has come for me at last. This Rajika has wind powers." She held out her wrists. "Take me. I can't beat the devil."

"Meriel..." I called a swirl of wind and, with a balletic movement, guided it around her.

It wove through her matted grey hair and the sack of her dress, and she giggled like a child, though she must have been in her seventies, perhaps older. The winds twisted upwards, clanking the bulbs overhead. Naehorn winced, covering her head as if the sound were sudden gunfire.

She grew mistrustful again, eyes darting around the cell.

"I have longed for someone to say my name again. Are you the devil wearing Rajika's skin?"

"I am her granddaughter. As much flesh and bone as you," I said.

Ezra stiffened. "Careful."

Revealing myself wasn't the cleverest decision I'd made, but sometimes, the only way to get what you needed was to take a risk. I couldn't expect the truth from Naehorn unless I was prepared to be truthful myself. "I'm Alisha Verma, a wind druid."

Meriel sank to the floor and covered her eyes with her four-fingered elven hands. "Prove it. Prove you are not in my mind."

I stepped forward to touch her shoulder, gasping when she clutched my hand with hers. How long had it been since she had known touch? I pulled my hand back, shaken. I could have done with Marina here with us. With her emotional radar, she'd have known how best to approach this conversation.

Instead, all I had was my courage and blundering self.

A flurry of emotions sped across Naehorn's face. Pain, anger and wonder. "It has been a long time since I had a visitor." She knocked on her own head, cackling. "I like visitors. Even the torturers. But they stopped coming, too."

"You killed my grandmother," I said. "You had a whole army with you. She only had her familiar."

"Was it me? Or was it a hallucination?" Naehorn eyed me with suspicion, clearly still weighing up if I was my grandmother or the devil. "Rajika had the whole might of the Celestial Library. She fought well that night."

My voice was cold. "She didn't survive."

An eerie smile played about Naehorn's lips. "Some would say she had the better life. A warrior's death. Her offspring thriving." She leaned forward to peer at me. "Is that you in there, Rajika?"

Urgency pulsed through Ezra's voice. "Alisha, come on. That's enough. Let's go."

"Alisha...Alisha..." Naehorn frowned. "Stay there! Don't come an inch closer."

I sighed and exchanged glances with Ezra. We hadn't moved.

She grabbed the stack of letters on her bed and tossed the first two aside until she found the one she needed. She scanned it and stabbed her finger at the lettering. "Alisha is a friend to the elves. A wolf helped rescue the elves."

"What is that?" I said.

Ezra's voice reverberated around the cell. "I agreed for her to receive a letter once every three months when I became Justice Minister and reviewed the conditions here. She has a cousin who has permission to write under oath of secrecy and prior checks on content. I deliver them myself, under her door. They go only one way. Naehorn herself has no writing utensils." His lips tightened. "I'm sorry, Alisha. It was on a need-to-know basis."

"You don't need to explain," I said.

He didn't owe me details about every aspect of his job, but it still hurt a little that he had kept it from me. I wasn't sure my grandmother's killer deserved that humanity, however harmless she now appeared. Or, indeed, in need of social contact and a psychiatrist.

"You did that." Naehorn looked at Ezra in awe. "You let me hear of the outside world. Why?"

Ezra gave a curt nod. "Because I could. And because the plight of another prisoner here made me reconsider the type of minister I want to be."

Naehorn scooped up the letters and grasped them to her bony chest. "My elves are still fodder in the Otherworld."

"You did that. You made them outcasts by your actions," I said.

"Did I?" said Naehorn. "Or is that just the world? One

day, the Chameleon Tale will come to fruition. One day, the dark will come, and the world will be remade anew. They made me the evil one, Rajika. But maybe it was you. Maybe you protected a system that should have been undone."

"My name is Alisha." If there were any secrets still locked inside her head, I feared they had all evaporated.

Naehorn moved into the corner of the cell, her movements skittish.

I tried once more. "You believe in the prophecy. When did you receive your most recent letter?"

"Two months, one week and one day ago." Her face became a grotesque mask of confusion. She wailed. "Or fourteen weeks, three days."

I did a quick calculation. The Kraglek ceremony had been mere weeks ago. "The prophecy is coming true, Meriel. I am the eternal girl. Your cousin's next letter will confirm it. She would have to be living under a rock to have not heard."

Naehorn clapped and then knocked on her head again with a closed fist. Was this what decades of isolation did to a person? "You. The eternal girl. Rajika."

I shook my head. "Alisha."

Naehorn gawped. "Alisha, a friend to the elves. Alisha, the eternal girl. I have dreamed of it. Of the eternal girl making a fairer world. No. No. You are lying. You are in my head. You are the devil. My powers might be gone, but I feel your power."

She wasn't alone. I sensed the power surge in the room, too.

It wasn't the devil. It was Death's sword whispering to me.

I slipped off my jacket, handed it to Ezra and drew Transcender from its baldric.

He gritted his teeth. "I hope you know what you're doing."

My pulse sounded in my ears, a flood of adrenalin as I

allowed my instincts to guide me or perhaps the link with the sword. Naehorn recoiled as I stepped forward, lifted her hand and added it to the hilt of Transcender with my own. The lightbulbs flickered. The whispers increased in volume, filling my head. Naehorn's vacant blue eyes grew wide and alert as she, too, heard the whispers. The language was unfamiliar, and the voices unknown, but I trusted the sword. It had saved me once. It would do so again.

The once elf-queen resisted as I pulled the sword away, but her strength was long gone. "More. Let me listen to more. Please. My dead elven friends. I need them."

"No," I said, resolute. "What did the voices say?"

Naehorn trembled, her eyes on the sword. "That you are the eternal girl, and to tell you what I know."

I stepped backwards in case she attempted to take Death's sword. "And what do you know, Meriel?"

She raged. "Those are *my* secrets. I held onto them for endless years. No one can take them from me. Not friend nor foe. I did that. You can't have them."

To be fair, she'd not been able to contact a friend since her imprisonment, or I was sure she would have blabbed like the grannies at temple. A samosa and a cup of chai amongst friends and, oops, what secret?

"What do you want in return?" said Ezra.

Naehorn gawped at him. "I want to see my cousin. In person. A real visit. With a picnic of my choice."

He rolled his eyes. "You've got to be kidding me. No."

She faced us with balled fists. "Then the secret stays mine. I will take it to the grave."

"You can have your picnic. Alone," said Ezra. "But I will allow you more letters."

Naehorn's nostrils flared. "One a week."

Ezra folded his arms across his chest. "One a month."

She grabbed a letter and stared at it, whispering to it like it was a friend. "One a month? We get to see each other once a month."

Ezra growled. "There can be no word of what happened here today, or all letters stop."

Naehorn nodded, eyes wide.

"What is the secret that you have never told a living soul, Meriel?" I said.

Her spine curved as the energy went out of her. "I was once obsessed with the prophecy. Like many others, I believe the book it speaks of to be in the Celestial Library. And I believe that book is the one Rajika died protecting. It is lost to the world because it is hidden amongst the stars. Hidden so well that not even future Custodians could find it."

I searched her face. "Why? Why is this book so important?"

Naehorn frowned. "You know this. You hid it, Rajika. You hid it because it is the only book in existence that reveals the true names of the gods. Not the ones we know them by. Not the ones in legends and fairy tales and temples. No. The ones that the Father of the Gods called his children. The names that, if a mortal knew and spoke aloud, would result in that mortal having control over the gods. That would result in their destruction as immortals. Because what are immortals if a mortal controls them?"

My heartbeat galloped. This was the answer to all our problems. If we found the book, we could keep the gods in check once and for all. Their meddling would end overnight.

Next to me, Ezra cursed loudly and colourfully. "Are we really talking about trying to control the gods?"

A cloud of uncertainty settled over me. But why hadn't Gaia told me of the book? Was it because she, too, would face the ramifications if I discovered it? Was she as much fixated on her own power as the rest of them?

Naehorn released a joyous cackle that spoke of schadenfreude and relish at the fight that lay ahead. Glee bubbled out of her like an engorged river. "So you see, that day in the Celestial Library, you did not end the fight with your cleverness and sacrifice, Rajika. You just pressed pause for another day."

"Where is the book, Meriel?" I said.

"Where you hid it. It came to me afterwards—the horse. The horse must have known. Only the horse can lead you there. A creature with wings. A creature of the air." Naehorn's face contorted. "Rajika. I am sorry I killed you."

I didn't correct her. I let her speak. Soon, she would be talking to the walls again.

She spat the words and, for a moment, became the warrior queen she had once been. "I stand by my reasons. The elves deserved more. I was never offered a seat on the senate even though the elven community is larger than the selkie one. Why did my kind end up doing menial labour when we are less prone to distraction than those ridiculous rainbow-making leprechauns and more trustworthy than witches?" She tore great handfuls of matted hair out, throwing clumps up at the bulbs before shrinking from the light. "When will a better world come? I can't wait any longer. I can't. Kill me, Rajika. Kill me with that sword, as I once killed you. It would be a worthy death. Let me be with my friends. I can't live like this."

"No. Your life is not mine to take." I slipped Transcender into its baldric and retrieved my jacket from Ezra.

He glanced at the lightbulbs, and a wordless exchange passed between us. He touched his moon charm, and the myriad of bright bulbs went out, their light extinguished, their angry buzzing silenced.

A sob of relief in the darkness. "Thank you."

As we backed out of the cell, I addressed the cowering shape of the once elf-queen. "One day, I will let you know what becomes of our remade world, Meriel. It's up to you whether you wish to live to hear of it."

9

E zra deadbolted the cell behind me. When he turned, our eyes met, and a world of meaning passed between us. "That was brave," he said. "I can't believe Gaia hid so much from us. Are you going to confront her?"

I bit my lip. "I don't know. I'm not sure if we can trust her. All the books in my parents' library taught me that the gods have two sides and many, many motivations. How could I forget that? I believed Gaia was good, but maybe she's not. Maybe she's like all the rest. Do you know what both worries me and gives me hope?"

"You can tell me anything."

"The elves aren't the only ones capable of dark hearts. If even Phinnaeous Shine and gods can fall prey to the dark, it shows we are all fallible. And we can all change."

We rode the lift to the main lobby of the hotel. Although only an hour had passed, it felt like days. Nodding our goodbye to the doorman, we slipped out onto the busy London street, where tourists had wrapped up warmly in thick scarves against the autumn chill.

I drew in a shaky breath, my head spinning from all we had learned and done, pinpricks of fear sending goosebumps up my arms. Maybe we'd made the wrong decisions. Maybe we'd trusted the wrong people. Maybe we had no chance at all to get the better of Phinnaeous and Cardea, especially if Gaia was untrustworthy.

And if Gaia was untrustworthy, did that mean Alma was too?

I didn't want to believe it. I liked how she brought Dad out of his shell and filled the house with love, but how could I be sure? Should I rush to him and pull him from his home? Or should I bide my time and delve deeper or lay everything out on the table with Gaia?

By now, we'd slipped into a side street. There was no need for the tube when I had a teleporting werewolf at my side.

My phone buzzed in my pocket. "Detective?"

"Did you see the news?"

I glanced at Ezra and put Rob on speakerphone. "We've been tied up. Ezra's here with me."

"Margola's poised to take over a human newspaper after a media magnate went missing. And he's not the only one," said the detective. "This case was all hush-hush for three days while local police investigated, but there are no leads. CCTV caught the man going into his office in the Shard, but he never came out."

"That's odd. Which paper?" I said.

"*The Evening Herald*," said the detective.

Ezra grunted. "Quite the booming readership. Margola must be rubbing her hands together in glee. At least the attention will be off Alisha. I can't imagine Margola will have time for *The Evening Herald* and *The Otherworld News*."

"I don't like it. This Shine Foundation for the Advancement of Peculiars and Humdrums is making my gut churn. Although I suppose it could be the vindaloo I ate last night," said the detective. "Phinnaeous Shine always complained about how he could only enter high society by shapeshifting. By hiding his values and the true nature of his power. And now, we see him funnelling people into humdrum roles. I don't like it."

"You're rightly angry at him for messing with your mind," said Ezra. "But he is guided by the Magical Constitution. He knows not to upset the fragile balance of London's ecosystem. Hell, he had a hand in writing most of those laws."

"Look, I can't be any blunter. As Justice Minister, you need to get your act together," said Rob. "Because from here, it looks like a near certainty that a peculiar has committed crimes against humdrums to move them aside for ill gain. What's more, Phinnaeous deliberately knee-capped my authority and access, and I have no more cards to play. You're going to have to get back into Wildwoods and sort out your own house, Neuhoff."

Ezra's voice hardened. "We're already on it, Detective."

"I hope you're right," said Rob. "I'll check in with you later, Alisha."

I hung up, looked at Ezra and then buried my face in his chest for a brief second. We were fighting so many fires at once. I needed desperately to sieve through my thoughts and sort them into something that made sense. But something clawed at me.

"We should check on Echo and the foxes," I said.

His grey eyes glinted. "We will. But we need to recharge first. There are too many moving parts for us to unravel. It's the law of common sense. Rest when you need to, or the battle will be over before it has begun."

"We can't go back to the cottage. It'll suffocate me. There's no air in there." Would I feel the same if I wasn't a wind druid? Or was it Gaia's protection spells I didn't trust?"

He pulled me towards him and kissed my nose. The sweetest gesture. "If we can't go to the cottage, we go home."

"To my flat? There's barely any furniture in it."

Grey eyes held mine. "No, hellfire. To the pack farmhouse."

"I don't know, Ezra. The wolves won't like me being there." My stomach swirled with anxiety. I'd rather go to Orpheus's vampire den. Our banter always made me feel better, and I could get six-handed Manfred to knead away all my stress.

He dipped his head to my ear, his voice a low growl. "They don't have a choice. It's about time they get used to you, don't you think? You're my queen, after all."

Butterflies danced in my stomach. "I like how you say that."

"I'll say it over and over if you want. Mine to love and mine to protect."

"Ezra, my head's too full. It's too much. I can't carry this all."

"You don't have to, hellfire. You've got me. We'll find a way through. But first, let me distract you." His stubble grazed my face as he kissed me, and then he teleported with me in his arms, already pulling my top over my head as we emerged in the loft space of the pack farmhouse that had once been Gunnolf's and was now his.

His hands were urgent on my body. He cast aside my jacket, slipped the baldric over my head and peeled off my T-shirt before taking a long, shuddering look at my breasts. The ones that I had found too small or too big at various points in my life but which he found perfect.

He unhooked my bra, taking his sweet time.

When he finally bent his head to kiss my breasts, I arched my back, needing more. Needing all of him. I raked my fingers through his hair, aching for his skin against mine, impatient that he was still fully clothed, but when I tugged at his T-shirt, he captured my wrists, holding me prisoner.

His eyes smouldered. "Patience, hellfire. Let me give you a few minutes you won't forget."

I bit my lip, feeling exposed but utterly turned on.

Ezra fumbled with the button of my jeans, tugged them

off, and then pushed me back gently onto his lumpy bed. Then he climbed on top of me, split my legs apart and pushed my knickers aside.

When his mouth found my softest parts, I moaned and clamped a hand over my mouth, not wanting his pack to hear but unable to stop my cries of ecstasy. He grabbed my buttocks, delving with his tongue, stopping only when I found my quivering release and then continuing my sweet torture when his coarse hands found the peaks of my breasts.

My eyelids fluttered shut, a half-smile on my lips as I let him have his wicked way with me, enjoying every flick of his tongue, every soft kiss and suck, every brush of his stubble and every rough and tender caress.

"My queen approves," said Ezra, his voice thick with lust and satisfaction.

"Yes, I do." I opened my eyes and leaned forward to give him a lingering kiss. "But it's not over yet."

His kiss was hard and demanding, an about-turn from how giving he'd been moments before.

"I bloody well hope not." He gestured ruefully to the bulge in his trousers.

I held his eyes. "Strip off. Now."

He raised an eyebrow. "The alpha gives orders. I don't take them."

"This time, you'll do as you're told."

Ezra undressed slowly, holding my gaze, until all that was left was his red-chequered boxers. Despite winter, his skin had a tawny sheen, and I wondered if that came from his wolf runs when he caught the dawn rays. His muscular arms and thighs, paired with a concave belly and strong shoulders, turned me on all over again.

How many times had he held me as we travelled between the worlds? I could live a lifetime in those arms and never be unsatisfied.

I drank in the sight of him. "The boxers, too."

He stepped out of his underwear and threw them at me playfully. But his eyes weren't playful. His eyes promised a delicious reckoning.

I stood, not a scrap of clothing on me, as I walked over to him, resisting the urge to pull the bedsheet with me. The extra inches, the grey hairs, and the slightly slackened midlife skin I saw in the mirror didn't matter at all when I could see myself through Ezra's eyes. And his nether regions gave me a clear indication of what he felt about my body. Let's just say the mast was up.

"Don't move an inch." I teased him by circling him, letting my breasts brush his back, trailing my fingers around the small of his back, over his concave belly and his pelvic bone, but stopping just short of touching him where he longed for it.

"You'll pay for that." He reached for my hips.

I gave a throaty laugh, enjoying my power over him, and then called the winds.

His eyes widened as I sent him sprawling back into an old armchair in the corner of the room, where a light gauze curtain danced in the breeze of the open window, and views opened up onto the woods the pack ran in.

I took a condom from his bedside drawer. Then I walked over to him, slowly, milking every second of the sparks flying between us. Kneeling in front of him on the bare floorboards, I ripped open the condom wrapper with my teeth and pulled it on him, stroking him.

His hands clenched the armrests.

"Hurry," he growled.

When I climbed on top of him, he groaned, his eyes closing as I moved. We found our rhythm, there, in the pack farmhouse, with the breeze drifting across us, on a tatty old armchair, his mouth on my breasts.

It had never felt so deep or so good.

His release matched mine as if we had been made to fit

like jigsaw pieces. Afterwards, sore and sated from our exertions, we untangled ourselves and flopped onto the bed, smiling.

He pulled the sheet over me with exquisite tenderness and pulled off the condom. "You didn't need to use a condom, Alisha. We know there won't be a surprise pregnancy."

I froze. We'd always used contraception, even though doctors had told me I couldn't conceive. I thought he'd understood that however unscientific my hopes were, I still longed to have a child one day.

A realisation hit me. "I thought you turned down your *perfect fertile werewolf mate* because you chose love for me over biology. But maybe I missed something. Maybe it also meant you don't want children."

He stared at me blankly. "How did you make that leap?"

My heart ached. "You're relieved that there won't be a surprise pregnancy."

Ezra frowned. "Alisha, you told me you can't have children."

"I know." I pressed my lips together. He was right. I had. But I hadn't told him my hopes that maybe the doctors were wrong and magic could happen. Even if we had to go at it like rabbits for a month, and I had to bicycle my legs in the air to give his little swimmers the best chance of reaching my eggs.

I hadn't told him that, even though I believed a woman didn't need children to be whole, I still hadn't buried my dreams of being a mother. That when Pan and Mami Wata had offered to cure my barren womb, it had taken every ounce of my strength to refuse.

Ezra pulled me into a hug. "Damn it, hellfire. All I meant is that we're in a committed relationship, so we can drop the condom if you want. I want to be as close to you as possible. If you got pregnant—after we've put the world to rights and made it safe for our baby—I would be over the moon. And if we can't have a baby, that's fine too. My world is perfect because you are in it."

A scuffle at the door stole the moment to roll Ezra's words over in my mind and decipher their meaning.

Maximillian, one of Ezra's pack, tumbled into the room. A slow grin spread across his face as he took in our tousled hair, flushed skin, and the clothes strewn across the room. "I thought I heard some bumping up here. It turns out it was more grinding."

I flushed. Being found in my birthday suit in the alpha's bed in the middle of the day wasn't an ideal start to this visit.

"Hi, Max." I clutched the bedsheet higher to protect my modesty.

"Get out, Max," growled Ezra. "I'll be down in a second."

Max ignored him, sauntered in, and sat on the bed, brushing a lock of silver-streaked hair from his forehead. His nose twitched. "I smell sex and anxiety. And I'm getting a whiff of Gunnolf, too. You've been visiting him again."

Ezra sighed. "Forgive this cretin, Alisha. Shifters drop their clothes anywhere, and it's easy to forget that most other people have boundaries."

He hopped out of bed and gave me a marvellous view of his naked bum as he hauled the shorter man out of the bedroom by the cuff of his shirt.

"Oi, hands off," Max said. "I came here to say there's a vampire in our kitchen looking for you both."

Ezra grunted. "Tell him we'll be down in a second."

"See you downstairs, Alisha," laughed Max.

With Max gone, I searched for my clothes. "Back to business then."

I dressed, trying to send our conversation to the back of my mind. Boxing up emotions was never a good idea, but what choice did we have? Still, my thoughts haunted me. What if our plans for the future didn't marry up? What if my love life had taken a wrong turn again?

Ezra tipped my chin up as I buttoned my jeans. "Orpheus can wait until we've talked this through. I'm not like your ex-husband, Alisha. I won't lie to you. I won't dismiss your worries. We're good together. I want us to work. You just have to open up to me."

The breakdown of my marriage had cost me so much. It had left me broken in ways I hadn't yet discovered. I didn't know if my wound about children would always be raw. If I gave voice to my dream of having children out loud, despite the obstacles, and Ezra pooh-poohed me, my heart would break into a thousand pieces. Could a forty-year-old woman still hope to have it all—all the things she had dreamed of as a child—a partner, children, a lovely home, purpose and fulfilment? Or should I have downsized my dreams by now?

One thing was clear: now wasn't the time to poke around in my wounds.

Knowing my luck, Orpheus was following every syllable of this conversation through the walls.

I collected my sword and slung it around my body. "Orpheus and the pack are waiting." I gave him a brave, let's-take-on-the-world smile. "We'll talk about it later. Okay?"

He hesitated, then sighed. "Fine. Have it your way. Look, it puts a spanner in the works that the vampire is here, but he'd have found out soon enough anyway. I'm going to spill the beans about our arrangement with Gunnolf. The pack deserve to know. It might get hairy downstairs. Literally."

A frisson of fear snaked up my spine. It was easy to forget this second family of his. Ezra was a man whose history and talents would have allowed him to be tether-less. But for all his lone-wolf nature, he believed in community and was loyal to a fault. That loyalty sometimes led him into grey areas of rules and morality. He'd bent the rules for me and Gunnolf. Would his pack protect or condemn him for what we did this morning?

I searched his face. "Are you sure the pack is loyal enough not to betray you?"

Blue crescent shadows under his eyes. "I would die for them, and they would die for me. Pack chemistry means the weaker wolves will always fall in line behind the strongest one. But I want them to have more than blind loyalty. Gunnolf hid so much from us, but I have my own way of doing things. I trust them with the truth."

He enveloped my hand in his, and we descended the three flights of stairs together. He could have teleported, of course, but a bit of low-impact cardio was never a bad shout in your midlife.

When we reached the pack kitchen, I breathed a sigh of relief that this time, no corpse lay exposed on the kitchen table and that Gunnolf, with his menacing, glowering style, was far away from here. The five remaining members of Ezra's pack sat around the table, nursing slopping beer and steaming coffee. Ezra had been considering increasing pack numbers, but for now, his core group remained.

"There you lovebirds are," Max's piercing blue eyes twinkled.

Ruud and Dominic smirked, respectively the smallest and burliest in size.

My romantic rival Rashida flicked her lustrous red hair like it was her star turn in a bloody hair dye advert. "Look what the cat dragged in."

At the window, looking out onto the woods, stood Orpheus in black trousers, a sleek jacket and a black shirt. His hands were folded behind his back, and his silver cufflinks glinted in the afternoon light.

Turning, his hooded eyes caught mine. *I went to the cottage and was worried. Where's the leopard? He should be by your side. At all times.*

I prefer to go to the toilet by myself, thank you very much. I've been meaning to come and see you, I said. *We've had our hands full.*

Orpheus looked down his Roman nose at me. *I'm all for sex marathons, but you'd think you'd have other things on your mind.*

"Welcome, Orpheus." Ezra frowned, his intuition alerting him to my silent repartee with the vampire.

"Neuhoff. I had to wait outside for a lifetime before your pack invited me in."

Ezra shrugged. "Sorry about that."

Orpheus scowled. "It's about time we spoke, don't you think? After all, the eternal girl isn't just yours to protect."

10

———————

The wolves exchanged uneasy glances. Only Deirdra, the friendliest amongst them, attempted to pierce the tension in the room. I made a mental note to save her first after Ezra if the wolves were ever in a precarious situation. I'd caused a fair bit of havoc the last time I was here and didn't know if the wolves still held my part in Gunnolf's incarceration against me.

"It's been ages, Alisha. Come and sit down." Deirdra patted the chair next to her. "We haven't had a chance to thank you properly for showing us the truth about Gunnolf."

I shuddered at a mental flashback to a freezer full of wolf corpses. "Happy to help."

The chair creaked as I accepted her invitation, and for a horrible moment, I envisaged it cracking underneath me.

It would serve you right to be humiliated, Orpheus said. *I've been frantic with worry since seeing your cottage. I haven't even been able to concentrate on my latest re-reading of* War and Peace, *and I hold you fully responsible.*

I grinned. *You're my friend, not my nursemaid.*

"Alisha is perfectly capable of protecting herself, as you

well know," said Ezra to Orpheus. "How about you sit down, and we'll get you all up to speed?"

"I prefer to stand." Orpheus stroked his beard like a grump.

Ezra sighed. "As you wish."

Rashida faced Ezra, ignoring me. She trembled with passion. The woman needed a lie-down. "When you moved in with *her*, you told us you'd be back daily, but we haven't seen you for days. We need you. And then Ravynne called from Baba Yaga's and told me you might not even be Minister for Justice anymore. What the hell is going on?"

She flicked me a filthy look like I'd made him my sex slave or something.

"That's what I'm here to talk to you about." Ezra's cool tone left no room for doubt. He was the alpha, and she had overstepped the mark. It was sexy as hell. He stood at the window next to Orpheus, sun-tanned wolfish muscle next to the vampire's pale sinew. "Phinnaeous Shine tried to take Death's sword from Alisha. Rayna, Lavinia, Orpheus and I disagreed, and we paid the price."

"Gunnolf trusted him," said Ruud.

"Gunnolf was wrong about a lot of things," growled Ezra. "Phinnaeous Shine has question marks over his head. Do you really think letting him have Death's sword would be sensible? He is already the most powerful man in the Otherworld. His position at Wildwoods, financial resources, networks across the peculiar and humdrum world, and magical abilities make him a formidable enemy."

"I never liked Phinnaeous Shine," Dominic bristled. "I've only ever seen him in a suit or robes and never in jeans. He's definitely dodgy."

This wolf has fewer brain cells than the rest if he thinks denim is a way to judge a man's value. I have known men in petticoats that are worth a thousand of him.

I masked a giggle with my hand. Orpheus's perspectives always made me smile.

Deirdra bit her lip. "I can't believe the Prime Sorcerer ousted half the senate. Why hasn't Margola Silver covered it in *The Otherworld News*?"

I scoffed. "Because she sees an advantage in it for her to align with Phinnaeous Shine."

"Look on the bright side," said Ezra. "If Phinnaeous Shine formally deposes me as Minister for Justice, I'll have more time to spend with the pack."

Rashida cast me a ferocious glance. "It's not your senate job that has been keeping you from us. Gunnolf lived here. We knew we came first."

"Rashida's right. You've been away too long this time." Max dropped his gaze. Challenging an alpha was dangerous.

"Enough." Ezra's voice cracked like a whip. "My choices have kept us all safe. Every decision I make is for the good of this pack. In case you haven't noticed, the gods and the Prime Sorcerer himself have been destabilising the fine balance between humdrums and peculiars, the one that has allowed us to live side by side for centuries."

"The Prime Sorcerer has thrown tantrums before, but usually they blow over more quickly than this," said Orpheus. "There can be little doubt that his integrity has been compromised. I'm tired of waiting it out. That's why I'm here." *And to check on you, Alisha.* "What happened at the cottage? Did Phinnaeous attack?"

"No," I said. "There's a new goddess on the scene. It looks like she means to kill me." *And there's more. A book in the Celestial Library that might give us power over all the gods.*

Then that's where you must go next, said Orpheus. *Because if you die, all is lost.*

A small part of me wondered whether he meant personally or professionally. Would a centuries-old vampire, who had become deadened to loss, really mourn me were something to happen?

Orpheus rolled his eyes. *You cretin. Have I not proven to you time and again that I like you more than other people?*

Rashida smirked. "Maybe the goddess had the right idea."

Orpheus gave her less regard than a mosquito. He pulled a rolled-up paper from his jacket and tossed it at Ezra. "You need to read this."

Ezra caught the paper with a frown, unfolded the newspaper on the table and leaned over me so we could scan it together.

HUMDRUM OFFICIALS IN SHOCK DISAPPEARANCE

The city of London stands united in shock today after the third high-profile disappearance of a high-ranking humdrum official.

Mere days after the Prime Minister's Private Secretary, Sir Johnny Ramsbottom, vanished in astonishing circumstances while relieving himself in the lavatories at 10 Downing Street, the city was faced with the disappearance of Ivana Humperdick, Governor of the Bank of England. According to leaked CCTV footage, Mrs Humperdick went into her million-pound shoe closet and never came out.

In the latest embarrassment for the security services, who are unable to identify a culprit, the media baron Sir Sonny Angleman has disappeared off his docked yacht in Greenwich. His cleaner maintains that Sir Sonny, who is married with five adult children, would retire to his cabin with some good-time girls every afternoon from 15.15 to 15.30 p.m. But when his visitors entered, they found only his favourite silken bathrobe on the floor.

That leaves the question, dear reader, who might be next? Who is the perpetrator, and what does s/he intend to do with the victims? And if humdrums can't protect themselves, should their peculiar counterparts step in?

Luckily, the Prime Sorcerer has been able to fill the gaps using peculiars who are already specialists in these areas through the Shine Foundation for the Advancement of Peculiars and Humdrums. I, too, dear readers, have been drafted in to help oversee the editorial direction of Angleman's newspaper empire. I am looking forward to the challenge. The Otherworld News *will, of course, remain my priority.*

Ezra straightened up and sighed. "It's as the detective said. Why does Margola always sound like she enjoys other people's suffering? You were right to bring this to us, Orpheus. I'd wager this is what has been keeping Phinnaeous busy."

I'd been around the block too many times to fall for the sheen of respectability that Phinnaeous Shine was trying to put on his sham foundation. "Rob warned us. The humdrum disappearances make Phinnaeous the saviour overnight when, in reality, he's the culprit. He's making moves to infiltrate humdrum positions of influence. His foundation is a sham. All that talk of equality, and it's all bullshit. Doesn't The Judge's Law in the Magical Constitution prevent him from doing this?"

"That law speaks about maintaining the power balance between magical communities. It makes no mention of humans," said Orpheus.

My heartbeat galloped. Maybe this was why Phinnaeous Shine and I had always been at odds with one another. I could never agree with one group having advantages just because they'd been born magical or despised because they belonged to one magical community like the elves.

But I'd lived most of my life as a humdrum. I could never turn a blind eye to their suffering. "But the Jailor's Law must help. It is forbidden to interfere with the compos mentis of another peculiar. Or how about the Protector's Law? A sentient peculiar who uses magic to harm a humdrum will have their magic drained ad infinitum."

Ezra's grey eyes darkened. "Laws are useless if you are

powerful enough to ignore them. This pack is full of seekers. We're bringers of justice. We don't look away when things get tough."

The pack murmured in agreement.

He had them in the palm of his hand. Ezra paced the kitchen and then came to a standstill. A fleeting glance at me before the truth fell from his lips. "This morning, I made a tricky decision, but it might give us the upper hand."

His sparse account of what had happened in Gunnolf's cell sent the wolves into a frenzy.

"He has no restraint. I hope you know what you're doing," Max growled.

"You let him out?" Ruud whistled in appreciation. "That took balls."

For Christ's sake. Orpheus's eyebrows shot up into his hairline. *Chaos reigns, and you two thought you should add to it?*

I don't think a vampire should really take the Lord's name in vain, I retorted.

"The druid was with you? It should have been me instead. What's she got to do with wolf business?" said Rashida.

"I hope you know what you're doing, Neuhoff. This is a dangerous game you're playing," said Orpheus.

Ezra nodded. "Do you really think we could win against Phinnaeous without the element of surprise?"

Orpheus's nostrils flared with ire. "Can you be so sure that the old alpha will do your bidding?"

"Will we get the chance to run alongside Gunnolf again?" said Deirdra.

Ezra raised his voice a fraction, and the wolves' raised hackles settled into meek obedience. "Right now, it's a waiting game. Gunnolf has forty-eight hours to see what he can uncover. We keep our claws sheathed."

I could cut the tension in the room with a knife. My priorities were clear. A goddess wanted to kill me. The Prime Sorcerer probably wanted to strip me of the sword that was my defence. Hopefully, by now, Echo and the foxes had retrieved the necklace. My next logical step was a trip to the Celestial Library to find the book my grandmother had hidden.

Still, sometimes life weighed so heavily that you needed to inject a bit of fun to get through the day. Sometimes, a little fun was needed for people to bond. It was my modus operandi every time there was tension in my classroom between pupils, and it wasn't any different with the pack.

A spark of mischief ignited in me. Here, on the outskirts of the city, there was little chance of discovery by humdrums, even without access to the shielding mechanisms of Wildwoods arena.

It had been a while since I'd had some sparring partners that wouldn't cut me any slack. "How about we all get a training session in?" I said. "That way, you get to sharpen your claws, and we can all let off some steam?"

"I'm game." Rashida peeled off her clothes, pointing her pert breasts at Ezra like blooming missiles. As if she'd been waiting for the opportunity to strip off since the moment we'd walked in.

Ezra rubbed his brow. "I'm not sure."

I grinned, standing up. "You chicken?"

You're a minx, said Orpheus. *If you were mine, I'd spank you.*

"Absolutely not," Ezra growled, his hand dropping to his belt buckle. "We could do with a training session to sharpen the skills of the lazy ones around here."

"Speak for yourself," said Max.

Ezra undid his belt and peeled off his T-shirt. "I'm a slickly oiled machine. Just you wait and see."

"Then here are the ground rules." I tore my eyes away from him. "We stay within the perimeters of the meadow outside the farmhouse. There are two teams and one object to retrieve. Orpheus, Max, Deirdra, you're with me. Rashida,

Dominic and Ruud are with Ezra. Anything goes, but no aiming to kill or maim."

Dominic stood, dwarfing the other men. "Sounds like fun. What's the object?"

I reached behind my back and unsheathed Transcender. "Death's sword."

Ezra frowned. "Bloody hell, Alisha."

"With so many after it, we might as well have a training exercise based around it. It might come in handy during a real fight," I said. "The first team to touch the hilt with a paw or hand wins. But here's the catch: for a team to win, every member of that team has to touch the hilt."

Orpheus's dark eyes glinted as he slipped off his jacket, removed his cufflinks and laid them on the crumb-laden kitchen worktop. "I prefer blood sports, but this will have to do."

I headed out onto the rickety patio as clothing rustled to the floor and bones cracked.

Echo would chide me for not including him in this ruckus. He liked nothing better than a bit of competition followed by lording his wins over the losers.

Glee bubbled inside me as I used my wind powers to propel the sword deep into the bark of a pine tree at the edge of the woods, a few inches up from ground level. The back door swung open as Ezra's copper-grey wolf came out to stand by me. Our teams lined up alongside us, there on the rickety deck bordered by orange dahlias. On my left, Orpheus cracked his knuckles with ferocious intent, Max as his silver-white medium wolf and Deirdra, small, coarse and copper brown. On my right, Ezra, copper-grey with his charm necklace about his neck. Burly, tawny, brown Dominic. Skinny, grey Ruud with his white muzzle and finally, Rashida, red and lustrous with a snow-tipped tail.

I was going to show that hussy what I was made of.

I tied my hair into a ponytail, a sure sign I meant business.

I sank my hand into Ezra's thick fur, caressing him behind his ears. Then I giggled, gave his head a slap—provoking a snarl—and fixed my eyes on the prize.

Ezra howled, and the other wolves followed suit.

"Let the games begin." I set off at a run.

11

—————

A woman running across a meadow in her midlife is a different prospect from a teenager doing the same. I wasn't balletic and free. I was a thundering moose holding my unsupported boobs, wishing fervently for a sports bra until my logical brain gave in to pure joy and instincts.

I was losing ground, holding back.

I released my hands from my chest and picked up my speed. About five hundred metres stood between me and Transcender.

It called to me—a soft hum of power like it had its own frequency.

Like we had a language all of our own, and the sword knew it was wrong to be separated from me.

I suppressed the sense of foreboding in my belly. With neither vampire speed nor four legs nor even my catalogue of creatures to animate a flying wonder, I was the slowest. But I had my wind powers. And there was a reason I'd chosen Orpheus. We made a good team. His telepathy meant we were sure to win.

Head for the treeline, I said.

His voice boomed in my head. *Where do you think I'm going, woman?*

My feet pounded the field. *Once you've pulled it out, I'll use my wind powers to guide it to each of our team.*

Ingenious plan, druid. I commend you. Orpheus surged ahead, almost at the sword.

Ezra will anticipate it. You might need to slam-dunk him if he tries to intervene.

It would be a pleasure. All in the name of sport.

Ezra didn't teleport in wolf form. The risks of getting lost in the folds of the world were too great. A wolf was more instinctual than logical, after all. Still, he and Dominic, as the largest wolves, had an intimidating speed and surged ahead, a fraction of a second behind Orpheus.

I unleashed a flurry of falling leaves to hide the hilt, hoping to disorientate them.

It was difficult to distinguish between the wolves. I'd only just learned the differences between them, and they blurred at this speed. Added to that, my eyesight wasn't the twenty-twenty of my youth. With difficulty, I picked out Ruud from the pack. I grasped a pocket of wind and lassoed it around his legs, jerking him back mid-leap and pulling him down to the ground with a thud.

He yelped, and a snarl formed on his lips.

I raced past, the thrill of competition bubbling in me. A spurt of confidence made me flashy. I called a whirlwind in my hand, growing it, tending to it, as I searched the field for Rashida. A flash of red and my legs fell out under me, and the winds fizzled in my palm as I, too, collapsed in a heap, my limbs tangling.

A jolt of pain in my lower back. "Oof. What the—"

The red wolf stared down at me. She bared her teeth, yellowed spit-drenched canines inches from my face, then shot off at pace towards the tree line.

I rolled over onto my knees, the scent of dirt in my

nostrils. I hauled myself up, a little humiliated but determined to get the better of her.

A little help, druid. Orpheus had found the hilt of the sword. He tugged it out of the tree, but he wasn't alone.

Ezra and Dominic circled him, snapping at his trousers, teeth bared. Ezra leapt, and his paw skimmed the hilt of the sword, making the score even. Next came Dominic, attempting the same move, but Orpheus couldn't be fooled twice. He boxed Dominic on the nose, and the wolf growled, all promises of friendly competition forgotten.

Dominic lurched towards Orpheus, and this time, it was our teammate, silver-white Max, who headed off Dominic. Dominic, larger in size and with more muscle, might have been the winner on paper, but Max was quick. He nipped his pack brother's ear, then darted around to bite his hind leg, and for a few seconds at least, Dominic's frustration and Max's courage kept them busy.

I was almost there. Spurts of wind against the ground propelled me faster and faster and cushioned my fall to the ground with that same power. It was like flying, then freefall. But then, that was what my life had felt like since I'd had true sight. Every day in the Otherworld was a rollercoaster.

But I wouldn't have it any other way. There was so much I still didn't know about my possibilities—ways to use my powers that I learned with every passing day, every battle or training encounter.

Something leapt at me from behind: Ruud or Rashida. Teeth locked onto the waistband of my jeans and scraped against the small of my back. So much for a bloodless sport, judging by the sting. I flicked my hand backwards, removing the irritant as if it were a gnat and pushed on, more determined with every step.

Ezra wasn't finished with Orpheus.

My mouth dropped open as he tore a strip of Orpheus's trousers and snapped at his pelvis like he did intend to take a bite out of his ding dong. Ezra pranced back and, with a leap, used the full bulk of his weight to throw Orpheus off balance.

The vampire's arms cartwheeled backwards into the dirt, and the sword flew from his hands. *Neuhoff isn't as placid in his wolf form. I'm mildly impressed.*

Deirdra darted into the fray, pawed and closed her mouth around the hilt seconds before Ezra reached it.

I whooped. The score stood at two for us. *Get to higher ground, but keep your eyes on the red wolf, Orpheus. She's a pain.*

Pine needles rained down as the vampire jumped into the trees.

A tornado curled out of my right fist and swept the wolves up and away from their drive to get Deirdra.

"Drop the sword," I said to her.

Her skittish eyes widened at Rashida's rapid approach, but she did as she was told.

I floated the sword to me on a breeze, almost lazily, while keeping Ezra, Dominic and Ruud at bay. Once, I would have struggled against one wolf. Now, I could keep the three of them in check without breaking a sweat. At least while Ezra was still holding back.

I opened my palm to receive the sword, eager to hold the familiar bejewelled hilt and lightweight blade that suited my frame. By my calculations, only Max would need to paw Transcender for us to win.

I stopped the tornado and reached out for the blade.

Only a few inches more. Rashida had no chance.

A rectangle of light opened next to me, and the red woman stepped out in a flowing dress.

Who in Dracula's name is that? said Orpheus.

The goddess who means to kill me. I threw myself towards the sword, knowing that only with it in my hands did we stand a chance against her. My heart pounded as I closed my fist around it.

A howl from Ezra sent shivers up my spine as he raced to my side.

But the red woman was there first.

"She's immortal and spreads disease," I called to the wolves. "Don't touch her unless you must."

Orpheus unleashed a flurry of Shakespearean curses. *There is never a dull moment around you.*

The red woman towered over me, her diseased fingers outstretched. "You escaped me last time, thanks to Gaia's tricks. This time, you won't be so lucky. Give me the sword, druid."

I shook my head. "I can't do that. Leave now. I am the eternal girl. You know I can harm you, just as I did Mami Wata. But it doesn't have to be that way."

A throaty laugh burst from her. "You gave her a small flesh wound. She was weakened and surprised by an octopus. You may have bested other immortals but never landed a killing blow, even with Death's sword."

Ezra bared his teeth, every sinew alert to her threats.

One by one, all the wolves except Rashida joined him. They surrounded me, lending their might to mine.

Was Mami Wata really alive and well? I channelled calm, although my inner banshee threatened to come out. Three women in my life had left me gifts. From Gaia, I had the sword. From Mum, the necklace. From Rajika, the book. And from Dad, my catalogue of creatures, and yet here I was, with every last aid stripped away, apart from the sword.

You have your wind powers, your intellect and your friends, druid. That is more than most, said Orpheus.

Stay hidden, Orpheus. Our only chance is to push her back into the portal. I set back my shoulders. "Gaia is on her way."

Orpheus's voice boomed in my head. *Agreed. Keep her distracted. We'll send her back and get you somewhere safe.*

The red woman's voice was a whisper of coiled anger. "Gaia and I were friends once. Sisters in joy. But why should I heal when everyone else destroys? How dare she give a mortal a sword that can take the life of immortals? We have known each other for centuries. It is an unthinkable betrayal."

"I know Gaia well enough to know she would never be disloyal unless she had no choice." Still, my doubts niggled. I closed my eyes for a fraction of a section to call to Gaia nevertheless. A prayer for help with her sister goddess here to kill me. *I need you.*

I need you, too. I won't let you down, said Orpheus.

I wasn't talking to you. I could get whiplash from multiple conversations. Multitasking really was a pain in the arse.

"Do you know who I am, druid? You should fear me," said the red woman.

I met her glacial eyes. "I do know, and I am not afraid."

Next to me, the pack itched to attack her, but I laid a hand on Ezra's hackles. If they touched her, who knew what disease she might spread.

"You should be. I am the convener of spaces. The gods are gathering, and when they do, there is always a trail of human blood and guts. You are the ants that walk beneath our feet. And you have displeased us. Why else did I abandon healing and choose instead to send plagues and diseases to humble you? The gods will make this world anew."

My heartbeat galloped. "This world is worth saving."

"Is it? The safe places you have enjoyed are already rotting. Your heroes are already making deals. Why are you holding out against the darkness when you are exhausted by the struggle? Hand me the sword. I will not say it again."

I gripped Transcender tightly between two hands, its dark blade ominous between us. "Maybe it's you who should be afraid."

"You overestimate yourself. You may have faced one god, but how would you fare against many, druid?"

That made me really mad.

How many times had I felt by a look or a careless word or

deliberate slight that I wasn't good enough, that I was somehow smaller or less worthy, that my opinions didn't matter or that someone else deserved my place at the table? If my mum's death had taught me one thing, it was that we had one life to carve out our place in the world and that those who spoke the loudest or were the most violent or most obnoxious weren't always the most worthy. Each of us had the power to make the world a better place, powers or not.

"Leave," I said. "You made a mistake coming here today."

The red woman edged closer, with malicious eyes and cascades of waist-length brown hair. "So full of hubris. My most fun enemies over the years have been those who talk a good game and then quiver at my feet."

Ezra snarled, inching dangerously close to her. He lunged for her, and my lungs constricted as she created a portal he fell clean through, disappearing and appearing again on the edge of the woods.

I kept my eyes trained on the goddess as relief swept through me that she'd not touched him. "Deirdra, check he's okay."

Deirdra darted away as Dominic took Ezra's place at my side, the natural beta.

The red woman continued, barely pausing the rhythm of her conversation. "When doors became my gift, I wondered if I'd been short-changed. Some goddesses tend the earth. Some hold dominion over hell. Others wage war or inspire with music and creativity. Then there was me—the goddess of *doors*. With time, I realised doors are special. We pass through them daily with little regard. We might scuff them or slam them. We put sticky hands all over them. But a door has power. A door can make a prison, a haven or an escape. Without them, we are trapped or unsafe. A door can appear anywhere if you know how to make one. Doors are portals. They are openings, and they are endings. They are fate. Are you so sure that fate will be kind to you?"

My palms grew clammy on the hilt. Where was Gaia? How long would it take her to get here? Behind the red woman, the portal glowed with no hint of where she had come from or where it led. I averted my eyes from Orpheus's approach, willing the wolves to play it cool and not give him away.

Rashida's whimper was timed to perfection.

The bloody cow.

The red woman twisted in the direction of the sound, spotting the threat and spoiling our plan. Her face twisted at the sight of the vampire. She reached out for me with blackened hands.

I won't let her hurt you. Orpheus sped forward, a blur of black and white, eyes locked on me as he blocked the red woman's attempt to touch me with his own body.

"No!" The scream ripped from my throat. *None of my friends are going to die today.*

I lifted my left hand, arcing Orpheus away from us. Then I sent a gust of wind to the goddess, trying to force her back into the portal. But with one hand clutching the hilt of Transcender against such a powerful opponent, it wasn't enough.

She stood there as though she were on the set of a 1980s music video, her hair blown about in a wind machine.

With no other choice, I lifted Transcender and slashed clean through the fingers of her left hand, recoiling as three blackened digits fell to the floor. Then my kickboxing instincts took over, and I dropkicked her into the portal, shining bright behind her.

The goddess lurched backwards, clutching her hand, her face twisted in rage.

Behind me, the paws pounded against the ground as Ezra and Deirdre returned.

The portal closed, and I fell to my knees, vomiting millimetres from the severed fingers. I wiped my mouth with the back of my hand, then cleaned Transcender's bloody blade on a mound of grass. Ezra's frothy muzzle prodded me to check I was okay as I buried my head in his fur, as anger and relief swirled inside me, a dangerous cocktail.

I jerked my head up. *Orpheus?*

I'm okay, Alisha. He came towards us, his smart clothes torn and dirty and his hair mussed.

I scanned his body. *She touched you.*

My flesh is already dead. She can't harm me. But thank you for caring.

I swallowed a lump of emotion as he extracted a handkerchief from his trouser pocket and picked up the red woman's severed fingers. I'd obviously missed the memo that immortal flesh was a delicacy for vampires.

He sighed. "I thought perhaps Marina could do some tests to ascertain the particular properties of these."

I nodded and struggled to my feet. "Let's go inside."

Ezra howled, and the wolves led us back to the farmhouse in the falling light, with the exception of Dominic and Max, who stood guard in case the red woman returned. Nausea rippled through me like a wave as I slipped on my baldric, ensuring a snug fit before placing Transcender in it. The sword belonged there, nestled against me.

And yet I knew. I might have lost it. I could never be that complacent again.

I turned my gaze away—ignoring Orpheus's revolted expression at their contorting bodies—as the wolves shifted back into their human bodies and pulled on their clothes. If anyone had told me that morning that I would trust Naehorn more than Gaia or that we would be relying on Ezra's murderous former alpha to retrieve intelligence on Phinnaeous, I would have laughed like a drain.

But the lines between ally and enemy had blurred. Why hadn't Gaia come to our aid?

Ezra spoke first. "It's unthinkable she came here. We're

lucky to have escaped. I would never have forgiven myself if anything happened to you." He paused. "Thank you, Orpheus, for shielding Alisha."

Orpheus pressed his lips together. "I rather think she shielded me. You must know she can't stay here. I can give her sanctuary at my club. You'll need to stay here with the pack in case the red woman returns, of course, Neuhoff."

I frowned. "How did she know I was here?"

Rashida's lips twisted into a malicious smile.

My restraint snapped like a brittle rubber band. I lifted my hands almost carelessly and created a breeze to send Rashida sprawling onto her arse even before she'd had a chance to pull her jeans on. Her legs flew up, and her tiny thong left nothing to the imagination. Either she'd not entirely shifted back, or it had been a while since she'd last had a bikini wax.

Granny pants for the win.

Orpheus choked with suppressed laughter as he collected his cufflinks and pulled on his suit jacket. *I missed your last catfight. I can't wait to see how this one turns out. What are granny pants?*

Ezra stepped in front of the fallen vixen, his voice firm. "There's no way Rashida could have known we were coming here."

Rashida rose to her feet, playing up her vulnerability for Ezra's benefit. Deirdra and Ruud rushed to help her while Rashida gave Ezra a simpering look.

Tread carefully, druid. The wolves will protect their own, said Orpheus. *Suddenly, we look quite alone. As it stands, the pack surrounds us, what with the two hairy, toothy ones outside.*

I stabbed my finger in the air. "That little whimper alerted the goddess to Orpheus's position. It's one thing lacking the courage to fight with us. It's quite another helping the other side."

"I was scared, Ezra. I'm sorry. I let you down," said Rashida.

I clenched my fists. "You can't really believe her. She put us all in jeopardy. Just because she doesn't like me."

Ezra stepped towards me. "We don't have time to be fighting each other, Alisha. We have enough enemies outside of these walls."

Neuhoff's wrong on this one, said Orpheus. *If one of my vampire clan had done that, I would have staked them myself.*

I frowned. "Ezra, if you let Rashida stay in the pack, how do you know she won't do that again? There's too much at stake."

Ruud stiffened. "You're going to let the druid tell you who stays in the pack? That's a step too far, even for you."

A vein throbbed in Ezra's jaw. "No one's casting Rashida out of the pack. Let's all take a breath here."

Rashida flashed me a victorious smile.

A stone settled in the pit of my stomach. My voice was flat. "You're the alpha. It's your call. You wait for Gunnolf. I have to go to the Celestial Library to find the book. It's the only thing that will stop the gods."

"You're not going alone," growled Ezra. "We'll do it together."

"She won't be alone. I'll accompany her," said Orpheus. "My knowledge of history could be an advantage."

Ezra glowered. "Of course, you'd be the first one to offer."

The phone trilled in the kitchen.

I wasn't surprised the pack had a landline or that it sounded like a relic. The farmhouse was old school. There was no dishwasher, just a growing pile of dirty dishes. No clothes dryer, just a washing line. A block of soap rather than one of those posh liquid soap pumps you get at hotels. A post box at the end of the drive. And threadbare towels that provided exfoliation rather than comfort. They would take the second skin off a snake.

Deirdra, who ran point on the larger network of seekers, left Rashida's side to answer it. She held the receiver to her ear, gave a tremulous hello, and then listened hard before the colour drained from her face.

"I'll let him know." She replaced the receiver with a clunk and turned to Ezra.

"What is it?" said Ezra.

"That was Armando from the Southeast London pack. He spotted two bleeding foxes next to a busy commuter area. They're with a leopard. He won't let Armando get close enough to help."

"Where?" My chair clattered to the floor as I stood. I had sent the foxes into the path of danger.

"Peckham Rye tube," said Deirdra.

My heartbeat accelerated. I darted a pleading glance to Ezra.

He didn't hesitate. He strode over to my side and addressed the pack. "Stay here in case Gunnolf returns."

In a flash, Orpheus stood next to us. "I'm coming too."

Ezra's lips tightened, but he nodded and offered a jerking hand to Orpheus. Then he pulled me hard against his chest as the three of us fell into the monochrome world towards Echo, my breath a rasp in my chest.

12

———

Evening had fallen when we reached Peckham Rye Station in the gritty south-eastern corner of the city. The streets thrummed with commuters on their way home from work, earbuds stuffed into their ears, scrolling through their phones as they worked or dazed decompression on their faces after a long day's work in the city. A few clutched clanking bottles of booze in carrier bags from the off-licence or sodden parcels of deep-fried battered cod and vinegary chips for dinner.

Armando, a gangly wolf with beanstalk legs and waggling square eyebrows that spoke a language of their own, met us outside the cramped, rundown station due refurbishment. I gave thanks for the dim lighting that had saved Echo, Fei Yen and Faeza from discovery for now. Orpheus would be able to wipe the minds of any humdrums who stumbled across us. He was always a safe pair of hands in a crisis.

"They're around the corner by the bins," said Armando.

I followed his gaze, every cell alert. "Do you know what happened?"

Ezra's mouth was a grim line. "We'll take it from here."

"Ministers." Armando nodded at Ezra and Orpheus but saved his lingering glance for me.

"Your reputation as the eternal girl precedes you, Alisha," murmured Orpheus.

I gave a bitter laugh. "Not much good if it doesn't keep my friends safe. My brother owns a flat around here. He wouldn't hurt them, would he?"

"Who knows what he's capable of," said Ezra. "We should be prepared for anything."

"The werepigeon is not much better than the pigeons that used to defecate all over Trafalgar Square before the mayor banned feeding them and introduced a hawk to intimidate them," said Orpheus. "Perhaps that's what your brother needs. A restricted diet and a predator to keep him behaving."

"I've caught their scent. We're not far," said Ezra.

We rounded the corner in silence. I scanned the street for CCTV in the twilight; our trainers light against the uneven pavement.

"There." I ran towards the slack fox body on the floor, recognising Fei Yen.

Her left foreleg oozed with blood, and when I looked closer, I recoiled to see the jagged broken bone. My heart plummeted. Her limb had come almost clean off. She wasn't alone. Naked Faeza in human form and a prowling Echo guarded her.

"Oh god. Is she okay?" I asked.

Echo unleashed a roar, which I hoped those without true sight heard as a miaow. "Thank the stars, you're here."

"She's not okay." Faeza stroked the fox's forehead, her face twisted in grief. "I've been through everything in my head, all the Chinese medicine in our supplies at Shanghai Moon, and I can't think of anything, Alisha. I can't think of anything."

I fell to my knees beside Fei Yen. "She needs a tourniquet."

"Take this." Ezra tore a strip from his T-shirt, threw it at me, and wrapped his jacket around Faeza's shoulders. Then he took off his charm necklace.

Faeza pushed it back towards him. A sob wracked through her body. "No, that trinket can't heal severed bone. Keep it. I knew we should stay out of Wildwoods business. I knew we should stay cocooned away from all the madness of the Otherworld."

The fox whimpered, brown eyes rolling in its head. Faeza rocked on her heels, trying in vain to pacify herself as Fei Yen bled all over the ground despite my efforts to stem the bleeding.

"Ezra, get Marina," I called over my shoulder as I tied the tourniquet.

The air molecules shifted as he vanished.

A growl rumbled through Echo's body. The leopard sniffed. "I can smell battle on you."

"I'll fill you in later," I promised. "What happened here, Echo?"

Mournful emerald eyes. "We almost had the necklace, but your brother had the ravens with him. The foxes are excellent fighters, but land mammals are vulnerable against a flock of predatory birds. It was horrible. One minute, the foxes were holding their own, and I was plucking off a bird one by one. The next, Faeza snarled in a corner, and Fei Yen became distracted by her reflection in a basement window. It was enough for her to lose her advantage. For her to lose a limb. I couldn't stop them, Alisha. The ravens were cavalry. He brought enough, so losses didn't matter."

I shuddered, noticing a dozen or more dead ravens in the alley. The ones Echo and the foxes had felled. Were some of these mine? The ones I had animated? Did the ravens mean the Ravenmaster had returned?

My throat constricted. She didn't mean to lash out. The love of her life was injured, and I would take any insult if it helped her through this. "Sahil did this?"

"Damn that necklace. And damn your brother." Faeza shook with anger that dissolved into tears. "My wife is dying."

"I had him in my reach, but before my jaw closed, I remembered my ancestral oath to protect the Vermas." Echo's emerald eyes filled with sorrow. "I couldn't rip his throat out."

My blood ran cold. "I didn't think he was capable of this."

Faeza's eyes were open wounds. "Please don't let that mistake cost Fei Yen her life."

The fox made a mewling sound, weaker than the whimper before it.

Echo's emerald eyes grew mournful in the twilight. He lay down next to Fei Yen, licking her sporadically, cleaning her limbs as if he knew she wasn't long for this world. "I failed you, Alisha. I failed the foxes."

"Step away, leopard. If it comes to it, it should be the lesbian lover who does the embalming, not you." Sudden anger pulsed through Orpheus's voice. "Look up, Alisha."

I followed his gaze and sucked in my breath. A flock of birds sat on a yellow-brick building dotted between the smoking chimney stacks. Seven ravens. Ravens were not an uncommon sight in London. Most city-dwellers would think nothing of seeing the odd one.

But I knew better. I knew ravens to be magical creatures. Intelligent scavengers with razor-sharp beaks and capable of following commands. After all, I had torn the Ravenmaster to shreds with ravens loyal to me.

It wasn't just the sight of the ravens that scared me. It was the eighth bird, who, by the formation on the roof, appeared to be their leader.

A werepigeon, grey-breasted, muscly and weirdly upright

compared to the ravens, replete with an orange beak and green-tinged head with fiery eyes.

It was always important for Sahil to stand out.

And now here he was, with his own sinister bird army.

"He'll answer for this." Orpheus crouched down as if he would spring up to the roof.

I met my brother's eyes, and he cocked his werepigeon head. Even without my catalogue of creatures, I could put an end to this. My wind powers were strong and targeted enough now for me to lasso him down or launch a twister to disorientate the birds before lobbing the heads of the birds one by one with Death's sword.

But I chose not to do that.

I wanted my brother to live. Not only because that was what Mum and Dad would want but because I wanted him to have a chance at redemption. I wanted us to be close.

Whatever he had done, I loved him.

But how could I reconcile that with the violence he had inflicted on Fei Yen?

"No, Orpheus. We stay together." I tore my eyes away from my brother and concentrated on keeping pressure on the wound. "I should never have separated us in the first place. Right now, the priority is helping Fei Yen."

"What about the Jericho necklace, Alisha?" said Orpheus. *It was too close a call at the pack farmhouse today.*

"We'll have another chance. If they make a move against us, we might have to fight."

Maybe my brother sensed the remaining love I had for him, borne of our childhood together and even our spats. Or maybe he was crapping his werepigeon pants at the thought of a twilight rooftop battle with me, the eternal girl, and my full magical contingent. It would have been a far more even match. In any case, a chorus of low croaks sounded as the ravens took flight. I glanced at the departing flock, led by Sahil, relieved we could concentrate on our wounded.

Yes, we were fighting for the future of the Otherworld and maybe even the right for humdrums in this city to exercise free will and not be beholden to the whims and egos of the gods.

But if we couldn't fight for one life, then none of it mattered at all.

I fixed my gaze on Fei Yen, who was fading fast. "Where's Marina? Orpheus, can you help ease Fei Yen's pain until she gets here?"

Faeza shook her head, her eyes glassy. She scrambled for a logical explanation, although at that moment, she was driven purely by emotion. "No vampire trickery. It will be harder for Marina to diagnose her." A pause and then a torrent of words. "We were only here out of love for you, Alisha."

Guilt gnawed at my insides. I heard the meaning behind her words and didn't blame her. For years after they'd left China, Fei Yen and Faeza had kept a careful wall between them and the organised magical community at Wildwoods. They'd built up a simple life, anchored by their shop, Shanghai Moon, only introducing new elements slowly. In case their lives fell apart again. It had taken nearly a decade for them to enrol in my English language class at the community centre. Such a small step, but for those who had been burned before, it had taken courage.

And yet, because of their friendship with me, they had—step by step—ventured deeper into the Otherworld they feared. Deeper into the secrets and battles. And now, one of them had paid the price.

Of course, tonight had reinforced Faeza's mistrust of others.

Of course, her trust had been shattered.

I hated myself for not protecting them better.

Tears filled my eyes. Fei Yen was my friend. She couldn't die. "Where are Ezra and Marina? What's taking so long?"

The revving of cars on the main road and the patter of

commuters rushing home suddenly brought it home to me that Fei Yen's mangled body had gone still.

Her whimpers had stopped.

Faeza wailed into the night. "I heal people all the time. Why can't I think of a way to heal my own wife?" Her screams crescendoed into the London night, unhinged and wild, like the fox hidden beneath her human skin.

Echo raised his beautiful head. "Calm yourself, Faeza. There's a slight rise and fall in her chest. She's unconscious, not dead."

My heart skipped a beat, and I wrapped my arms around Faeza. An explosion of relief overcame me as Ezra returned with a flushed, dishevelled Marina, still in her work scrubs and clutching her medical bag.

My voice cracked. "Hurry. She doesn't have long."

Marina's professional experience kicked in. She darted a sombre glance at Faeza, whose screams had subsided into a wordless flow of tears.

"I'll take good care of her. I promise." Kneeling beside Fei Yen, Marina reached inside her medical kit with deft hands. "Ezra, hold up my torch. I need more light to work. What caused this?"

"A werepigeon and raven attack," said Echo. "They concentrated their efforts."

Seconds felt like hours as we all held our breath.

Marina took a brief look at Fei Yen's pupils, followed by her gums to check for oxygenation. Then she pressed her stethoscope to the fox to monitor her heart and respiratory rate, counting under her breath all the while. She checked for unseen lacerations and adjusted my tourniquet. Eventually, she laid her healing hands on Fei Yen, just as I had seen her do to Elvira as the witch lay dying, with an empath's touch rather than a veterinarian's, perhaps dulling Fei Yen's pain.

I swallowed the lump in my throat as she turned to us.

"Ezra, you can switch the torch off." With a calm voice

and infinite gentleness, Marina addressed Faeza. "Her breathing is shallow. Alisha did a good job with first aid, but the bleeding hasn't stopped, and there is a heightened chance of infection, given the weapon was a bird beak. We need to get her somewhere warm, or she risks pneumonia. And the partial amputation… There is no time to lose."

Hope filled Faeza's tear-stained face. "But she'll live? We'll take her to your surgery, and you can fix this?"

Marina's shoulders drooped. She reached out for Faeza's hands and jerked slightly, frowning, before caressing Faeza's hands in soothing circles. "An injury like this is tricky in a non-magical creature, and it's complicated further by Fei Yen's shifting ability. Once closed, it will have to heal exquisitely well, or it risks being ripped open when she shifts into her human form. I'm sorry, but I think she needs more than my surgery can offer."

Faeza snatched back her hands as if she had been burned. "There's nothing at Shanghai Moon to help. And now you are saying your vet surgery can't help either."

"I want her to have the best chance," said Marina softly.

"The empath thinks the fox's best chance of survival is Wildwoods," said Orpheus.

Marina chewed her lip. "I hate what Phinnaeous Shine did to Rob, but I think this is the only way. Fei Yen's injuries are complex."

"But Wildwoods is a viper's nest at the moment. We should take the fox to Rayna," said the leopard.

"Rayna won't be able to work without the medical equipment in the Wildwoods infirmary, together with the healing plants in her office," said Orpheus.

"Fei Yen can't speak for herself right now, so this is your choice, Faeza. If you agree, I will teleport you there. The infirmary is always well-manned. I will speak to Phinnaeous." A flicker of doubt in Ezra's gravelly voice. "He won't turn away a peculiar in need."

Her face was wan, her body drenched in her own sweat and her wife's blood. "All this time, we have avoided that place. And yet, it holds the key to Fei Yen's survival." She slumped. "What else can I do but agree?"

I nodded. "Fei Yen must live. Orpheus, you'll accompany us? You hold more sway with Phinnaeous than any of us."

The vampire inclined his head.

Marina crouched down to the patient. "There's a blanket in the compartment of my bag. We can use it as a makeshift hammock. Keep her as still and supported as possible. To save her limb, we'll have to be quick."

I found the blanket, and when Faeza lifted Fei Yen onto it, I cushioned the injured fox with a light breeze, keeping the air flowing while Ezra and Orpheus hoisted her and took an edge each between them. In her fox form, Fei Yen weighed little more than a spaniel.

We stood in a circle, each linking to the other: Ezra, Fei Yen and Orpheus, Faeza distraught and supported by me, Marina and a cowed Echo, who for once didn't have a song falling from his lips.

Ezra whisked us through the greys and blacks of the eerie twilight, where ghosts roamed and souls departed. He led us back to the place where, for me at least, magic had begun. A place that the foxes feared but which held the key to their interrupted happy ever after.

13

A sliver of a moon shone in the sky over Wildwoods as we emerged in Crystal Palace Park. A grinding noise filled the air as the sphinxes, Mammatas and Rhokon, turned their stone heads towards us.

"You can't be here, Alisha. The Prime Sorcerer was very clear. Your rights to Wildwoods have been revoked," said Rhokon. "As have yours, Ministers. And yours, leopard. And yours, empath."

Ezra's tight jawline revealed his fraying temper. "That is disputed. There has been no full senate meeting to revoke our rights. You are acting on one man's whims."

"Preach, dog," said Echo. "As Aretha Franklin would say, R-E-S-P-E-C-T."

Rhokon sighed, the gloomier of the two. "I miss the days when we only had to worry about dark elves, not pop-culture-quoting leopards. In any case, the yew tree will not let you enter, nor will we."

"Speak for yourself." Mammatas's stone body shuddered with emotion. "Have you brought us a picnic in that blanket? The wind has carried the smell of cold meats to us across the park from the high street all day. It's torturous being imprisoned in our stone bodies without so much as a slice of bloody sausage."

Annoyance drifted across Rhokon's terracotta-painted face. He rolled his eyes, and for a moment, I feared his stone eyeballs would get stuck in opposing positions. "What's tortuous is lying next to you for over a century with you constantly mistaking everything for cold meats. That, you dingbat, is a dead fox. You can't expect to gain entry to Wildwoods with such a poor offering, druid."

"She's not dead," cried out Faeza.

"The eternal girl will always be welcome at Wildwoods," said Mammatas. "Don't you sense the vibrations of the arena, the yearning of the vaulted cabin, the swaying of the trees beckoning her home? The Prime Sorcerer may retain his crown, but magic flows away from him. That's why he's so angry. He can see his demise in the withering of the leaves."

God, how I hoped that was true. Right now, the odds seem stacked against us.

"Of course, the leaves are falling." Rhokon's voice, dry as sandpaper, thundered through the park. "It's autumn, you baboon."

Mammatas's head turned through the degrees until he faced Rhokon. His head curved downwards. "First, you call me a dingbat, now a baboon. You know very well I'm a human head on a lion's body. And you say *I* have bad eyesight."

I can sense the fox's blood draining. It disperses on the wind, said Orpheus.

I cut the sphinxes short. "Thank you for your advice, friends. Our injured fox needs help. We will try our luck at the yew tree."

Rhokon's unblinking eyes found me. "I wish you luck, druid."

I urged the group onwards, tugging Faeza along with me. "Let's go."

The sphinxes' voices followed me.

"She called us friend, did you hear? The Prime Sorcerer never calls us friend, and we've known him for much longer," said Rhokon.

"You should think about that," said Mammatas.

Berries and twigs crunched underfoot as we made our way to the gnarled yew tree with its rune. Echo bounded ahead. Above us, a starless night sky peeked through barren, late autumn branches.

"She'll be okay," I said to Faeza in the crook of my arm.

How often had I taken their effortless love for granted? The way they finished each other's sentences. How they spoke in unison. How they saved the last dim sum in the takeaway box for the other. And took joy in wearing matching qipaos for date night. Their silent teamwork borne of their decades together. Their laughter for each other's foibles. Their reliance on one another, as if without the other, as a buoyancy aid, life would not be worth living.

Women so grounded, that takeaways, a new set of tarot cards and attending night class made them happy.

Women who had moved continents so they could lead a quiet life together.

Faeza's voice was barely audible. "We had tickets to The Butterfly House at The Horniman Museum on Wednesday. She was so excited."

I pressed her hand. "You'll go another time."

Her face was wan in the moonlight. "What will become of my life if she doesn't survive?"

I shook my head. "You mustn't talk like that. She can hear you. You must hold onto hope."

"What good is hope?" said Faeza. "Hope is like children wishing for the tooth fairy, Santa or a trip to Disney Land. It has no basis in reality. I decided long ago in China to never make promises I couldn't keep."

"Hope is more than that. It's not sparkle and fairies. It's

grit and determination. It's holding the hand of a loved one and pulling them out of the dirt. It's clinging on through clawing fear to fight for what you need. You can't give up hope, Faeza." I squeezed her. "I'll do my part, I promise."

We neared an oak tree that made a natural den, its boughs plentiful and deep, and a hollow in its trunk that offered refuge if the situation deteriorated.

I called the others. "Set Fei Yen down here while we negotiate terms. Keep her out of sight and calm. Faeza and Marina, stay with her."

Ezra and Orpheus lowered the makeshift hammock with care and joined Echo at my side. We continued to the yew tree. My heart ached to know that, even if I did press my hand to the rune, I would feel no warmth of acceptance. Wildwoods would not materialise for me today, not after my snubbing of Phinnaeous Shine.

How often, over the expanse of time, had a woman been punished because she had said no? *No, I won't fold your socks. No, I won't laugh at your jokes. No, I won't dress how you please. No, I won't sleep with you. No, I won't bear you children. No, you can't have this piece of me.* Only to have men take revenge.

The Prime Sorcerer deserved a well-aimed kick to his sausage and eggs. I would show him that he couldn't push us around. That he couldn't remake the magical community in his image.

That victory would taste so sweet.

Sadly, tonight was not that night. Tonight, I'd nod and agree and do what I had to so my friend received the care she needed.

Echo's tail swished. "I will take the high ground in case a battle ensues to be of better service to you."

I scratched him behind the ears, knowing how sore he was to have let me and the foxes down. "You and I stick together from now on. I shouldn't have sent you on a mission alone."

"Sometimes I wonder if you need me at all. You sliced off the red woman's fingers, and there's not a scratch on you."

The fingers will make a wonderful display at my club, said Orpheus.

Quiet. Me and my cat are having a moment. "I need you, Echo of Maharashtra. You'll always be my kitty."

He purred and nuzzled his head against my waist before leaping into a nearby tree, his golden rosette coat blending in with his surroundings, his emerald eyes scanning the park for trouble.

He didn't have long to wait.

Ezra stopped short yards from the yew tree. "We have company."

There stood Phinnaeous Shine—alerted no doubt by the sphinxes—encased in darkness. As our eyes adjusted to his dark robes, midnight skin and play of shadows, he cupped his hands and brought a sparking ball of light into being as if it were the simplest thing in the world. His wizardry had always been spectacular, but magic couldn't take the tar off his dark soul.

It took a hell of a lot more than party tricks to impress a woman in her midlife.

His hair had grown unruly, and his neutral expression had given way to a simmering venom. "So the prodigal sons and daughters come scurrying back, as expected. You will receive a cold welcome here." Dark eyes found Orpheus. "I expected it of the wolf. He is, after all, sleeping with her. But I am disappointed in you, old friend. There is still room for you at my side."

Orpheus nodded. "I appreciate the olive branch, Prime Sorcerer, but if the centuries have taught me anything, it's that friends fall out. Perhaps you might see the error of your ways."

Phinnaeous blanched. "How dare you? It seems you, too, have fallen under the druid's spell. We must curb her power."

Echo roared, causing Phinnaeous to jerk his head warily in the direction of his perch.

"Enough," I said. "Enough willy-waving and rhetoric. Let our actions speak for themselves. I might not fully trust you, Phinnaeous, but I believe you care for peculiars."

He played with the ball of light as if it were a yo-yo. The message was clear. Any one of us could be hurt by it. "My title is Prime Sorcerer."

What had I done to make him hate me so much, other than be myself? My anger burned bright, but I swallowed it. "If you care for peculiars, Prime Sorcerer, you'll agree to care for an injured *hu hsien*. She needs treatment in the Wildwoods infirmary."

"I had long heard rumours of *hu hsien* in London." His gleaming eyes settled on the hilt of my sword, visible through my ponytail. "Let me see her."

My mouth went dry. I called over my shoulder. "You can come out."

Faeza and Marina, a bright speck in the woods with her rainbow hair, carried the hammock between them. Blood had pooled through the fabric of the blanket, leaving a dark stain.

"Closer," said Phinnaeous. "Closer." He peered inside and then smiled at Faeza. "How wonderful. And by your nakedness, I assume you are *hu hsien* too?"

Faeza nodded.

"Remarkable."

My gut twisted. "Will you help?"

"Yes, for a price," said Phinnaeous. "Give me the sword."

Ezra cursed. "We can't trust him."

Faeza twisted to look at me. Her whisper tore at my heart. "Please."

I wouldn't do it, Alisha. Some people covet death. Perhaps the limp fox is embracing her end, said Orpheus. *Without the sword, you are a fangless mewling against the gods. And fangs are very important.*

"Take your time to decide. The injured fox will thank you for it," said Phinnaeous.

"There's no other way, Alisha." Marina kissed the lucky clover on her wrist, followed by the cross at her neck.

We needed all the luck we could get.

I looked at Marina and then at Echo, my eyes softening. My friends had got me so far. They had never abandoned me.

How could I abandon them? There was only one thing I could do, however much it pained me. It was the thing that Mum had taught me, and Dad, and Marina by fighting for the life of every hamster or guinea pig that crossed her vet's table. Even the Earth goddess Gaia, by the way she took the time to make piping hot potato curry and chapatis for the latch-key children on her estate.

Every life mattered.

I pulled Transcender from its baldric. The baldric that the foxes had made me.

Maybe it would always have come to this moment.

If I did this, it could be that I wouldn't hear Mum's voice again. It could be that the next time a god came for me, I would be defenceless. But all the same, looking at Faeza's pleading eyes, I knew I couldn't trade my life for Fei Yen's.

"No," said Ezra. "The sword is the only protection you have."

"My friends are my protection." I gave him a small smile, though my breath quivered in my chest.

I turned over the sword in my hand one last time, feeling the smooth, mammoth-tusk hilt that Gaia's lover Death had fashioned for her, and ran my thumb over the deepest blue jewel adorning it. Its obsidian blade glimmered in the moonlight, and a rush of whispers filled my head.

How I wished I could listen to them.

I swallowed the lump in my throat. Echo jumped down from his perch with a thud and padded alongside me, a low rumble in his throat as we approached the Prime Sorcerer.

I handed the sword to Phinnaeous Shine.

He extinguished his ball of sparking light at long last and searched my face as his hand closed around the hilt. "That wasn't so hard, was it?"

He held Transcender up to the moonlight.

My sword was now his.

Phinnaeous placed it into a pocket inside his robes. It vanished like it had never been there at all. Then he refastened his robes and looked up. "I always get what I want."

"Questionable," purred Echo. "You didn't get Rajika Verma."

I kept my tone even, although my hate for him swarmed like bats in my belly. "You will call us to pick them up when she is healed and keep us updated on her progress?"

He bent to scoop Fei Yen up in his arms. Unceremoniously. As if she wasn't a fragile thing made up of bones and flesh and wisdom and love. Phinnaeous's eyebrows shot up, quick as an arrow. "Them? The injured fox comes with me. No one else."

Faiza stifled a cry. "She can't go in alone."

Phinnaeous shrugged. "Then she doesn't come in at all. I don't need the eternal girl's spies in my hallowed halls."

"Please, Phinnaeous," said Ezra. "This woman is no threat. You can see she just wants to care for the fox."

The Prime Sorcerer shook his head. "I had high hopes for you, Neuhoff. Such wasted potential."

"It's okay. It's okay." Faeza pressed a kiss to Fei Yen's furry head. "Stay strong for me. We'll be together again soon."

Phinnaeous grimaced. "Out of my way. We have work to do."

He shouldered Faeza as he passed with the precious bundle, and the yew tree shuddered, giving us a glimpse of Wildwoods before it disappeared again and Fei Yen with it.

We stood, aghast, as the hooting of a night owl punctuated our thoughts.

"He has to be removed," said Ezra.

Orpheus nodded. "Yes, Neuhoff, he does. Let's hope your plan with the old alpha works. We need to find a way into Wildwoods and take it back by force if necessary."

"Finally. That's what Rob has been trying to tell you," said Marina.

Echo's emerald eyes glinted. "If the red woman returns, Alisha will be in danger without the sword."

There had been no other choice but to give it up. The foxes were my friends.

I frowned, spinning in the circle. The night was dark, but my eyes weren't that bad. "Where's Faeza?"

My stomach clenched as a fox's screams pierced the night air. Not just any screams. Heart-wrenching shrieks of grief and separation. Ezra's jacket lay discarded in a heap on the damp ground.

Faeza—in her fox form—emerged from within its folds. Her gut-churning wails continued, and she spun as if driven to despair. Her skittish brown eyes were no longer focused on one point. Her brown-red coat and bushy tail weren't as bristly as Fei Yen's. Whereas Fei Yen had patches of white on her neck and the tip of her tail, Faeza's tail and legs had been dipped in black ink.

But as we watched, a change took place.

Her wails peaked, and at that peak of anguish, a snowy white erased the vibrant red of her body. It covered the fur of her jawline, the backs of her protruding ears, head and tail, and the whole expanse of her neck.

A contagion.

Until no red remained, save for a small patch around her eyes, a sliver on her chest and upper legs.

I stifled a cry of surprise before reaching out for her. "Faeza."

She took off, in her new incarnation, driving straight through a hawthorn hedge in her mania.

"What just happened?" Shaking, I checked the hawthorn bush to make sure she wasn't stuck in there.

"My best guess is stress. Let her go," said Marina. "She needs some space to process what happened. There is nothing more we can do tonight."

I picked up Ezra's jacket from the floor and hugged it to me. "There's no hope of visiting the Celestial Library without the foxes to facilitate the Shanghai Moon portal. Let's go home to the cottage."

His grey eyes met mine. "Yes, hellfire, let's." He growled. "Cat, you're with us. We'll drop you and Marina off on the way, Orpheus. But this taxi service is only to win brownie points with my love, so don't get used to it."

Orpheus sniffed. "I hardly need your help, Neuhoff. Although I'm embarrassed to say my Lotus is still parked at the farmhouse. Perhaps it might be better if Alisha stayed with me tonight. Just for safety's sake."

"No. The cottage is fine," I said flatly.

I blocked out that I'd wanted Ezra to throw Rashida out of the pack, and he'd refused. I blocked out my gut feeling that, despite his protestations, he didn't want children. Blocked out how I might still have Death's sword if Sahil and his deathly troupe of ravens hadn't attacked Fei Yen. Blocked out the foxes being alone tonight.

Right now, I needed Ezra.

I went to him, my hand flat against his chest. "Let's go home."

14

A new day dawned, but the cocooned cottage, still wrapped in Gaia's vines, made me lose all sense of time and space. I woke, wrapped in Ezra's arms, still heavy with sleep, before scrambling for my phone on the side table.

I groaned and switched on the lamp to chase away the dark. "Crap. It's gone ten o'clock."

Ezra splayed his hands on my hips and pulled me on top of him. His hair flopped in his eyes.

His smile gave me butterflies. I loved him like this, all unkempt and musky before his shower. The side of him that was mine alone before he pulled himself together for the world outside.

"If we're already lazy layabouts, then a few minutes more makes no difference." He ran his hand along the back of my neck and pulled me closer, biting my bottom lip before deepening his kiss, stealing my breath.

Heat pulsed in my core.

Despite everything, he so easily made me the centre of his world. Memories from the preceding night flooded back: The red woman at the pack farmhouse. Sahil attacking. Fei Yen slack and bleeding. Handing Phinnaeous Shine the sword. And Faeza's grief-stricken wails.

I kissed Ezra—our lips entwining for a delicious moment, mountain air and smoky warmth, his body hard against my softness—before rolling off him. "We should check on Faeza to see how she's holding up."

He sighed and propped himself up on his elbows. "You're always thinking of others. But the greatest threat right now is to you."

My intuition sparked, triggered by a flashback to the meadow outside the farmhouse that afternoon. "Actually, I don't think that's right. The portal goddess had every chance to kill me. But it was the sword she wanted."

I spooled my thoughts back to the red woman's initial attack at the cottage.

"Do you remember how it played out the day she first came here?" I asked. "She and Gaia talked about once dancing in the heavens together, being friends and how Gaia had betrayed the gods by giving me Death's sword."

Ezra nodded. "Her words are burned in my brain. She threatened you."

"That's just it." I chewed my lip. "Did she?"

He sprang out of bed so we faced each other, his face tight. "I remember what she said word for word, Alisha. She said 'the druid thinks it matters what she wants. All that matters is that you die.'"

"Ezra, I think she was talking about Gaia." My blood ran cold. "Not me."

"No." Doubt flooded his face. "It's you. It's you that Gaia said the gods considered to be a wart, a thorn, a verruca."

I huffed out a laugh. "Yeah, thanks. I got that the first time. But my English teacher's radar tells me that we misunderstood. That switch from *she* to *you* midway through means she was talking to Gaia all along. The red woman could have killed me at the farmhouse, but instead, she was fixated on getting the sword. It's Gaia she wants dead." My lungs constricted. I'd felt abandoned by her, but what if something had happened? "We have to speak to her."

A padding of feet as Echo nudged the door to the bedroom open. "Well, thank the stars. Signs of life in here at last. I thought you'd gone into hibernation."

I crouched to stroke him. "You should have woken us."

The leopard leapt onto the newly vacated bed. "I thought I'd eat my way through the supplies of fish and steak in the fridge first. I like a hearty breakfast. But then the unnatural darkness started to get to me. I can't be out there alone in this tomb. I'll wait here while you two freshen up. I can be your radio."

Half an hour later, after Echo had made our ears bleed with a medley of The Lighthouse Family and The Bee Gees, topped off with massacring Madonna's "Vogue," we said goodbye to Ezra.

"I'm going to seek out Gunnolf," said Ezra. "Just to make sure he hasn't absconded on our deal."

"And we will visit the Earth goddess before checking on the foxes," I said.

Echo's tail swished. "So you can tell her of the threat to her and ask about the book the dark elf lied to you about."

He hadn't been impressed with Meriel Naehorn's tale. But why would he be? He liked to think of himself as the fountain of all knowledge on my grandmother, and it pained him that she'd kept a secret. There was no possibility of him believing a word her murderer said.

Ezra sighed and pressed a kiss to my forehead. "Be safe, Alisha. Echo, stay close. She might need you." He set his phone to loud for me, even though he hated it. "If you need me, call. I'll be there in a flash."

Echo and I took an Otherworld taxi to Tooting Broadway. The market bustled with life. We veered past fruit and vegetable stall holders touting fresh produce into Gaia's rundown estate.

Plucking out a hair each in payment, I wondered how a bald person might pay before hopping out of the claw-marked taxi.

"Come on, Echo," I said.

I didn't need to ask the leopard twice. He loved Gaia, perhaps even more than me. He bounded ahead of me through the open door of her flat while I lingered to admire the abundance of blooms in her front garden so late in the year. For those who knew of her existence, the garden was a loudspeaker announcement, a flashing billboard sign, that the Earth goddess lived here.

I worried that Cardea would find her.

Suddenly nervous, I pushed open the sunshine-yellow door and called out, "Gaia."

"I'm in here, druid," said the goddess. "Just cutting up Chanakya some lamb."

I headed for the kitchen. "Don't go to any trouble. He's eaten already."

Echo purred. "Don't listen to her. My stomach is a never-ending pit, and my hunger pangs are the bane of my life. You can leave it on the bone, goddess. I fear I am getting soft in this city life. I miss the hunt. The thrill of the chase."

The goddess chuckled. "I can throw the lamb shank up in the air for you. You can give it a shake and pretend it's real. I won't judge you. It's never been in my nature to be judgemental, whatever Cardea said. I love all god's creatures. Apart from vampires. Those toothy, death-ridden abominations can rot in their coffins for all time."

Pleasure infused her cheeks with red as she turned and caught sight of me. She pressed me against her bosom.

Any closer, and I would have been motor-boating those puppies.

"Gaia," I said. "I'm sorry to turn up out of the blue. The

place looks so clean, and here I am, foisting a lamb-shank-throwing leopard on you."

Her smile dulled. "My door is open for as long as I'm here and probably afterwards unless the council boards it up, which is a real possibility, given the crime rate around here. Anything not nailed down wanders off, and then suddenly, you find it in your neighbour's house without a flicker of remorse. Like the pink Wellington Boots with the rainbow rubber sole I found in Flat 28's kitchen." She shook her head. "Still, it's better than the days when men would bludgeon each other to death over a cucumber. The first one ever grown really was a coveted item."

Given lamb bones crunching wasn't the best soundtrack to a conversation, we settled in the living room, leaving Echo to his chomping. This time, the ceiling lamps and photo frames had been dusted, the thin green carpet hoovered, the armchair cushions plumped, and the magnolia walls had a new coat of paint.

Gaia adjusted her simple green sari before lowering herself into the armchair. A look of satisfaction filled her worldly eyes. "My latch-key children did the paint job. They wouldn't let me lift a finger. I sat in this armchair, and they even made me a cup of chai. It was awful, of course. Not brewed long enough, and the spices were unbalanced. Plus, the milk curdled. To be honest, it tasted like cow urine. Nothing like the chai at my beloved café. But they will learn. My strays always do. All it takes is a little faith. Like everything, really."

I grimaced. Despite her pride, this time, her home didn't feel as homely. Like it had been sanitised. The sort of feeling in a house just before an estate agent covers the furniture with dust sheets.

I perched on the armchair opposite her, a chest set between us. "Gaia, I have something to tell you."

"I know, child. You called for me, remember? I listen to a

thousand voices, a thousand neighs, a thousand bleats and woofs and hisses. I hear the falling leaves on God's green earth, the anger of the winds, the crumbling of the coastlines and the melting of the ice caps. Of course, I heard you."

A stone weighed on my heart. Her very presence made me feel safer. How I wished I could trust her. "You didn't come."

She pursed her lips. "You doubted me."

I fidgeted, twisting my wrists. Anything to avoid the censure in her knowing eyes. "So you know what happened?"

"I know it all. That you are no longer welcome at Wildwoods School of the Wondrous and that it is starting to become clear who really stands with us. That you released the old alpha and visited the dark elf. That Cardea found you at the farmhouse, and you sliced off her fingers without missing a beat, completing your transformation from classroom teacher to warrior. That you don't have the necklace and you lost the sword. That one fox is hurt, and the other is unhinged. That you have good sex with Ezra."

I flushed with embarrassment. Her list was disastrous, but what really concerned me was whether she had seen us getting jiggy with it. Heaven help us; how good was her hearing? And could she see, too?

Gaia grinned, her face folding into creases. She knotted her thin hair at her nape, exposing her plump midriff as her sari blouse rolled up with the movement of her arms. "An inspired move, using your wind powers during foreplay. That was a favourite trick of mine during my youth. Just think, during your divorce, you thought you might never have good sex again."

I wiped my clammy hands on my jeans. "Will the red woman hold it against me that I slashed off her fingers?"

Gaia chuckled. "I doubt she was expecting that, but never you mind. Cardea's innate healing abilities mean she can regenerate. She has that in common with flatworms, lizards and sea slugs. Lucky her."

"She had every chance to kill me. I'm starting to think she's after you, not me."

A sad smile twisted her dry lips. "That could be."

"But you will protect yourself? I'd hate for what happened to Ra in that warehouse to happen to you."

"And yet the sun still shines. And the ravens still fly. Even the water goddess nurses her wounds."

I frowned. "So you can't be killed?"

"Of course I can, Alisha. Did I slip into Aramaic again? But killing an immortal is not a finite act. Our life force ebbs and flows like a river. Sometimes it's dormant. Sometimes it's volcanic. Sometimes, it is trapped in a stone relic or needs a spark of untarnished life to metamorphosis. Centuries can pass in between. But one thing is clear—immortals experience death differently to mortals."

Her answer did not satisfy me. The Gaia I knew would never be sanguine about her fate. The Gaia I knew would be plotting and planning to ensure that light won out. That darkness didn't envelop us.

She registered my furrowed brow. "The roads we travel are never smooth, but eventually, everything falls into place. Just believe, druid. Believe as your grandmother did before you."

Something about the way she said that gave me pause. I was tired of the Earth goddess's secrets. Tired of the piecemeal way in which she gave me information. Like I was just a pawn on a chessboard or cavalry on a battlefield. A piece to pave the way but ultimately discarded. She'd met me when I knew nothing of the Otherworld, armed me with weapons, and filled my head with morsels of wisdom, but how much had she left out?

I went quiet inside. "How many times did you meet my grandmother, Gaia?"

Gaia's eyes flashed like the burning of a distant sun. "After all this time, you still doubt me, Alisha."

"There is a book. A book of names." I hesitated. "Names that belong to the gods."

She held my gaze, her hands fluttering to the armrests of her chair. "Yes, there is."

A breeze rustled her hair. It wasn't one I had raised. It was a show of power from the goddess herself. Who knew what her real form was? What did I really know about her? Maybe she could grow as fast as her vines. Maybe she didn't have a human form, and this body of hers, the old Indian grandmother, wasn't hers at all. Maybe she had chosen it because it was the form I'd most trust.

My insides quivered.

Echo sensed the change in atmosphere and came to my side when once he might have chosen hers. His emerald eyes swung from me to Gaia, whiskers twitching as he assessed the danger.

Gaia issued a stark command, all warmth gone. "Ask what you want to ask me, granddaughter of Rajika Verma."

I laid a hand on Echo's back to calm him. "Do you know where the book is?"

On the sideboard, the cacti plants sprouted new prickly leaves. "I asked your grandmother not to tell me. A god's life is long, and motivations change. I wanted it safe even from me."

Bile filled my throat. "I am asking again, Gaia. How many times did you meet my grandmother?"

"Guard your tone, druid. Even my patience can wear thin. No one is irreplaceable. Not even you."

Echo growled. "Perhaps we have outstayed our welcome."

Gaia softened. "Time is short, and I don't want to part on these terms. Come here, Chanakya." She tweaked his ear with her weathered hands, a gentle chastisement, then scratched his chin. "You couldn't hurt me if you tried."

He purred and rolled onto his back, exposing his belly. The traitor. "My apologies, goddess. I suspected as much, goddess. Thank you for the lamb shank."

A cloud of melancholy settled over Gaia. "You know, I've been in this flat for decades. I know its every nook and cranny. Every pockmark on the wall, every bit of peeling wallpaper, every hissing pipe and dripping tap and every creaking floorboard. It's not perfect, but in a long life full of change, it has been a buoy in the ocean." She sighed. "Very well, druid. I'll tell you how many times I met your grandmother." She held up two crooked hands and then closed one. "Ten times, perhaps. Or maybe five. I lose count."

Her sharp eyes made me doubt that very much.

"Rajika and I always made sure to be alone," she continued. "Yes, that includes you, Chanakya. Sometimes, women need to be amongst themselves. It's the way the universe balances out all the time men spent in Roman baths. But it is my very last meeting with Rajika that is emblazoned in my mind."

I leaned closer, entranced by the story, and when I looked closer, it was as if the events themselves played out in Gaia's irises like these weren't memories she spooled through but a film reel.

"You'd just turned one," said Gaia. "Rajika had just come from your father's house, where she had been babysitting you and Sahil. Your parents had umm-ed and aah-ed about leaving you children in her care, and they'd finally bitten the bullet. Your grandmother wasn't very involved, you see. The Custodian of the Celestial Library is always an obsessive, and she was no different. Your mother worried she would no longer know how to change a nappy or mop up drool. But Rajika pushed them out the door."

"Where were my parents going?"

"To a Duran Duran concert. Your mother was wild for Simon Le Bon, I believe. It was your parents' first date following your birth."

Echo's handsome face flattened in sorrow. "That was the day Rajika died. She left the children in my care. I got to the battle late. I took out my fair share of elves and fought to get closer to her, but Naehorn's second in command gave me this." He tilted his head to indicate the three-inch scar at the corner of his eye. "He was a wily old fellow with a hammer in one hand and acrobatics that left me dizzy. By the time I'd despatched him, your grandmother was too weak to speak. She breathed her last as I stood over her. The winged horse was there too."

"A lot of good people died that night, and a future was lost in which your grandmother, not Phinnaeous Shine, would have shaped the Otherworld," said Gaia.

Echo growled. "Afterwards, I found Naehorn plundering an inner vault. She could not escape me."

Gaia sighed. "Your grandmother knew a time would come when this world would fall into darkness. We had spoken of the prophecy many times before and of your family's place in it. The night she babysat you children, when she realised the elves had found a way to penetrate the defences of the Celestial Library, she made a decision. Call it intuition. Or perhaps call it a happy coincidence that she'd wrestled that night with how to help you claim your magical destiny, although your parents seemed more interested in a humdrum existence. Whatever the reason, she made a detour on the way to the battle. She knocked on that door right behind you."

I spun around, the fine hair on my arms rising. The sunshine-yellow front door suddenly seemed like a relic from the past. "What did she say?"

"She told me that, sooner or later, your parents' natural caution would lead them to bind your magic. She said that if anything were to happen to her, I should find the right time to tell your mother that your only chance of living to a ripe old age was for you to embrace your magic."

Forty was pretty ripe. I was more bruised banana than tart apple. "Why didn't she ask you to approach my father?"

"She wanted their marriage to be harmonious. And that if Rosalie could be convinced, then Joshi would follow. A mother would always be swayed to difficult choices if she felt she was protecting her children." Gaia picked at the threads of her sari. "And Rajika was right. Your father did ask witches to bind your powers. And it was your mother I spoke to and colluded with about keeping you safe. Your mother planned to speak to your father at last and confide in him about the Jericho necklace. But that night, her car crashed."

Grief settled over my chest, a weighted blanket. I missed Mum so much. "Why are you telling me all this now?"

"Because I might not get another chance," said the goddess.

"You've kept so much from me. You didn't tell me about the book of names."

She huffed. "Humans are always so keen to know everything at once, but if you did, your skull would explode from the sheer magnitude. Be grateful I hand-feed you pieces of knowledge as if you were my own pet goat."

Echo honked with laughter as Gaia's feet. "You have a delightful sense of comedy, goddess, that sneaks out in the most unexpected places. I wonder why you have never tried your hand as a comedian."

"Actually, there's not many things I haven't tried in my long existence. I did a comedy show at the Globe Theatre in the early seventeenth century before a performance of *A Midsummer Night's Dream,* and the audience pelted me with rotten tomatoes. I was tempted to turn them into a forest in revenge, but the actors had spent so long learning their lines it didn't seem fair. That taught me there is as much honour in withholding my power as there is in using it."

I thought of the gifts I had lost or had yet to find. The ones given to me by Gaia, Mum and Rajika. "Will I get the sword back? The necklace? Will I find the book?"

"The fates have not yet decided, druid. But mark my words, the key to this whole adventure is friendship. We will only succeed if every cog plays its part."

A shiver ran up my spine. "And you, Gaia? Are you a cog, too?"

Her sari rustled as she leaned forward. She picked up the queen from her chess set before setting it down in the middle of the board and then knocked it over with a sigh. "We are all cogs, Alisha. Every thought leaves a ripple that can become a wave. Every action has a counteraction."

"Goddess, do you think I should have punished my brother for what he did to Fei Yen?"

Gaia shifted in her chair. "The werepigeon was always going to be important for this story. My approach has always been to shower wayward beings with love, but history has shown it doesn't always work. Look at nature. Heavens, even *The Lion King* had it right. Families are meant to support each other. Hurting a family member only leads to hurting yourself."

"Isn't there a leopard movie you can quote?" said Echo. "This emphasis on lions is tiresome."

"You can tell me what tiresome is when you get to my age, Chanakya," chided Gaia.

He bowed his handsome head.

"As I was saying, druid. You made a choice about the werepigeon." Her eyes glinted. "I pray in time that your generosity and openheartedness will pay off. And truth be told, it is always dangerous to take direct vengeance for a crime. Far better to leave that to a higher authority. Judgement Day is a hoot for those of us with clean souls. We can sit back and watch the others get their bottoms spanked. Until then, the only thing a mortal can do is their best." A weighted pause. "You will do your best to retrieve the sword, the necklace and the book, druid, won't you?"

I gulped. "Yes, goddess."

She dusted off her hands and gave an excited giggle. "Good. I'm glad that's sorted. Now, who wants to join me for some chai at the café? Who knows when we'll get another chance? My pension just landed in my account, and I have pennies to spend."

"And if the red woman comes?"

The goddess heaved herself up from the armchair. "I pledged once never to succumb to darkness. That pledge means many things. Today, it means not being afraid to go out in search of the perfect cup of chai."

15

Gaia linked arms with me, and we ambled towards her favourite café. She frowned at Echo as he sharpened his claws on a sycamore tree.

"Hurry along, you two," she said. "Any slower, and I'd have to transform you into a tortoise, Chanakya. I'm afraid there's no way for you to avoid the rain shower today, but if I hurry, my own feet will remain dry. I'm immune to human afflictions such as colds and bladder infections, but I hate wrinkly wet toes."

The sky had grown heavy with gunmetal clouds during our visit. They lined the horizon, threatening rain, yet Gaia ventured out in her sari and sandals without a coat. The Earth goddess clearly had an ingrained sense of weather patterns and didn't need a weather app like mere mortals.

"Are you sure Echo can come into the café?" I said.

A mischievous glint sparked in her worldly eyes. "Oh yes, anything goes when it comes to me. I'm a minor celebrity in these parts. He'll walk right in with us, and they'll serve him a lovely saucer of salted *lassi*." Sure enough, she'd waved to half a dozen people in as many steps. By the looks of it, it was possible that the Queen of England had copied her waving technique. "When I say minor, I mean on par with Amitabh Bachan's fame in Mumbai. I just prefer not to boast."

My phone buzzed in my pocket. An unknown number flashed on the screen.

Gaia gave a sad smile and pushed open the door to the café. "Our small window of opportunity has closed. Never mind. I can drink an extra cup on your behalf. You better answer that. That robed devil won't wait. Good luck, druid."

I nodded goodbye and held the phone to my ear. "Hello?"

Phinnaeous Shine's voice, caustic and gruff, travelled down the line. "Druid."

"Prime Sorcerer." I kept my tone muted and calm, although my heartbeat raced. "Do you have an update on Fei Yen?"

"The patient will live." His voice was matter-of-fact, making me wonder what he was hiding.

I exhaled with relief. "Thank you. I will let her family know."

"If by that, you mean the other fox, you need not look any further than Crystal Palace Park and its immediate vicinity. Judging by the police presence just outside of Wildwoods this morning, she has gone fully *hu hsien*."

A pang of guilt. Had Faeza, in her grief, lost her grip on her humanity? Is that why her red coat had transformed? What did going fully *hu hsien* mean?

I gripped the phone tighter. "I will handle it."

"Be sure you do, Alisha Verma. You brought this trouble to Wildwoods. I won't let you undo all my hard work."

My thoughts whirred. Just like the chess décor at Wildwoods this term, Phinnaeous plotted his steps meticulously. With any luck, Gunnolf reported back to Ezra by now.

I asked the one thing I knew would help calm Faeza down. "Can Fei Yen come home?"

"That depends on Neuhoff. Bring him with you." The line went dead.

The warmth of Echo's body weaving around my legs couldn't neutralise the iciness that gripped my heart.

Emerald eyes and his golden coat stood out against the grey London asphalt. "What's wrong?"

As a humdrum, the world plodded along. Groceries to buy. A lesson plan to write. Laundry to fold. Socks to pair. The floor to mop. Dinner to make. A bed to fall into before the cycle started all over again.

As a peculiar, the world unravelled quicker than I could string my thoughts together. Could I learn fast enough to stay afloat and rival the most powerful beings in the Otherworld?

Time to put on my big girl knickers. I took a deep breath and then let loose a loud belch to call an Otherworld taxi. "We're going to need our friends and my catalogue of creatures. We're going to Wildwoods."

WE ARRIVED in Crystal Palace mid-afternoon. Usually, the park playground and its meandering paths—past ponds and through woods and the painted dinosaurs so loved by children—would have been busy at this hour. But as the goddess predicted, the heavens had opened, and the driving rain had chased away pleasure seekers from both the park and the bustling triangle with its parades of shops and restaurants.

Thank the heavens because police sirens blared across the area in Faeza's wake.

Six of us took shelter from the rain underneath a bus stop: Ezra and Orpheus, Marina and Rob, Echo and me.

I took a deep breath. "Thanks for coming."

A curt nod from Ezra. "We've been through worse. We'll be fine if we work as a team."

Orpheus gave the slightest shrug. "Sometimes it is better for a lone individual with killer instincts to just go in and do the job."

I glared at him, raising my voice over the din of the rain. "There will be no killing today. What's the situation?"

Rob gave me an apologetic look. He tilted his head in the direction of an Indian restaurant a few doors down. "Faeza's running rampant in there. I told the blues and twos to back off and give me a thirty-minute window to sort it, but we cocked up. Marina and I thought we could handle it ourselves. We didn't want to disturb you while you were with Gaia. We got the diners and staff out of there and managed to close and crowbar the door. *Hu hsien* can use their paws as hands. One woman ran out screaming about deformed London vermin. It's all gone tits up."

Marina limbered up like a pro wrestler attempting to intimidate an opponent. "I brought my tranquilliser gun, although I hoped to go the easier route with some empathy. But I couldn't get close enough."

Her growth had been exponential, from our first encounters with Echo to leaping through the crumbling shards of the Celestial Library to an out-of-control hu hsien. Marina's instincts had adapted. She was more likely to run towards fire than from it. But after Sahil's mauling of Fei Yen, I was hyperaware of the need to protect my friends.

Marina continued. "I don't blame Faeza for flipping out. She's been through the mill; bless her. It's very unusual for an animal to turn white overnight. Like humans, dogs and cats go grey, but it's usually a long process. I didn't expect to find her one tail had become six, either. Or for her to look so wild. You don't find that in the Merck Veterinary Manual. Turns out a *hu hsien* isn't as easy to capture as your typical garden fox."

"I had to Taser her when she literally tried to suck the life out of some suited and booted men dipping their poppadoms in mango chutney. It only made her angrier."

"The poppadoms or the Tasering?" said Echo. "I like meat myself."

Orpheus's face was even paler than usual, his mouth a grim line. *I never realised I would be attached to such a ramshackle outfit. I like to be on the winning side.*

Oh, mark my words, sunshine, I thought. *We'll win.*

A vampire is a creature of the night, Alisha. He smirked. *We are very proficient at night-time pursuits.*

Christ alive, Orpheus. Can you concentrate?

Rob rubbed his stubble. "I reckon my general grubbiness saved me. She seems not to like powerful-looking men."

"I expect I'll be a prime target then," said Orpheus, provoking a snort from Ezra.

I took a deep breath, drawing on my classroom skills to get my rabble working closely together. Ezra deferred to me. I loved him for it, but I also recognised my growth as the eternal girl meant that, more and more, our wins had been led by me.

I could do it again. I just had to believe in myself.

"Rob," I began, "how long do we have until the police move in?"

He checked his watch and winced. "Ten minutes. The restaurant manager is pushing them to move in sooner. He's worried about a tandoori paneer and chickpea dish the chef has in the oven."

I nodded and stepped out of the shelter of the bus stop to peer into the window of the Indian restaurant where the *hu hsien* fox crashed into blue velvet chairs in a fury. Her brown eyes had turned an eerie green-violet mix. Her patchy red-white body, with its snowy throat and jaw, sent a frisson of fear through me. But it was her six white tails I feared the most, changes marking her change to soul-devouring *hu hsien*, the part Faeza had kept locked away since leaving China.

Although Dad would have told me that, in India, extra appendages signalled great luck.

But then, Dad's interventions weren't always helpful.

A vague plan forming in my mind, I returned to my friends, my hair damp with rain, and dropped my hand to my satchel to feel the familiar outline of my catalogue of creatures. "We have to get Faeza back under control for her own sake, and this community, and we have under ten minutes in which to do it. This is what we're going to do. Rob, you keep the bobbies back as long as possible and arrange for the CCTV footage in the local area to be wiped clean."

The detective nodded. "Consider it done."

"Orpheus, find any witnesses and wipe their minds," I said.

"You don't want me on your main team?" He struck his chest. *You wench.* "I'm wounded."

I got the feeling you were a little blood-lusty. You're lucky I didn't bench you. I turned to Ezra. "You stay in human form. Your teleportation skills mean you're the only man safe in there, but you'll still have to be careful."

Grey eyes on mine. He exuded calm and focus, his trust in me complete. "You're the boss."

"You, Marina and Echo are with me. We're going to make Faeza remember her humanity."

Echo gave a roar of approval and bounded ahead.

I led them towards the restaurant with fast strides. Within seconds, the rain had soaked our clothes to our bodies. "We don't show any fear. Animals can sense that."

Marina locked and loaded the tranquilliser gun and shook out her rainbow hair as if this was cosplay, but her alert gaze and set jaw showed determination. "Let's do this."

I faced the restaurant and the fox within. "The tranquilliser gun is a last resort. We must get through to her, or she'll enter this state again when she's awake."

Ezra and I exchanged glances before he slid out the crowbar holding the door shut. Inside, Faeza turned her eerie green-violet eyes on us and rushed to the front façade of the building, enraged at her captivity. Her ears were erect, and her six tails fanned out behind her, as magnificent as a peacock's spread. The glass shuddered in its frame.

Anxiety fluttered in my chest. "Now, Ezra."

He flung open the door, retaining the crowbar in his hand.

"Get in, quick." I raised my hands, creating a wind buffer to hold the charging *hu hsien* back and a small passage for my friends to slip through before rushing in myself. Indian spices filled my nose: cardamom, cumin, chilli and coriander. Baskets of naan and smashed curry plates littered the floor. "Marina, stay in the corner."

She leapt onto a rickety table with her tranquilliser gun at the ready, eyes trained on the target. Behind her, embroidered pictures of gods and maharajas on black cotton lined the walls, their gold frames lopsided and hanging precariously.

Ezra slammed the door shut to prevent Faeza's escape. With the door closed, my wind powers dropped in strength, and the fox leapt over the buffer, flying towards Ezra with snarling vengeance.

My blood cooled.

"Echo!" I shouted.

Ezra lunged for a chair to fend off Faeza. He could have easily shifted—a fox stood no chance against a wolf, even a *hu hsien* fox—but he didn't want to hurt her. He understood more than most how sometimes the beast controlled the person. How it was easy to lose control. How it was her love for Fei Yen that had driven her to this, not her hatred for men.

A man who understood love and hate was worth his salt.

But Ezra didn't need the chair as a barrier.

Echo leapt in between, my brave leopard, tail flicking angrily as he faced off against the fox, his teeth bared, his claws sharp. "Yes, my fox friend, you know us. And if you calm down, I'll round up a poodle for you to nibble on. Or a

German Shepherd that's more to your liking. Although adult ones are as bristly as a toilet brush." He lifted his nose to the air and sniffed. "Or perhaps a lamb curry with egg and potatoes if my nose doesn't deceive me."

"Will you stop talking about food?" said Ezra.

"Actually, he's giving her cause to stop and stare. We have to keep her in this state. It's vet 101—if you can't use force with an irate animal or create a bond, a distraction is the next best thing," said Marina. "He's not my magical consultant at the surgery for nothing."

I knelt on the carpeted floor and flicked through my catalogue of creatures, my fingers deft. "Buy me a few seconds."

Echo opened his mouth. A tuneless, garbled version of Madonna's "Crazy for You" flooded out.

The fox's tails went poker-rod straight. Her high-pitched howl made me wince.

Ezra winced. "Christ, make that stop. You've done it now. She looks like she wants to tear our heads off."

"At least it wasn't Britney Spears. Some things are too holy for Echo to ruin." Marina raised her tranquilliser gun with a sigh. She'd been head-over-heels in love with Britney in our youth.

Ezra pelted Faeza with naan. With every hit, the fox grew more determined to reach him. "If he was after songs about going crazy, he could have chosen Gnarls Barkley. At least that would have suited his range." He teleported to the other side of the restaurant, confusing the fox. "Hurry up, Alisha."

"She's stressed in here," said Marina over Echo's crooning. "She may be an urban fox, but this environment isn't helping. Her brain is flooding with cortisone in here. We have to remind her of the natural environment."

"Got it." I bit my lip and turned the pages as fast as I could.

There. There it was. I knew I'd seen them in there.

I smoothed out a colourful double spread in the new catalogue. On it, Dad had painted dozens of butterflies of various British species in all their glory.

Hadn't Faeza said that butterflies were a love she shared with Fei Yen?

This had to be my way to tug her back from the brink—a reminder of her absent, injured wife.

I swept my hand over the page, confidence brimming with every passing second. There were red admirals, black with red stripes on their wings, and painted ladies, which were orange with black tips and white spots. There were washed-out meadow browns and deep-red peacocks with blue eyespots and black marks. There were reddish-orange small tortoiseshells and green-veined whites, which Mum had excitedly shown Sahil and me in the garden one summer. There were holly blues and small coppers, each painted with such exquisite detailing that I almost didn't want the page to empty.

Because life meant death, and here, with Dad's skills, they were preserved forever.

But I knew.

I knew this might be the way to make Faeza remember who she was.

I dug deep, my focus already anchoring to the page. "Ezra, teleport Echo out of here."

"How rude," said Echo. "Maybe she wants to hear the end of my song."

"Nope. I think she's all right," I said. "Wait outside. Leave me and Marina alone. You'll know if we need you."

Ezra swallowed hard, his Adam's apple bobbing in his throat as if his protective instincts made this difficult. "Be careful."

He disappeared with Echo, leaving the three of us women alone.

The *hu hsien* turned its snarling form towards us. Me on the floor, Marina poised on the table.

"I hope you know what you're doing," said Marina.

I reached into the page and found the threads of the butterflies. It wasn't like the first time with Tielbu when I'd had to rummage to find his essence. When I'd been unsure of myself and my talents. It wasn't like with the bees in my bedroom when I'd accidentally done the job. Or like the rooster or the woodpecker, birds I'd conjured from the white of the page as lone creatures. Nor was it like the ravens at Wildwoods or the sea creatures down in the depths of the London sewer system that I'd animated from a place of crippling fear.

This time, I knew what I was capable of as sure as I knew my face in the mirror.

I knew this skill was as much a part of me as my own breath.

That the butterflies would flow from the page as soon as I reached into it.

And so it was.

I closed my eyes for a fraction of a second as the *hu hsien* neared, her six white tails in my peripheral vision. My breath slowed as I sensed the dimensions in the page and the butterflies hidden within it that only I could reach. Only I could give life to.

Beneath my fingertips, there on the grubby floor of the Indian restaurant, as the rain splashed the pavement outside and a distraught Faeza considered how to hurt us, I sensed the butterflies: their tiny legs, abdomens and thoraxes, heads and antennae, their glorious wing veins and scaled wings.

I gave them a purpose in my mind's eye: dance for the *hu hsien*, then be free.

Then I pulled my hand up with the flourish of a ribbon dancer, a movement so fluid that the butterflies flowed from the page, flying up, over and around the fox.

The fox stopped in her tracks, just like I'd hoped she would, captivated by their individual beauty. Her eyes flickered from green-violet back to brown, and her six tails became one, although her colour remained the red-white mix of her trauma.

Marina breathed out in awe. "It's working, Alisha. It's working."

Faeza was no longer a *hu hsien*. She was the common garden fox she'd become when she'd left China.

The butterflies continued their flight across the room, dipping and diving, sometimes settling on the blue fabric chairs or orange raw silk curtains that framed the window, before taking flight again when the fox neared them.

Marina eased herself down from the table to stand at my side and set aside her tranquilliser. "Let me try to soothe her the wholesome way."

I nodded.

We linked hands, two middle-aged women trapped with a stressed fox and a whole host of butterflies in an Indian restaurant in the Crystal Palace triangle.

Somehow, we were back to the beginning of our Otherworld journey. Back to a cornered creature in a small space, with the person I loved most in the world at my side. Except this time, we knew so much more about how to survive.

Although my bladder still threatened to do me a disservice.

"I know you're worried," I said as the fox darted me a glance. I raised my hands, feeling a stream of air from the kitchen that I could perhaps commandeer if the fox soured, my voice soothing but firm. The teacher voice that Faeza knew so well. "I know you are hurting. But I heard some news about Fei Yen this afternoon."

The fox stilled, poised to react, and in her stillness, the potential for destruction lingered.

I didn't miss a heartbeat. "She is going to be fine."

Was that what the Prime Sorcerer meant when he said Fei Yen would survive? I didn't know if I was telling a lie, but at this moment, it was the right thing to say.

I followed it with a second assumption that would pierce through Faeza's pain. "She can come to you, Faeza. Fei Yen can come home to Shanghai Moon."

The fox drew a shuddering breath, and its legs gave out from underneath it.

At the window, Ezra slumped with relief while Echo's emerald eyes gleamed with pride.

Marina rushed forward, and with her first empath's touch, the fox curled up into a ball, its head in her lap. There it lay, relaxed with every touch of Marina's fingers.

But then, I wasn't surprised. Powers or no powers, my best friend had always radiated love.

"There, there," Marina said. "You see? It's all going to be okay. You and wifey will be together again soon. No one can tear you apart. You belong together like yin and yang. Like noodles and soy sauce. Like a bra and knickers set." Her hands worked their magic. On she cooed, like she did with the animals in her surgery and with me when Mum had died, her whole person engaged to her core with the other's suffering.

And just when I thought our time was up, the fox whimpered and dragged herself into a corner, away from prying eyes.

Faeza emerged in naked human form, her shoulders crumpled, her soft brown eyes full of tears. "Is it true? Is Fei Yen okay? I can't imagine a world without her."

"Welcome back, Faeza." I nodded. "She's out of danger."

Marina rubbed the four-leaf clover on her wrist. Just as well that Faeza didn't know her as well as I did, or she would have realised things weren't as clear-cut as we had promised.

"Can I see her?" Faeza asked.

"We'll head to Wildwoods to pick her up just as soon as we've found you some clothes." Marina nipped to the backroom and returned with a waiter's uniform for Faeza to wear.

Faeza sobbed with relief, cowering behind a chair to protect her modesty. "I'm so sorry for all of this."

"We understand," I said. "You are our friend. We're here for you."

Marina said, "That's what friends do. Help each other. You let go of all that guilt. How many times have you helped us?"

"But look at what I did. At what I tried to do." Faeza pointed to the disarray.

"I wouldn't worry about it." Marina helped her dress, holding out a pair of ill-fitting shoes that would have to do the job. "I'm pretty sure this place has seen worse after a group of lads stop by for a Saturday night curry after getting wankered at the pub. Their toilets have definitely seen worse, judging by the stink back there. I turned the oven off, by the way. I'm afraid the paneer is a charcoal dump, but at least the kitchen's not on fire."

Faeza's overplucked eyebrows knitted together. Her fingers jittered as she buttoned up the uniform and discarded a stranger's name badge from the lapel. "I haven't been that thing for such a long time. I'm all desire, rage and vengeance in that form. It's like the darkest parts of me are amplified. It was the thought of Fei Yen being in that place. All alone. The place we are scared of. At the mercy of people who don't care for us. Who probably don't even know what item number she likes from the Chinese takeaway menu. Who don't know she likes a hot water bottle in bed at night or how to read her daily tarot cards. Who don't know that we can't survive without each other."

I embraced her slight figure, hoping I could keep my promise. "Let's go bring Fei Yen home."

She gave a shaky nod.

We collected our belongings, placed her in the middle of us, linked our arms through hers and walked out of the restaurant to join Ezra and Echo. The butterflies followed us out into the rain in barely-there splotches of colour. They vanished, clinging to the undersides of nearby foliage, waiting for the skies to clear.

16

A balding man with a pot belly, the Indian restaurant manager by the looks of it, meandered through the dispersing police blockade as we exited the building. He flicked Faeza a curious look, dressed as she was in his restaurant's uniform. His eagerness to get out of the rain and back to his business meant he forgot about her the moment he looked away. I hid a smile. From the man's calm demeanour, Orpheus had done his job.

Echo nuzzled my legs. Emerald eyes gleamed with pride. "You did well, Alisha."

Ezra nodded and stole a smoky kiss from me. "That was incredible."

I beamed. "Why, thank you, kind sir."

He smiled at Faeza. "You gave us quite the scare there."

The vampire stalked towards us, leaving the detective to scamper behind him. "We did your bidding, Alisha. No one in this area will remember what they ate for lunch, which words they uttered or what their humdrum eyes witnessed."

"There's not a single functioning CCTV camera in the area." Rob winked. "What are the chances."

Marina planted a smacker on his lips. "Oh, clever you."

Orpheus raised an eyebrow. "We have therefore abided by The Founder's Law and maintained the secrecy of the Otherworld."

"We make a crack team, mate," said Rob.

"Hmmm." The vampire glowered. *I feel like a prize bull stuck at a parade.*

Sorry about that. The night is not over. You'll have plenty of time to shine.

He was like a show-off pupil in the classroom, reluctant to take a back seat. I should have realised that when I had my first ride in his gleaming Lotus and visited his gentleman's club. How many people owned a sprawling townhouse in Charing Cross, complete with Renoirs and Constables on the wall and a live-in, six-handed masseur in the basement?

The thin line of his lips twitched. *I heard that.*

Damn it.

"Orpheus, you did keep those fingers for me to examine?" said Marina.

The vampire nodded. "They're in the fridge with my blood bags at my club."

"Excellent," said Marina.

I prodded them along. "Come on, let's press on towards Wildwoods. The last thing we need is to answer twenty questions—or worse, get banged up for the night in a South London police station awaiting our fate."

"We have a teleporting werewolf, Alisha. No cells can hold us," purred Echo.

Ezra grinned. "Actually, Echo, I think you'd find you'd be placed on your own in Battersea Dogs Home, and before you ask, yes, they do have a cat section."

Echo flung up his head. "Oh, the indignity."

Faeza's fragile bones shivered under the waiter's uniform, her energy spent. I left her in the care of the others so I could have a private moment with Ezra.

I sought his eyes, concern filling my voice. "Phinnaeous

didn't just want me to find a way to stop *hu hsien* Faeza. He wanted me to bring you to Wildwoods."

Ezra tucked me under his arm, shielding me from the brunt of the rain. His jaw clenched. "He's probably about to confess. After we parted ways this morning, I had a fruitless search for Gunnolf. Then Deirdra called to tell me that he had turned up at the farmhouse." His whisper was urgent. "Gunnolf held up his side of the bargain, Alisha. He did it. He followed Phinnaeous and has evidence to tie the Shine Foundation for the Advancement of Peculiars and Humdrums to the disappearances of the humdrum officials."

My skin prickled. Not with fear but with relish. "We finally have confirmation that Phinnaeous is rotten to the core."

"It's all in plain sight on the Prime Sorcerer's home computer. All he had to do was to wait until Phinnaeous was in an orgy with his succubi house slaves and then crack a simple password." Ezra snorted. "ALL-HAIL-THE-PRIME-SORCERER, apparently."

I knitted my fingers through Ezra's. "Ugh, what kind of person uses a shouty, self-obsessed computer password? Most people use a variation of their pet's name."

"Gunnolf found research on all the victims. Folders dated before their disappearances. Clear evidence that they were targets. Neither of us believes that Phinnaeous actually has the stomach for bloodshed. He's happy enough giving the orders, but he prefers other people to get their hands dirty. We think the victims could be at Wildwoods. That the foundation was a front to channel peculiars into high-profile jobs."

I frowned. "Why would he do that? Peculiars are getting on just fine in this city, with the exception of the elves, and that's his doing. Why would he want to meddle in the humdrum status quo?" I blew out my breath in a whoosh.

"Even if the victims are at Wildwoods, he's not exactly going to keep them indefinitely, is he? He'll have to get rid of them."

Ezra kneaded the back of his neck with his free hand. The past few days had been hard on us all. "You could be right. We can't put anything past him. Gunnolf wanted to have a poke around Wildwoods. He swears we're missing something. I talked him out of it. It's too dangerous. We've got grounds to question Phinnaeous now. I'll send in a group of seekers to figure out the rest."

"But how? He couldn't have gotten into Wildwoods anyway. His rights to Wildwoods were revoked at his sentencing, long before ours."

"He'd found a way. You know how resourceful he's always been. As Justice Minister, he was privy to secret information I am still getting to grips with. The night of the Battle of the Celestial Library, Meriel Naehorn and the dark elves tunnelled into Wildwoods. Some say the elves' black hole magic managed to let them get the better of the yew tree. The yew tree eventually registered their presence, of course— it's how Lavinia was alerted to what was going on—but by that time, Meriel and her elves had already infiltrated the Celestial Library. Back then, Wildwoods had its own portal to the library. Senators and the most experienced pupils had free access to see if the library would deem them worthy to walk its hallowed halls." He shuddered. "But everything changed that night. The portal was destroyed, but Gunnolf suspects the tunnels are still a vulnerability, even though they have been sealed."

"Bloody hell. That's how they got in? My grandmother might still be alive if Wildwoods' defences had been better. But no matter. We don't need to sneak around. It's all above board. Phinnaeous did wrong, and he'll pay for it. There'll be a new Prime Sorcerer, and everything around here will calm down. Apart from my brother. Oh, and the maniacal red woman. Oh, and the napping Father of the Gods."

"I take it Gaia didn't help this morning."

I plucked the wet T-shirt from my chest, thankful that my waterproof satchel protected my catalogue of creatures at least. "Actually, she did. She was honest with me, I think, and angry that I'd question her loyalty. She confirmed the book of names exists and admitted that my grandmother had asked her to give Mum a message when the time was right for us to step into the Otherworld."

He brushed the rain from my cheek with his thumb. "That's heavy."

"She didn't seem overly worried about the red woman. Maybe murder between the gods is child's play." I shrugged. "If it's possible that the Ravenmaster was resurrected, it's possible for all of them. Or maybe her past friendship with the red woman protects her. But she was sadder than I've seen her before. As fixated on drinking chai, of course, but a little untethered. I couldn't put my finger on it. She said friendship is the key to solving everything and warned us it would rain."

His mouth twitched as our trainers squelched on the muddy path. "Helpful."

I stopped. Orpheus and Rob waited with Marina, Faeza and Echo a few hundred yards away by a crooked elder tree. "Ezra, you took Gunnolf back to the dungeons, right?"

A grimace. "Not exactly. You should have seen him. Even in a few hours, he was a changed man from the one we saw in The Ritz dungeons. Turning into his wolf meant he had access to faster healing again, but it was more than that. It was like he'd found joy in just being a seeker again. He was getting a thrill out of it. Maybe he can serve his time and then find a way to be happy. Not an alpha but as an ordinary wolf, running free under the blue sky."

My heart thudded in my chest. "Ezra, where is he?"

"I gave him until midnight to stretch his legs one last time. We ran through the woods as a pack, hellfire. It felt amazing.

Like we were one breath. Like we were functioning as a family for once. And it felt good, Alisha. I thought, why can't I grant him a couple more hours' freedom? It won't hurt anyone. So when he's back inside, he remembers what he has to live for."

I gulped. Gunnolf was still a murderer.

But I held my tongue, understanding the strength of Ezra's bond with the disgraced alpha.

Ezra continued. "Come tonight, he'll be serving out his sentence—a reduced one for the help he has given us—and Phinnaeous Shine will be banged up in that corridor, too."

We approached the group and filled them in.

Orpheus squeezed the bridge of his Roman nose. "It is trying when a man you once admired turns out to be a knave. Luckily, my affections are limited to a small number of people, so I'll get over it."

The detective slumped with relief. "I got to say, I'm pleased it has come to this. After I lost my mind—"

"Your cabbage phase," said Orpheus.

Rob frowned. "—and then to have the PM's office refuse to take my calls, I thought we were never going to get to this point. I love my job. I love working with Wildwoods, but with Phinnaeous at the helm, I wondered if I'd have to jack it all in."

"That's why your aura's been all confused," said Marina.

Faeza trembled. "We have to get my wife out of his clutches."

I nodded, determination filling every syllable. "We've got Phinnaeous Shine where we want him. Flinar was right. Handing over the sword brought it home to me. I can't stay out of this fight. None of us can."

Maybe our success in bringing Faeza around had boosted my confidence. Or maybe I sensed that Phinnaeous's efforts at harming communities he valued less were finally unravelling. Either way, the time had come to take him down.

"Let's go put an end to this," I said. "We'll bring Fei Yen home. Once she is safe, Ezra will arrest Phinnaeous, and we will retrieve Death's sword and restore normality to Wildwoods. Phinnaeous Shine might be strong, but we're stronger still as long as we work together. Who's with us?"

Echo growled. "All of us, obviously. We are warriors, not limp cheese sticks."

A murmur of assent ran around the group.

Ezra's grey eyes darkened. "Tonight, we show Phinnaeous Shine he's unworthy of Wildwoods."

A thrill of apprehension surged through me as we neared the sphinxes. Whereas they remained statue-still on the approach of humdrums—although the rains had cleared the park—their terracotta heads reacted immediately to our presence, turning to fix us with solemn stares.

"Druid," said Rhokon. "What brings you back here on this miserable evening?"

"Rhokon. Mammatas." I inclined my head respectfully. "Please summon the Prime Sorcerer to the yew tree."

Mammatas's stone head tipped skywards as he unleashed a spine-tingling roar. "It has been done. Fare well, Alisha Verma and friends."

Orpheus sighed. *I have known those stone relics for decades. It is the second time today I've been relegated to the minor leagues.*

Get used to it. It had taken a while, but I enjoyed being a leader. After all, big boobies were as conducive to good leadership as big cojones. It was silly to determine someone's value by their body parts.

We left the sphinxes in our wake and strode towards the yew tree. With each step, I grew more convinced we had justice and right on our side and maybe even the element of surprise. After all, the Prime Sorcerer intended his call about the *hu hsien* rampage to be a curveball. He hadn't expected us to solve it so quickly, and while he had summoned both Ezra and me, he wouldn't expect us to turn up en masse at his door.

I silenced the voice in my head that told me to invite Rayna and Lavinia to the party, who brought their own formidable skills and had been as slighted by Phinnaeous as we had been. Instead, we forged ahead to the familiar clearing and lined up in a semi-circle with barely a foot between us, instinctively knowing we should stick together.

The ground shuddered as the Prime Sorcerer emerged from Wildwoods, along with two others.

I squinted in the fast-fading light and slowing rain in the depths of the park where the boughs blocked out the light, even though autumn had removed the curtains of leaves and made them a golden carpet instead.

The Prime Sorcerer uncurled his body. His eyes were a wasteland of emotion, a searing emptiness that made my blood run cold. He wore his usual robes like he had almost every time I'd seen him, as if his ego needed him to project his power at all times. The sort of clothing choice Marina would link to small-cock syndrome.

Actually, I've seen his penis in a Swedish sauna, and he's in donkey territory, said Orpheus. *Unless he was hiding an inflatable under his towel.*

My eyes deciphered the shadows. Two gagged figures— one large, one small—cowered on either side of him. Both appeared to be bound at the wrists. A shimmering gold chain linked all three at the waist.

"That's Fei Yen," Faeza squeaked and edged forward in her too-big shoes.

Ezra restrained her, his voice a harsh cut of grief. "There is more to this than meets the eye. Leopard, do my senses deceive me?"

Echo's tail swished, his body dark with the rain. "The old wolf is here. The one who killed his own."

I squinted and prayed Gunnolf hadn't been captured.

There was Fei Yen, shivering in a nightdress from the Wildwoods infirmary, her feet bare and squelching in the mulch. A thin blanket covered her shoulders, and her fearful eyes were fixed on Faeza as if she had at last found her anchor.

My heart plummeted.

On the other side of Phinnaeous, bruised and bloodied, his shoulder hanging as if it was dislocated, was Gunnolf in human form. His expression was downcast as if he'd already accepted defeat, as if it made no odds for him to put up a fight, even though the Prime Sorcerer was outnumbered.

What does the old wolf know that we don't? said Orpheus. *He must drop the defences he erected long ago and let me into his mind.*

Try and get in, Orpheus. I don't have a good feeling about this.

I stepped forward, blocking my anxiety for Fei Yen, and focussed on Phinnaeous. "Let them go."

Ezra joined me. His hands hung loosely at his sides, but every cell pulsed with energy, itching to unleash violence. "You heard the lady."

Phinnaeous smiled at me. "Well done for controlling the *hu hsien*, druid. It can't have been easy." A pause. "I think I hold the cards, Neuhoff. Don't you?"

Anger, true and raw, surged through me.

I could call the winds. Send a tornado to sweep up the Prime Sorcerer and land him in the ocean, where Kraglek could finish him off. I could smash him against the yew tree and end this where we stood. Or create a ring of confinement so Ezra could enter and pull him limb from limb. Hell, Echo could sink his teeth in, and Faeza and Fei Yen go all *hu hsien* on him. I wouldn't blame them.

I'd sit back and enjoy the spectacle. Not from vengeance but because Phinnaeous Shine had earned a reckoning.

But the three of them were linked by the shimmering chain. Even as I fantasised about violence, even as I sensed the unity in my group of friends—Ezra's rage, Echo's impatience, the seething anger of Orpheus's voice in my head, Marina's worry, Rob's determination and Faeza's sheer animal distress—even then, Phinnaeous sank deeper than I thought he would go.

That was the thing about bad people. They'd sink to unimaginable depths. Depths that good people wouldn't sink to. At first, it made them seem unstoppable.

A wizard's going to wizard.

Phinnaeous chanted, and in an instant, two swords—both the spitting image of Transcender—appeared above Fei Yen and Gunnolf's heads, angled to drive down into the backs of their necks.

Faeza whimpered uncontrollably, held only in check by Marina's touch.

"Do something," hissed Marina.

"Damn wizard magic," growled Echo.

Beads of sweat broke out on my forehead and mingled with the rain. Ezra and I exchanged glances. It was impossible to differentiate between which sword was an illusion and which was a reality.

That tricky bastard.

The point of the sword fell lower, drawing blood from Gunnolf.

Phinnaeous's dark, stony eyes fell on Ezra. "You set a seeker on *me? Me?*" the Prime Sorcerer said. "And you thought I would be too foolish to realise? My boy, it is a mistake you will pay dearly for."

He knew. He knew what we had done.

"Please." Ezra's voice broke, and it gutted me.

"I never thought you capable of this, Phinnaeous," said Orpheus. "It is beneath you."

Phinnaeous stopped muttering his spell, but the swords still hovered dangerously close to doing irreparable damage. "Peculiar and humdrum history books alike will laud me for bringing about a new world."

"Why are you doing this?" I said quietly.

"Your mind is fractured between humdrum and peculiar desires, druid. It is weak. I wouldn't expect you to understand, but I will explain all the same so that, eventually, you will realise I was right all along. My equality foundation has one aim."

I raised my chin, goading him, hoping to distract him from his spell. "On the tin, it said equality for peculiars and humdrums."

He offered a watery smile devoid of warmth. "To pave the way for peculiars to live out in the open. Even now, carefully selected peculiars have been inserted into key positions to influence policy and narrative to pave the way. Aren't you tired of shapeshifting in secret, Neuhoff? Aren't you tired of living in the shadows, Orpheus? Aren't you all tired of pretending we are ordinary? Just think. Just think of a whole generation of Wildwoods students who never know the pain of hiding their identity, of pretending to be someone they are not. Who can show their true brilliance. Who rule society because they can employ their innate skills. Isn't that a world worth fighting for?"

Ezra swallowed his emotion, flipping the switch in his mind between beta pack member and warring alpha. He growled, his wolf close to the surface, and Gunnolf jerked in response, sensing the power of the alpha.

"Your morals are muddied, old man," said Ezra. "You tire of life or are incapable of seeing its beauty. The whole ethos of the London Otherworld is equality. You would overhaul that on a whim, without the senate's backing, through backroom deals, shifty plans and criminal behaviour. You have broken multiple laws and conventions according to our Magical Constitution. Put down your weapons, release your captives and surrender yourself."

Phinnaeous's laughter rang through the air. "How naive you are, Neuhoff. The Otherworld has never been about equality. Your position of privilege prevents you from seeing it. There have always been underlings. The elves. The commoners. The people who refuse to open their eyes and see the world in all its peculiar beauty."

"Or maybe I have never seen them as underlings," said Ezra.

Gunnolf flicked moist eyes away from Ezra and to Orpheus for an extended minute.

Enough with the bullshit.

"Let them go," I demanded.

Phinnaeous's lip curled. "It's not as easy as that, druid. I thought I'd give you a taste of how difficult it is to lead a community. You see, you point fingers at my choices when the world is not black and white. Each path is full of sludge and covered with thorns. And to demonstrate that only one of these captives will go free today. Some lessons are hard. The decision is yours. Take as long as you need. I'll wait."

We huddled together, drenched bodies whispering frantically.

"Do something, Alisha," said Faeza. "Please."

"It's my fault," said Ezra. "He is my father in all but name, whatever he has done."

"The obvious answer is to hit him with all we have," said Orpheus.

"I've had it with him. How we ever worked together, I don't know. The only answer is to kneecap him and feed him to the leopard," said Rob.

"I'm fussy about my meat, thank you very much. I have no doubt he tastes like a stringy turd," said Echo. "What's more, I've done all the possible calculations while you have been talking, taking in the angles from the trees, the speed of our warriors, the trajectories needed and our innate weapons. It brings me no pleasure to say that the combination of the magical chains and swords at their neck, plus the injuries of the captives, mean—"

"That we stand no chance." I bit my lip. I'd made the same assessment.

Faeza wrenched her hands together. "You promised. I can't lose her."

I met Ezra's eyes. "You know the answer."

He nodded, and when we turned back to Phinnaeous, his face crumpled with anguish. "We choose to free the fox."

Phinnaeous smirked, and the chain around Fei Yen's waist and wrists dissolved, as did the sword illusion above her head. "Go."

She scrambled forward in her muddy nightdress, her face wan and eyes wide with suffering, her chin-length hair limp. Faeza cried out and ran towards her, arms outstretched. As they collided, the thin blanket around Fei Yen's shoulders fell.

I gasped, realising her left arm had been amputated just below the elbow. A wave of nausea hit me. "Marina, Rob, stay with the foxes. Get them to safety."

I turned back to Phinnaeous.

"You think me a monster, but once I caught the wolf rummaging around Wildwoods, it would always have ended this way. The *hu hsien* is an exquisite creature. Her deformity does not diminish that. But this murderous wolf escaped his prison." He turned Transcender in his hands. "The law is clear, Neuhoff. A peculiar who evades or escapes custody leaves only one solution." He wrenched the gag from Gunnolf's mouth. "Any last words?"

The pain in Gunnolf's eyes revealed he knew what was coming, but he didn't resist. He raised his eyes first to the moon and then to Ezra. "Son, I love y—"

Ezra raised his hands. "Don't."

Phinnaeous's eyes gleamed, and so did Transcender's black blade. He sank it into Gunnolf's neck—judge, jury and executioner—and pressed the sword clean through.

Ezra's despair rang through the air, a howl of anguish, as his uncle's body dropped to the ground, convulsing. Blood puddled there, thick and viscous. Ezra teleported to him, ripping off his necklace so the thistle charm could work its magic.

"Heal, Uncle," he said.

"It's okay." Gunnolf dropped his hand from his bleeding neck, his voice barely a croak. "I should've listened."

Ezra knelt beside the dying man, his jeans darkening with blood, and pulled Gunnolf into his embrace. "Shift, Uncle. Shift and run free."

Gunnolf groaned, bones cracked, and in an instant, the body Ezra cradled was no longer a man's but a wolf's.

A rasp of wheezing breath, and the black wolf finally lay still.

There, in the rainy mid-afternoon park, without even the moon to call him home.

Ezra bent his head for a long moment. Then he closed the wolf's eyes and laid him aside with infinite gentleness. When he stood to face Phinnaeous, fiery embers blazed in his eyes.

"You'll pay for that." His voice cracked with grief.

Orpheus sped towards Ezra, clamping him with his arms. "Don't be stupid, Neuhoff. We need to regroup. Tend to the injured and the dead."

"Take your hands off me," spat Ezra. He teleported to Phinnaeous.

I raised my hands and lassoed him back with a loop of wind. My gut wrenched as he strained against me. I wanted him to have his revenge, but not like this. Not in a fit of rage.

Phinnaeous still had all the resources of Wildwoods at his disposal. We would not win the fight. Even the sphinxes would side with him. When we took our revenge, I didn't want him to be painted a saint.

All his nefarious deeds needed to be out in the open.

A sardonic smile as Phinnaeous flicked his gaze between us. "The law is on my side, Neuhoff. I wasn't the one who released him from his chains."

The shapeshifting weasel turned on his heel, past the yew tree, where we couldn't reach him. Only when he was gone did I release my hold on Ezra.

He fell to his knees in the dirt, mere yards from his uncle's lifeless wolf body.

I lay my hand on Ezra's shoulder. My heart ached for him. Nothing would ever make this all right. "I'm so sorry."

Raw, fierce emotion pulsed through him. "I did this. If he'd been safe in prison, this never would have happened."

"You gave him the chance to shift into his wolf again before he died. You know what type of man he was. He didn't want to die in a cell. You said it yourself. He wanted to run wild under the blue sky."

His Adam's apple bobbed. He dragged himself up and attended to his uncle's body, rearranging his limbs into a more comfortable position and straightening the black wolf's back, which had crumpled as he fell. As if Gunnolf could still feel. As if he still breathed.

"He promised me he wouldn't come back here." He shuddered as he stroked the dead wolf's brow. "He wanted to earn redemption. To put his life on the line. For me. I loved him. In spite of it all."

A chill ran through me. I'd seen the look in Gunnolf's eyes, too, when he'd looked at Ezra just before he'd died.

It wasn't the look of an uncle to a nephew.

It was the look of a father to his son. A passing on of the torch. An apology. And maybe even relief.

I tried to guide Ezra away from the body, just a step or two, but he resisted.

Orpheus and Echo joined us, their heads bowed.

The vampire spoke first, his eyes hooded. "We'll coincide it with the Wildwoods Halloween Ball, just to be safe."

Emerald eyes glowed in the fading light. "Let me be the second to give you my condolences, Ezra. That dog was a murdering double-denim-wearing monstrosity, but he was *your* murdering double-denim-wearing monstrosity."

"I know how he did it," said the vampire. "Gunnolf opened his mind to me through that ordeal. The Prime Sorcerer caught him inside the walls, but the tunnels are still well hidden. His last gift to you, a kernel of knowledge to help us prepare to defeat Phinnaeous." His nostrils flared in disgust. "The man who presided over the Pragmatist's Law and campaigned against it being rewritten has himself been meddling—no, colluding—with the gods. The red woman is in Wildwoods. The red woman who creates portals through which unsuspecting humdrums have walked into Wildwoods, only to be replaced by peculiars. That is the missing piece of the puzzle Gunnolf found out tonight. That is why he was killed and what Phinnaeous Shine didn't want us to know."

I clenched my fists, spitting fury. "That hypocritical dickhead."

Ezra's face was painted in shades of grief and rage. "For this, Phinnaeous Shine will die."

I nodded, aching for him. "Gunnolf gave us a second gift. He gave us a way in. Thanks to him, we know about the tunnels. We'll take back the sword and make Phinnaeous pay." I swallowed hard. "What makes you think Wildwoods won't sound the alarm when you're in there?"

"You're the eternal girl, hellfire." Ezra's bloodshot eyes found mine. "Your presence has been predicted in Wildwoods lore since the dawn of time. Phinnaeous is just passing through."

I swallowed the lump in my throat at the sight of the foxes intertwined, the detective and Marina hovering over them. Then I crouched beside Ezra and placed a hand on his shoulder.

Usually, he'd yield to my touch, but this time, he stayed stiff, pain making a shell of him.

"Let's get Fei Yen and Faeza home," I said. "Try to rest, everyone. In the morning, some of us will be taking a trip to Baba Yaga's. It's time we all joined forces and put an end to this."

Ezra scooped up the dead wolf in his arms, face grim. "First, I'm taking my uncle home."

He disappeared between the worlds, carrying his heavy load.

Somewhere far away, a pack of wolves howled.

17

Ezra ran through the night with the pack as they processed Gunnolf's death before cremating him at dawn—per his uncle's preferences—in a quiet ceremony while I watched from the sidelines. His sadness had turned increasingly to fury that wouldn't be sated until Phinnaeous Shine got his comeuppance.

Phinnaeous might have played a blinder, but he didn't have friends and allies to back him up. Not like I did. And with Ezra in pain, I turned to the woman I should have trusted in the first place.

His witchy aunt Lavinia, whose offer of help I had refused.

Knowing how stubborn she could be, how wily and difficult to win over, there was only one thing for it. I had to sidle my way into her good books by attending one of her glittery, Spandex-filled exercise classes at Baba Yaga's Gym. Usually, I would have chewed off my own fist rather than attend, but I'd snubbed her invitation to join forces. I was happy to eat humble pie if I needed to, all for the love of Ezra. All because, even though I found Lavinia hard to trust, there was no doubt that she had the best interests of the Otherworld at heart.

A woman of my age realised that humility wasn't a weakness.

Admitting mistakes and course-correcting could be the difference between happiness and despair.

We arrived en masse, without prior warning, just in time for the women—plus a drooling, rat-triggered Echo under my stern eye—to join Lavinia's Zumba class and for the men to join Isadora's boxing class. I hoped Ezra could take his anger out on punchbags in the boxing class this morning.

There was no doubt he'd save plenty of ire for Phinnaeous himself.

After solitary hours training to wield Death's sword—before Phinnaeous Shine got his greasy mitts on it—communal exercise did have one upside. It served as a reminder that training alone wasn't half bad when you'd been forced to wriggle in Lycra with a bunch of frazzled, panting, hip-winding women.

Latin music filled the room, its beat irresistible, if that was the sort of thing you liked.

I mean, I might have enjoyed watching Enrique Iglesias crooning in a dark room, but dancing to the stuff was an entirely different matter. Especially when I contrasted the mood in the room full of pulsating yummy mummies with the dark memory of the preceding day.

Fei Yen. Gunnolf. Missing humdrums.

The red woman working with Phinnaeous.

Wildwoods, a tool of a dark-hearted wizard.

It was too much to bear. No wonder I looked like a constipated hippo in the mirror reflection.

Whoever thought mirrors were a good idea when exercising, thereby highlighting all the wobbly bits, had lost their minds. I would have hit an endorphin high much sooner with blinders on.

Still, to each their own.

Lavinia shimmied and ground her hips with gusto, ensuring the class knew she might be of pensionable age, but she certainly didn't require a knee or hip replacement. She could rival a twenty-year-old in hip thrusts. Echo prowled after the rat familiars, his emerald eyes dwelling on a particularly chunky one, my warning about eating it stinging in his ears. Marina happily leaned into the bootylicious aspects of Lavinia's routines. Rayna was there too, floating around like a butterfly, stopping only to blow her nose now and then to show her distress at the Wildwoods ousting.

It was a different story for me.

I lumbered along, bumping into disgruntled participants with as much panache as a goblin in a row of perfect ballerinas. I slicked away my sweat, but the salty liquid found its way into my mouth. Not to mention that my knickers had snuck their way up my bum crack. I pronged them out just when they began to slice me in two.

Echo rolled about on the gleaming wooden floor for attention from anyone who would look his way.

The hussy.

After the class, Lavinia approached us. "Empath, you showed your Cuban heart today. Magnificent."

She towelled her dry neck, making me wish I had one for my own sopping one.

No doubt, the old dear would have been one of those witchy P.E. teachers at school who'd made me feel like a dumpster fire when I didn't ace everything sporty.

Lavinia tutted. "I've been telling Rayna she should come to the gym more often now she has more time on her hands. There's more to life than snotty children. Think of Baba Yaga's as your home from home; now you don't have Wildwoods."

Rayna's eyes widened with incredulity.

I didn't blame her. Lavinia's manner wasn't exactly delicate.

"I'm sure the Wildwoods situation will be resolved in due course, Headmistress," I said.

Lavinia's hazel eyes were coy underneath a helmet of stiff, silver curls doused in oodles of hairspray. The spider to my proverbial fly. "So you have come for my help, after all, druid. During our phone call, I got the distinct impression that you assumed you'd be just fine without allies. What changed your mind?" She adjusted her hot pink crop top. A walking, talking advert for age being just a number, if I ever saw one. "Let me see. Could it be a rogue goddess has attacked both the love nest you share with my nephew and the pack farmhouse? Could it be the fact that, for all our sacrifices in losing our esteemed senate positions the night of the vote, you handed over your sword to Phinnaeous without a whimper? Is it because, dear druid, your own brother mauled a *hu hsien* fox? Or that my dear nephew lost another family member last night and that Phinnaeous Shine is working with a goddess with admirable taste in dresses with pockets?"

I sighed. "You are well informed by your rat spies."

The witch folded her toned arms. "Nothing stays a secret around me, Alisha. I unravel secrets in my sleep."

"That must be why your face is so haggard." Echo padded towards us, his ears pricked in our direction. "Or perhaps it is because when a lady of a certain age trains her body, her wrinkles move from her bosom to her face."

I peered closer under the bright studio lights. He was right. A certain haggardness had set in her facial area. The anti-ageing potions and spells didn't seem to be working as well anymore.

Lavinia's posture sagged. "You mock me, leopard, but I have held my position since Rajika Verma's time. It is hard on the soul to be turfed out of Wildwoods and the senate. And without inner satisfaction, my potions haven't been working nearly as well. What's more, the Earth goddess seems to be muscling in on our protection racket. The coven income has taken a hit. Although how flour rituals and koi are going to do the job of protection spells and a squadron of witches, I don't know."

I almost felt sorry for her.

Then I remembered she'd once told me how much of a giggle she and the coven had keeping fit at Baba Yaga's so when the time came, they could break bones.

Maybe it was time another peculiar had the chance to fill the role of Defence Minister. Or maybe the reason Lavinia has held the position for so long was she was good at it, the little voice inside my head said.

I swallowed my pride. "We've worked together before, Lavinia, to stop Ra and the Ravenmaster. But it wasn't enough. The old gods are rising, even the ones we've vanquished before. And Phinnaeous Shine's tentacles of power have reached too far. You and the rest of the coven are skilled operators—both on the battlefield and strategically. You were right. We need to join forces."

Truth be told, I didn't trust Lavinia as far as I could throw her. With my limited upper body strength, I couldn't even throw her far. Safe to say, I'd tread carefully. But she had the lady balls to stand against Phinnaeous and the gods and had shown herself to be a friend to humdrums before. Yes, she might have hankered after both a vial of Ezra's blood and Tielbu, but for now, the old saying rang true: the enemy of my enemy is my friend.

"I see you have learned that practicality is central to a woman's ability to survive. A woman needs trusted sisters. She needs a grand library so her wisdom grows with her age." Lavinia gestured to the umbrella leaning in the corner of the studio. "She needs a weapon close at hand and to know when to stand her ground."

"So that's a yes?" I held my breath. Gaia had said that extending the hand of friendship could be the difference between winning and losing the coming trials.

Lavinia's lips curved into a pearly smile, and her whole body relaxed. "Of course it is! This really is marvellous. I am pleased we can work together. We're going to bring that swine Phinnaeous to heel. And more importantly, we can help Ezra find peace. He is my nephew as well as your sheet warmer, Alisha."

Whatever Lavinia's manoeuvres, they'd always shared a bond. Ezra certainly had a soft spot for her. Family meant everything to him. Heat warmed my belly. If he ever had a family of his own, I knew he'd put them at the very centre of his life.

"As soon as the men are here, we'll lay out our ideas," I said.

Lavinia's hazel eyes glimmered. "They'll be here any minute."

In the absence of chairs, she flung out some crash mats for us to sit on, then bade the stragglers to her Zumba class goodbye.

I flopped on a mat, and Echo curled up next to me while Rayna and Marina chose a mat each.

"Headmistress," I said, "I was sad to hear what happened. I feel responsible. If you hadn't voted my way…"

Rayna sniffed. "Sadly, I'm not headmistress anymore. But it's far better to be ousted with my head high than to be one of the cowering fools still at Phinnaeous Shine's side. Orpheus told me about your fox friend. I wish I could have helped. To think of how many regenerative plants are in my Wildwoods office, wilting from lack of care and affection."

"I'm glad you have no regrets."

Luminous studio lighting brought Rayna's blue crescent under-eye shadows into sharp focus. "If I'm honest, watching you grow has made me wonder how to pursue learning of my own at this stage of my life. As much as I miss the school, my ousting freed up time to work with the elven community. It's been quite the revelation. They're a wonderful folk, Meriel

Naehorn notwithstanding, of course. They think very highly of you."

"I'm glad to hear it," I said.

"Have you met our friend Flinar?" said Marina.

"Of course. He's a fine ambassador for the elves," said Rayna. "Not so long ago, his vision of elves welcome in the Wildwoods community would have seemed farfetched, but who knows if we can oust Phinnaeous? Speaking of progress, I dare say neither of you has reached your magical potential. Take you, Alisha. I have a feeling you might be surprised if you accompany me on a trip with the elves to Stonehenge. It's a place of great power, especially for druids."

I nodded. "I promised Flinar I'd come."

"Count me in too. Somewhere spiritual sounds like just the ticket to clear the cobwebs out of my head. I've been so focused on healing everyone else, including Rob, that I've forgotten how to care for myself. I mean, just look at my roots." Marina pointed to her scalp, where an inch of strawberry blonde roots poked out above the vivid rest.

Lavinia returned, a bubble-gum pink balance ball in hand. She perched on it cross-legged, like some sort of zen magician on a makeshift throne, high above the rest of us. "Let's cut straight to it, shall we? We should have known Phinnaeous was problematic."

"He ran from Wildwoods during its hour of need," said Rayna.

"He's a ruthless narcissist," I said. "I don't think he'd notice a personal flaw if it hit him between the eyes."

Echo lifted his head from my lap. "The entitled way he pursued Rajika Verma."

"He messed with Rob's mind as if it was putty," said Marina. "And keeps succubi house slaves. It can't be legal."

"He is a walking, talking reason to keep men at arm's length," said Lavinia. "My nephew being the exception to the rule, of course."

"Oh, I don't know. In every pool of the population, you'll find both sparkling gems and stinking turds," said Marina.

"My ex-husband was a gambler," I said. "And he looked at his phone more than he looked at me."

"I dated a man before my dear husband who thought monogamy was a wood," said Rayna. "I gave him another chance when he said he respected women who were breadwinners. But then a literal moth flew from his wallet."

"That's nothing. I had a promising start with a romantic interest who couldn't find my G-spot," said Lavinia. "Even when I gave them a map."

"I have had so many mating partners, I am unlikely to recognise them on a re-encounter. It is most troublesome. How do I know the orifice is going to be worth it?" purred Echo.

I coughed politely. "Shall we get back on track? Clearly, we all believe he needs to be stopped."

Right on cue, Ezra, Orpheus and Rob swept into the studio straight from their boxing class.

They walked towards us in sync—and quite possibly in slow-mo—like they'd stepped off the pages of a men's magazine—three men of different builds. Jameson, the shortest, with his angular face, military buzz cut and stocky build, wore joggers and a white T-shirt pooled with sweat. Orpheus, tall, slim and pale, moody by nature, incongruous in cycling shorts that showed his ample package and a grey vest. And Ezra. Marginally shorter than the vampire but stronger, with well-defined muscles, floppy brown hair and an arse that could crack a walnut. Evident in the barely-there red shorts he was wearing.

Lavinia bounced off her gym ball and reached up to throw her arms around Ezra. "My dear nephew, I was so sorry to hear about that dirty old wolf. I didn't show it, but I quite liked our healthy sparring over the years." She tweaked Ezra's cheek. "He did love you very much."

A vein throbbed in Ezra's cheek. "I appreciate that."

He came to sit next to me on my mat.

Lavinia returned to her perch while Rob joined Marina. Orpheus and Rayna ended up with Echo between them.

"If you mark your territory, leopard, I will box your ears," said the vampire, brooding eyes in an alabaster face. "Bodily fluids yank my chain."

Rayna gave a sad smile. "Never mind, Orpheus. We're all feeling out of sorts since the Wildwoods ousting."

Lavinia tucked her legs up onto the gym ball with impressive balance. She must have had a core of steel. "Each of us here today has paid the price for not compromising our values. Wildwoods is the heart of our community, and yet, we are now unwelcome there. That man always did advocate keeping the power between a select few."

"I don't remember you making a fuss about that as long as it suited you," said Orpheus.

"Yes, well, vampire, the tides turn. Vampires shrivel in their coffins, and sometimes someone padlocks them. You know how it goes." She beamed at Ezra. "We have plenty of manly muscle around here already."

"I think you'll find that the red woman escaped your nephew at the cottage. Hardly stellar work," muttered Orpheus.

"I assume that is why you went so hard at me in the boxing ring?" Ezra raised an eyebrow. "Although I seem to remember the red woman escaped you at the farmhouse as well as me."

"Nephew, releasing Gunnolf to entrap Phinnaeous was an inspired move. I didn't think you had it in you. Perhaps there is more of me in you than you think."

Ezra's lips tightened. He still doubted himself.

Lavinia adjusted the waistband of her yoga leggings, and I felt the tug of power between us. She muttered a spell under her breath, and somewhere, a tinkling bell rang. "There is something you must all see."

Into the studio came Ignacio, the fat rat who had been Elvira's familiar while she had lived.

"You may make your report, Ignacio," said the witch.

A flurry of squeaks of varying lengths and pitches followed.

"Did you see that, Rob? Remarkable," said Marina. "What did he say?"

Lavinia turned to the group. "That various hotspots of medieval diseases are popping up in London, courtesy of the red woman. Luckily, medical advances mean there haven't been fatalities yet, and he rather hopes it stays that way. The rats shouldered a lot of blame for the Black Death. The ancestral guilt still weighs on him."

I sighed. "Is there any god in this city that works for the betterment of humankind, apart from Gaia? All this provoking of suffering so that people return to prayer in their misery. It's manipulative."

"It's the way of the world," said Orpheus.

Ignacio ventured closer to us and handed Lavinia a rolled-up newspaper.

She patted him on the head, her hand hammer-heavy rather than caressing. "You may leave."

He scampered away on all fours and disappeared into a crack in the wall.

"Did you see this morning's *Evening Herald*? The pertinent section is buried away on page ten; now Margola's in charge, of course." She flung the paper our way.

I skimmed the newspaper, my gut twisting. The tally of missing humdrums had risen. Again, Phinnaeous Shine's Equality Foundation had stepped up to fill the positions. "How many are missing now?"

"Seven," said the detective. "The PM's private secretary, the newspaper magnate, a judge, a front bench politician, the deputy commissioner of the Metropolitan Police, the Governor of the Bank of England, and a hedge fund manager have all disappeared into thin air."

Lavinia flashed a pearly white smile. "Luckily, I have a plan."

Ezra raked a hand through his hair. "The thing is, Alisha does too. But by all means, Auntie, let's hear yours first."

Hazel eyes narrowed. "You doubt me, nephew?"

"Not at all. I know your strengths, Aunt Lavinia. My parents would still be alive if you'd been there the night they died." A pause. "But there is only one eternal girl. She is who we have been waiting for."

Ezra having my back was hot. I had a right mind to drag him into a broom cupboard there and then, but those rats probably had peepholes in every corner of the place.

Probably best to spare those of us with sensitive hearing our blushes. I've already had to bite my knuckles through one of your marathon sessions. Aloud, Orpheus said, "We are waiting with bated breath to hear your plan, Lavinia."

Vampires don't breathe, do they? I mean, if you did, with all the decaying of your body, it would be pretty stinky, wouldn't it? Unlikely a bit of floss or spearmint would fix that pong.

"First, I will send the rats to claw back the necklace from the werepigeon. As they say, a rat is worth a thousand birds," said Lavinia in true defence minister style. "Then we'll head to Wildwoods via the skies, raining a million bullets from our umbrellas before taking back the sword, freeing the humdrums, capturing Phinnaeous and surviving the red woman with a mixture of spells and cunning. Easy peasy."

"Actually, I'd rather you leave the family matters to me," I said. It was one thing me going after my brother, but Lavinia was a crude instrument. "And given Wildwoods is a school, I would have thought raining down bullets is a little risky."

Lavinia frowned. "Yes, well, there's always casualties in war, Alisha."

"I've never heard that one before," said Marina. "That a rat is worth a thousand birds."

Lavinia arched a thin eyebrow. "Yes, well, all that fluorescent hair dye likely caused a deterioration in your mental faculties."

Ezra shook his head ruefully. "Don't mind her. She doesn't play well with others."

"My bluntness is one of my best attributes, Ezra. I don't give a damn how many noses I put out of joint. Unless it's Roger Federer, of course." She winked. "The day he wins another Grand Slam, I'll offer myself to him with whipped cream on my cupcakes. But the rest of the world can like it or lump it."

The witch believes she has her hands back on the reins, said Orpheus.

Don't worry. I'm keeping some information back. Lavinia might know about the necklace and Death's sword, but she doesn't know about the book of names. Neither does she need to know. *And yes, Orpheus, I know you've already deciphered that little thought buried away in my brain.*

What are friends for? said the vampire.

"As for Phinnaeous, the sequence is quite clear. One, we isolate him. Two, we give him an opportunity to come quietly and sling him in the dungeons after a cursory trial. Three, depending on his response—" Lavinia drew a sharp line across her throat. "He meets with an unfortunate end, courtesy of my umbrella-wielding acrobatic coven sisters and a murderous crew of rats. Whichever way you think of it, he won't be head of the senate. Wildwoods can start a new page. And I can replace that terrible black-and-white chess décor with some cheerful pink."

Rayna's mouth slackened. "You can't mean to bring about his death. We have been colleagues for years."

Orpheus shrugged. "He crossed a line long ago."

Ezra's quiet voice interjected. "We owe him no leniency. Neither did he offer it to Gunnolf."

"I can't believe I'm here for this hitlist talk. I'm a healer, not a fighter," said Marina.

"I can't sanction action against him, but I can pretend not to have heard this conversation," said Rob

I cut through the noise, my voice clear and quiet. It was time to end all this. "Are you ready to hear *my* plan?"

18

I woke in a tangle of sheets, my face pressed against the pillow. Ezra's arm lay heavy across my back, a comforting weight. I slid out from under his arm and made a mental note to find my set of satin pillowcases. With all the late nights, I had to find a way to be kind to my middle-aged skin. There wasn't much time for a three-step routine these days.

The cottage, still in its cocoon, disoriented my sense of time. I checked the clock on my mobile phone and planted a soft kiss on Ezra's lips.

"Hi." He stirred, though his eyes remained closed. His initial smile faltered. "It's the day of the Wildwoods Halloween Ball."

"Yes, it is. I'm going to pop to Shanghai Moon. Give me a ride in your arms? I want to make sure they know they are loved...just in case we don't make it out of Wildwoods tonight."

His grey eyes were pensive. Then he propped himself up. "Okay. We'll go see the foxes."

Fifteen minutes later, after a cursory wash and a hasty coffee too bitter for my tastes, we travelled through the monochrome world with Echo in tow. Thankfully, the leopard had become accustomed enough to teleporting that he no longer vomited, at least when we crossed short distances. But when we emerged in our old neck of the woods outside Fei Yen and Faeza's tea and occult shop, his muzzle was wet with drool.

A closed sign hung on the door, but we rang the bell to their apartment.

Long minutes passed before the foxes came into view from the stairwell at the back of the shop. They wore matching silk pyjamas with tiny, knotted buttons and waved a tentative hello to us as they came in tandem to unlock the shop door. As if they never wanted to be parted again.

The bell jangled as Ezra, Echo and I entered the shop.

"Welcome," they said in unison. "The tarot cards said we could expect visitors today."

I caught my breath at the empty sleeve where Fei Yen's lower arm had once been.

She followed my eyes with a sad smile. "It's not so bad. We've had to adapt before, and we will adapt again."

Faeza pressed Fei Yen's hand. "My love will heal her." Faeza swept her gaze around the shop to the pharmaceutical drawers, the endless jars of Chinese herbs, and the ornate crystals. "She's in the right place for healing. It's what we do here."

Fei Yen nodded. "That's right. Your love will heal the parts of me that really need healing."

"I wish it hadn't happened," I said. "I wish I hadn't sent you after him."

"I seem to remember we insisted." Acceptance drifted across Fei Yen's face. "We can't change the past. We can only change the future. I must thank you for giving up Death's sword so I could be treated and for bringing Faeza back from her *hu hsien* self. We are fortunate to call you a friend."

Faeza nodded. "Not everyone would give away their advantage so willingly, not for unregistered peculiars."

"But what we really are missing is our night class. All this eternal girl business is one thing, but a regular intellectual workout amongst friends works wonders for the psyche," said Fei Yen.

I laughed. "Your English has far surpassed my class."

Fei Yen's smooth, tired face broke into a genuine smile. "Why do you think we are so comfortable there? You make us feel at home. Come now. Come upstairs. We have been listening to K-pop and watching a new anime series while we recover. We even ordered dim sum for breakfast."

"Nothing but the best for my love," said Faeza, her eyes only for Fei Yen.

"Nonsense," admonished Fei Yen. "I can hear the wolf's belly rumbling from here."

Ezra grinned. "You're not wrong, but we can't stay."

"Speak for yourself, dog. I can smell the distinct scent of pork and shrimp wontons. My mouth is watering," purred Echo.

Ezra raised an eyebrow. "Oh, that's why your mouth is wet."

My heart expanded in my chest. It felt like we were in the eye of the storm, and yet I was so glad we'd taken this moment to stop by. I still had one more thing to say.

I addressed the foxes. "We have a plan to take down Phinnaeous Shine tonight. You must stay here and stay safe." I glanced at Fei Yen's empty sleeve. "If things go wrong, I want you to know you couldn't have done any more in this fight. I think of you as family, and I am so sorry for what you suffered."

"Oh, Alisha, suffering is part of life. None of us can escape it." Fei Yen sighed.

"We will make the werepigeon pay," growled Echo.

"It's not just your brother, Alisha. I keep thinking we knew we couldn't trust Wildwoods," said Faeza.

Fei Yen's soft voice filled every crevice of my soul. "There are good and bad people everywhere, dear one."

"I hope one day you can trust Wildwoods," I said. "We're working on it. Just promise me one thing—never, ever open the portal to the Celestial Library to Phinnaeous Shine. Send him anywhere but there. There is something amongst the stars that he can't get his hands on."

"Is Gaia going to help you?" said Faeza. "After all that's happened, it would be good to have a goddess on your side."

I tried to hide my worry. "I went to her flat last night to tell her our plans, but it was empty, and for once, the door wasn't ajar."

"I'm sure she'll turn up when the time is right," soothed Fei Yen. "She always does."

We said our goodbyes, and when the door jangled closed behind us, I turned.

The foxes walked back towards the stairwell, heads leaned together in a world of their own.

A STARLESS BLACK blanket of sky floated above us. Excited whispers reached our ears as a stream of peculiars filed through the park. The Wildwoods Halloween Ball was underway, a night of magic, music and ritual that had become a highlight of every registered peculiar's family calendar. The rules of the ball—to not come as yourself and to wear a mask —made it the perfect night for our mission.

"Stay away from the main pathway and keep your voices down," I said.

I love a woman who takes charge, said Orpheus. My dear mother, now deceased, did a fine job of controlling six raucous brothers. I considered turning her when she was on her deathbed, but I was afraid she'd be so angry she'd stake me herself. So I buried her, although I missed the church service, of course. But the priest accidentally flicked some holy water at me. I'm still not over it.

I glared at him. *Shh, I'm trying to concentrate.*

We were a motley crew of Lavinia's coven, Ezra's pack (minus Rashida, who I had vetoed), a vampire, two druids, an empath, a humdrum and a leopard. Although you wouldn't have known it to look at us. Not with the masks and ornate costumes we had on. There were villains from film history like Pennywise the Clown, Thanos and the Joker. Plus, biblical choices, such as Lucifer and Lilith. Some had opted to dress up as figures from mythology like Loki or literature like Dorian Gray. Orpheus, unwilling to abandon his usual black garb, had gone for Hades with a fiery mask.

But this wasn't any old Halloween party.

For Wildwoods Halloween Balls, costumes weren't just ordered online, borrowed from charity shops or cobbled together with odd bits from around the house. That may have been the starting point, but it didn't end there. The costumes underwent a change, tweaked by spells and potions or by the innate talents of the peculiars. Hidden pockets of magic changed a familiar voice into a cackle, lengthened nails into gruesome claws, added fangs where there had been none or a snout where a nose had once been.

It was thrilling and terrifying. My heartbeat grew wild with the new sights and sounds, this overt display of all the weirdness and possibilities of the Otherworld.

Only Echo remained recognisable. We'd dressed him as three-headed Cerberus, though he'd protested at being disguised as a dog. The two additional heads fanned out from his own, their eyeballs moving unnaturally, but to those with true sight, there was no hiding that this was the leopard. For that reason, he'd promised me to slink in the shadows and only show himself if all hell broke loose.

And I bloody well hoped it didn't.

The plan was to pull things off quietly.

Ezra and I trudged ahead of the others. I was dressed as Catwoman in an outfit that held in every wobble without the need for control pants. I'd tucked a dozen pages from my catalogue of creatures into my bra.

"Do you really think the school won't give us away?" I said.

"It knows what's in its best interests. I don't think it will turf us out," said Ezra. "I've been weighing it up, and it all comes down to one thing. Do you know why Wildwoods has survived this long, through endless iterations of the Sorcerer's Senate and generations of Custodians of the Celestial Library, despite being in one of the most surveilled cities on earth?"

I adjusted my mask, the weight of the world on my shoulders.

"Wildwoods is a whole complex ecosystem. It adapts. It changes. It protects itself. It could have taken your sword in the vaulted cabin, Alisha. It could have withdrawn my Minister's rights to teleport within the grounds of the building, but at that moment, when Phinnaeous Shine challenged you, it didn't help him. It let us escape." He adjusted his costume, a gorilla's head over a tuxedo.

The effect was comic rather than horrifying, and Phil Collins's drum solo from "In the Air Tonight" involuntarily filled my head. I wasn't the only one.

Up above, Echo hummed the tune and leapt from tree to tree. "The wolf is wiser than he looks. But if all does go to the dogs, we can take comfort in taking everyone else down with us."

"Here we are," I said in hushed tones.

Meriel Naehorn's tunnels lay cleverly concealed by thick and glossy laurel hedging deep in the park on a route hidden from the gaze of sphinxes. It had taken some literal digging and a broken nail at twilight, but we'd found them, just as Gunnolf had done before us.

I turned to face my friends and allies. "Are we ready?"

"We are, druid." Lavinia's voice was muffled underneath her Alien costume. She'd hidden her umbrella in the pocket of her leg. "Lead the way."

"Remember, everyone, take off any mental blocks you have erected. Orpheus needs to be able to read your thoughts. He is our walkie-talkie in there. Far more subtle than the real thing." My pulse sounded like a drumbeat in my ears. "Marina and Rob, stay here and keep watch. We might need your healing powers and links to the police."

Marina had dressed as Morticia Adams, her rainbow hair sprayed black. "If anyone comes this way, we'll go incognito as horny teenagers, and I'll snog Rob's face off."

Rayna had gone as Medusa. She wore a shredded Roman gown and a magnificent headdress that teemed with coiled snakes. At my word, she touched the earth at the tunnels, ripping out the remaining undergrowth and fashioning a bulbous growth of vines to conceal the entrance once we had slipped through.

Closing my eyes, I sent a silent prayer to Gaia. Just to let her know where we were. It would be nice if she could do the same. "Good luck, everyone."

I dipped into the dark tunnels, with Ezra close behind me. We trudged, our backs crooked in the small space, our minds whirring. We didn't dare light the way, but soon, Orpheus and Echo joined us up front. Their eyes were more accustomed to the dark. Fifty metres, a hundred metres, two hundred metres, I lost count. The sniffles, breathing and footsteps of my friends filled my mind until we came to a stop before a boulder. With brute strength, Ezra and Orpheus heaved it aside.

We found ourselves in the back of the obelisk that towered in the arena, the one from which Sahil, Marina and I had jumped at Ezra's request when we laboured to discover our powers.

Rock music swelled, together with the raucous noise of exuberant partygoers.

Echo's Cerberus heads nodded in time with the beat. "It's a live band playing 'Time Warp' from *The Rocky Horror Picture Show*. How can I concentrate when my whole body wants to join in?"

"Calm yourself. We're on the battlefield now," I said with quiet authority, expecting the Wildwoods to catapult us out of there any second.

But it didn't.

I did a head count. Fifteen of us, all accounted for.

The yew tree hadn't raised the alarm. The arena hadn't submerged us. The sphinxes hadn't been released from their stone forms to rip us limb from limb. The party continued, and no one paid us the slightest bit of attention.

Maybe Ezra was right. Maybe Wildwoods had chosen a side.

My courage solidified. As we approached the school, we walked unhurriedly to blend in with the partygoers. I was on standby to animate Dad's bat drawings should we be discovered. I figured some circus-style bat displays would allow us enough time to escape if need be.

Orpheus had been so excited by the idea it made me wonder if he had a hard-on for bats.

I heard that, he said.

I grinned. *You were meant to.*

We queued for the cable cars alongside revellers and deliberately split up our group when the time came to ride up to Wildwoods. Echo took his own route up. He climbed the trees up to the cabins, waiting for a moment of need, his emerald eyes trained on my every move. My protector and friend.

I'd been warned that Meriel Naehorn was a popular choice of costume since the Battle of the Celestial Library, but nothing prepared me for the sight of young peculiars dressed as her. There were fallen angels, mythological monsters, dragons and creepy dolls.

The Wildwoods cabins looked bleak in their chequered chessboard décor against the starless night sky, a glowing banner with blood-red writing attached to each one. I scanned them, momentarily indecisive. Palm Reading. Zombie Pumpkins. Ouija Ghouls. Apple Bobbing. Dinner with the Dead. Conjuring Circle. Murder Mystery. Séance Catacombs. Vault of Horrors. Witch Doctor Wilds.

We exited the cable cars, and I murmured in Lavinia's alien ear, "Fan out with the coven and find the red woman. Use the chaos to blend in. Don't engage her. The rats have been briefed?"

She nodded and laid a hand on my arm. "You are braver than I thought."

Then she whispered a word I couldn't decipher, prompting the rats to run down the trousers and arms of the witches. The coven scattered in different directions across the rope bridges.

I refocused on my task. For my plan to work, I didn't need to be stronger than Phinnaeous. I just needed to understand his psyche.

That was the thing about middle-aged women, especially those who had lived ordinary lives. We might be easy to overlook, but we saw things. We noticed a slight change in expression or tone. Or whose step was light and whose was heavy. We noticed who commanded the energy in the room and who faded into the background. We knew who created joy and who sucked it away. We knew who took the prime cut of meat from the buffet for themselves and who left it for their loved one. We knew who was incapable of anything but arrogance and selfishness.

Phinnaeous Shine was that man.

He might have been a shapeshifter, but I knew him down to his bones. His narcissism would be his death knell.

Narcissists believed they held all the power when power could never be one person's alone. Power was meant to be shared. Even if one person captured it, it wasn't static. Eventually, it flowed to the next recipient. The Prime Sorcerer's battle was lost before it had even begun.

And he didn't even realise it.

I bit my lip. I knew he favoured spectacle. It wasn't enough for him to win. He wanted everyone to see him win. Death's sword would not be in his office or the Wildwoods vault or guarded by the animals in Helio Woodwink's bestiary.

It would be hidden in Phinnaeous Shine's robes because he thought himself invincible.

Our main showdown wouldn't be in one of the smaller cabins. It would be in the vaulted cabin at the Nightmare Masquerade. The cabin topped by the king piece from chess. Because Phinnaeous Shine liked to think of himself as a king, even though the queen was the most powerful piece on the board.

"We're going into the Nightmare Masquerade," I said. "There are seven captives, so there needs to be at least seven rescuers inside. No one dies. Ezra, you're with me. The rest of the group needs to split up in there."

Ezra, Orpheus and Rayna nodded. The vampire mentally dispersed the message to the wolf pack, and I led the way through the excited throngs into the vaulted cabin.

A chill ran through my bones when we stepped into an absence of light. Only a slither of moonlight through the stained-glass windows allowed me to discern the mass of costumed bodies pulsating to a cover of Radiohead's "Creep" by the live band. The door shut behind us with a shuddering vibration, and the music ground to a halt.

The mass of bodies turned to face us. "She's here."

Their whispers turned my insides to jelly.

19

They know we are here, said Orpheus.

The whispers died down. *No shit, Sherlock. Are the rats in place?*

Yes, said the vampire. *Lavinia's coven has swept every corner of the school. She says the red woman and the captives must be in here, but the door to the vaulted cabin has been magically sealed. No one is getting in or out.*

Well, that's just peachy.

Ezra and I steeled ourselves as the crowd parted.

A spotlight traced Phinnaeous Shine's path into the room. Shimmering on his arm was the statuesque goddess of hinges, thresholds and, more recently, disease and portals. She wore a Venetian mask and a red sequinned, full-skirted dress.

My hands tingled with power, but I balled them up, not wanting to risk casualties. I ignored Phinnaeous and glared at Cardea. "Where is Gaia?"

"Preparing to commune with the gods. We do talk, you know. Like squabbling siblings, we find a reason to come together eventually. Even if it takes us centuries. Not that I owe you any explanations." She pulled her left hand from her pocket. Thanks to me, only one blackened finger remains. The middle one. She flipped me the bird.

I didn't feel an ounce of guilt. At least her manicures would be cheaper.

Phinnaeous gave a sly smile. "I knew you'd both come. You just couldn't let sleeping dogs lie."

"How could I miss my first Wildwoods Halloween Ball?" I couldn't wait to wipe the smug expression off his face. *You were right, Orpheus. He thinks too much of himself to wear a costume. The sword has got to be in those robes. Tell the rats to wait for my go.*

"I wasn't expecting theatre tonight. It didn't say that on the ticket," said a woman.

"It's cool the eternal girl and Ezra Neuhoff want to be a part of it. I wish they'd speak up, though. I can barely hear what they're saying," said her friend.

Ezra bristled, his sole focus on the man who had killed his uncle. "Why is it that there are no other senators here with you, Phinnaeous? You must know they only voted for you out of fear, not admiration."

Tux or no tux, I had a feeling he was going to change into his wolf tonight.

Phinnaeous smirked. "That's always been your problem, Neuhoff. So idealistic when it's not idealism that drives progress. It's ambition." He laughed. "Did you really think Wildwoods would keep your presence on its soil under wraps from *me*? How do you think I found Gunnolf? Even now, Helio's beasts are rounding up the traitors."

My hands went limp. *I thought Wildwoods was on our side.*

Orpheus's deep voice filled my head. *Phinnaeous clearly doesn't know his history as well as I do. I'd wager that Wildwoods is playing both sides until it knows who will come out on top. This school's primary aim is the preservation of itself and its pupils.*

I bit my lip. *So he doesn't have the others?*

He's trying to destabilise you. I've done a tally, and so far, he only has you and Neuhoff, said Orpheus.

Cardea's blue eyes were like ice chips. "It was Gaia who taught me that victory and defeat aren't confined to the battlefield. Sometimes, an everyday choice is what reveals our mettle. An impossible choice. That all started with Eve, obviously. We all knew she was going to eat the apple. But what about you, druid? What cloth are you cut from?"

"A loin cloth?" a small voice piped up from the crowd—a voice I recognised.

"Mirabel." My heart clattered. "Leave this to the adults. It's not safe."

She ignored me and came to my side in her Wednesday Addams costume. "Do you know where my parents are? They were just here, and I can't find them anywhere."

"Go and ask Lost and Found." I focussed on Cardea.

"I'm not a shoe. Can't you come with me?" said Mirabel.

"Just give us a second, kid." Ezra guided her back into the crowd as Phinnaeous addressed the room.

Clearly, he relished the spotlight. His voice boomed like a circus maestro. "Wildwoods, I promised you something special at our sacred Halloween Ball. Tonight…" He waited for a drumroll from the band. "We're going to play Trick or Treat with the eternal girl."

The vaulted cabin erupted into rapturous applause.

He dropped his voice so only Ezra and I could hear. "There's more than one way to kill a legend."

"Behold, mortals, the might of the gods." Cardea strummed the air with her diseased fingers, which, quite frankly, would have been more impactful if she'd had a complete set.

My stomach lurched as fourteen identical white doors appeared in the vaulted cabin between the parted sea of spectators. The doors faced each other in pairs, seven pairs to be precise. They lit up like lights on a runaway.

The revellers gasped.

"Bravo, bravo! I wonder if they flew this sorceress in from abroad?" said someone.

Orpheus's sigh reverberated around my head. *Like lambs to the slaughter.*

"Welcome to your real test, Alisha Verma," said Phinnaeous, like a maniacal game show host. "Behind each of these fourteen doors is a person. Seven peculiars and seven humdrums. Only half will live. You must choose who to save. And there'll be a time limit, of course."

The glint in his eyes dared me to save the humdrums because if I did, he could demonise me.

My heart raced. So that's where the captive humdrums were. But who were the peculiars he had trapped alongside them? Hadn't it always been his suspicion that I would never be a fully-fledged peculiar? That I would always put humdrums first?

Hold on. Echo and Lavinia are almost here, said Orpheus.

A ripple of excitement ran through the crowd.

"It's a cracking good show," said a man in a Frankenstein costume. "I love shows with magic, acting and philosophical questions all thrown in. They're never going to be able to top this next year."

"I wonder if the pretend victims will fall into a barrel of goo. Wouldn't that be fun?" giggled a woman.

I clenched my fists, stalling Phinnaeous with a question I already knew the answer to. "Why are you doing this?"

"All my life, peculiars have lived in the shadows. It's time for a new world in which we are in charge." His lips curved into a chilling smile. "And the gods like my vision."

In Cardea's cornflower eyes, her love of chaos glinted. When mortals suffered, the gods thrived.

Ezra's grey eyes on mine were unwavering. We'd made

tough choices before, such as choosing between Gunnolf and Fei Yen, but that had been a ruse. Phinnaeous had intended to kill Gunnolf all along.

This time, we weren't falling for it. We weren't making a choice. The determined set of Ezra's jaw told me he felt the same.

Every single captive mattered. Each one deserved to go home.

Phinnaeous waved his hands, and a glowing red countdown appeared on the drum kit on stage. "You have a minute to free your choice of seven. Then, the remaining doors will burn."

Fourteen doors between the two of us. A quick mental calculation told me that left us less than ten seconds for each door, and who knew what state the victims would be in behind them.

A woman dressed as Velma from *Scooby Doo* giggled with excitement. "It's like the Salem witch trials. The perfect Halloween theme."

He's clearly lost his mind, said Orpheus. *Fate has had the last laugh after his cabbagification of the detective.*

"You run afoul of the Magical Constitution, Phinnaeous," growled Ezra.

"Wasn't it you who said that new times call for new rules?" said Phinnaeous. "Ready yourself, druid."

Cardea's skirt swished as she and Phinnaeous took up position on one side of the runway of paired doors.

"Begin," she said as the fourteen doors sizzled and the seconds on the clock ticked down.

My stomach twisted in knots. *Tell the team to hurry.*

Ezra sprang into action. He grabbed my waist and teleported us to the furthest set of doors.

They were flat, with no depth behind them, making it hard to imagine how a person could be held captive there. We lunged for one each. The golden round knob burned my hand, but I yanked it open, my eyes widening at the depth behind the door. A small square of space existed contrary to the physical laws of the universe. A gagged Sonny Angleman stood there, his legs and arms bound tightly. I wrenched him out at the same time as Ezra flung Ivana Humperdick into the central aisle.

The crowd went wild with clapping and whoops.

Orpheus and Ezra's wolf pack—still in their human form—surged forward to help as Ezra and I ran to the next pair of doors, desperate to reach every soul trapped within them. Someone dragged out Margola, bound and gagged. My hands burned as I pulled out an angel. Orpheus freed a fellow vampire.

For the love of coffins, said Orpheus. *They're the volunteers from the Shine Foundation for the Advancement of Peculiars and Humdrums.*

But this was supposed to be my trial. I wasn't supposed to involve my friends in this rescue. Phinnaeous and the red woman wanted me isolated and alone.

Our disregard for the rules had a penalty.

The clock sped up.

Incoming, said Orpheus.

The stained-glass window at the top of the vaulted cabin shattered. With a roar, Echo landed with a thud in the midst of the doors, still dressed in his Cerberus costume. That was the thing about having a leopard protector. He could climb to great heights, and he would stop at nothing to stand at my side. He snarled at Phinnaeous, tombstone teeth bared.

Behind him, Lavinia's coven flew in through the broken window on their umbrellas, weaving through it in impressive formation despite the tight space, and joined us in yanking open the scalding doors.

Phinnaeous's expression transformed from malicious joy to a mild sense of panic. "Get Helio in here, now!"

But the crowd remained in situ, paralysed with

uncertainty. Perhaps it was my friends' arrival or the breaking of the storied stained glass. They began to sense, at last, that perhaps this wasn't a show after all.

The goddess's tone was haughty. "Calm yourself, wizard. They're not going to succeed."

"I'm affronted that my lack of opposable thumbs prevents me from participating in this team sport." Echo hissed, impatiently waiting for the rest of us to open doors before he and the rats dragged the still-bound and gagged victims to the central aisle.

I whipped around to do a head count—how many were safe now? Nine, ten?—then jerked my head to the clock. Ten seconds left.

Part of me didn't believe they would let souls perish here. That Phinnaeous Shine and a goddess who had once been gentle enough to be Gaia's friend, could let anyone burn. It was unthinkable.

But in the Otherworld, the unthinkable became possible.

Hadn't Ezra warned me? *Magic isn't just for party tricks, not in my world,* he had said. *It's blood and sweat, and sometimes it's dead bodies and running away in the night.*

Five seconds left. *Send the rats now, Orpheus.*

The rats sprang into action, doing my bidding, sneaking into Phinnaeous robes for Transcender while commotion raged, but it was the goddess who caught my attention.

She flicked her luscious cascade of hair out of the way, and with a spiteful look of foul play, she touched the last two doors closest to her. A surge of heat warmed my skin as she turned the once-white doors transparent. I sucked in my breath at the sight of Mirabel's parents Briar and Juniper Elmstorm, trapped, each in a chamber of their own.

Then, those final two chambers burst into flames.

Despite there still being precious seconds on the clock.

A primal scream built in me. *Don't let Mirabel see this, Orpheus.*

I ran towards Juniper, flinging my hands up, desperate to contain the fire with my wind, but it was airtight. I clung to the handle, heat blistering my palm, but it wouldn't open, even with Lavinia's help, her spells useless. I beat at the door with my fists until my arms grew heavy, horror driving me on. Nothing worked. Behind me, Ezra and the wolves attempted the same with Briar, but the heat drove them back.

"Use your powers," I said.

Orpheus's sombre voice in my head. *Their powers are insufficient. They will fare no better than if the selkie were still trapped.*

Juniper's confusion turned to terror; her hands flapped in a desperate attempt to still the flames, but her fire fairy powers weren't up to the task. She writhed in pain, locking her eyes on the door opposite where Briar was imprisoned. His face twisted in pain as the flames licked his legs, but he fought to remain stoic, mouthing *I love you* to his wife. He might have been a fire chief, but his paltry fire talents meant he relied on humdrum tools to fight fire. With no fire extinguisher at hand, he was in trouble without our help.

"It isn't pretend. That's a real goddess. Those are real flames. She's killing peculiars!" a man in an Edward Scissorhands costume cried out. "The Prime Sorcerer is watching them burn."

In an instant, the sense of revelry evaporated.

The noise levels crescendoed amidst a stampede of panic. Peculiars battered the door to the vaulted cabin, clamouring for release. Rayna, still dressed as Medusa, ran towards the vaulted door, vines spiralling through the broken stained-glass window and already attaching themselves to the door to make it yield.

Wildwoods gave way.

Not because of the vines but because the school had decided to act. Outside, the sphinxes Mammatas and Rhokon shepherded the surging crowd away from danger like they, too, had abandoned their allegiance to Phinnaeous.

Phinnaeous flushed. He understood his mistake at once.

He'd been so determined to paint me as the villain that he had given his own dark heart away. He reached into his robes for Death's sword. Horror clouded his face as, instead of Transcender, he found one of Marina's strap-on dildos instead. He dropped it with a look of revulsion and melted into the crowd, shapeshifting as he went.

"I'm going after him." Ezra ripped off his tuxedo, transforming as he ran, with Echo close behind him.

The rats, skilled in spells and illusions, handed me the sword. Its obsidian blade glinted in the glow of the flames, whispering to me of power and revenge. I spun to face the red woman. "Stop it, or I will cut you down where you stand. You can't want this."

The red woman smiled. "But I do want it. I want all the chaos." She glanced at the sword. "That sword belongs to the immortals. It would have been Phinnaeous's offering to me for my help tonight."

My voice was steely. "Come and get it."

Cardea's face twisted. She opened a new portal and stepped into it.

"Stop," I said. "Don't leave them to burn."

The portal closed, but her voice still found me. "You thwarted the gods. What else did you expect but pain?"

And then it was over for all but Mirabel's parents.

I fell to my knees, shaking, as Juniper and Briar burned. The witches stood in a semi-circle around the burning couple, helpless, their heads bowed. Witches knew well the pain of burning—the futile horror of it.

Their gags meant their daughter couldn't hear their screams.

It was over in minutes, but I couldn't stay.

Instead, I staggered out into the night and vomited. The

rope bridges still thronged with costumed people. In the smaller cabins, Halloween lovers still partied, oblivious to what had transpired.

Phinnaeous Shine could be anywhere by now.

I turned to find a grim-faced Orpheus, who held Mirabel against his chest.

The fairy lifted her tear-stained face. "Are they dead?"

My chest constricted. I nodded. "I'm so sorry, Mirabel."

Her face crumpled, and she slammed against my chest. "I don't understand. I don't understand why they were in there. They were only just with me. We were going to the apple bobbing tent." A sob. "Where will I go?"

Orpheus passed Mirabel a handkerchief. "She trusts you. Take her home, Alisha. Rayna and I will see to things here. Neuhoff and the leopard will return soon enough, and The Ritz will have one more prisoner."

I hugged Mirabel to me. "Do you want to stay with me tonight?"

She hiccupped. "Can I stay longer?"

My heart hurt. "Of course." I met Orpheus's eyes. "You'll have to wipe the humdrums' minds and take them to the detective. Marina can check them over and soothe any emotional turmoil."

The vampire inclined his head as the coven approached. "We have Wildwoods back because of you, Alisha."

"Orpheus is right. Your plan was a good one." Lavinia smoothed her hand over her umbrella. "No battle is won without losses. Come, Alisha. I'll take you home. Mirabel can ride with Chandra."

I swallowed the lump in my throat. Had it been a good plan? The rats as the pawns, my thieves and illusionists. Lavinia as my rook, supporting the advance, her weapons always sharp. Orpheus as the bishop, sliding between us all, our mind link. Echo as my castle, my refuge, leaping through medieval glass in service of me. Ezra as my knight, even at great cost to himself. Me as the queen, finally able to move freely across the board. Now, we'd toppled the opposing king.

But Mirabel's parents had died, and I didn't know if she'd ever be okay again.

20

I took Mirabel home to collect some things. She'd cried through the night, great hiccupping sobs that receded into silence and then resurfaced again. I held her, knowing only one thought had helped after Mum's death.

"Your parents are a part of you," I said. "Their DNA, their values, the memories you made together. None of that goes away. You carry them with you."

The two of us arrived at the cottage in the early hours of the morning in an Otherworld taxi.

My phone already pinged with breaking news that the missing humdrum high-fliers had been mysteriously found in the basement of a London pub, with no mobile reception and empty crates of wine beside them. A paparazzi had managed to snap a dishevelled picture of the sorry lot.

Journalists speculated that one of their number had invited them to a networking afternoon, replete with wine-tasting, but they'd locked themselves in by accident and then polished off all the alcohol to drown their sorrows. Or their livers.

No journalist bothered to ask why none of them had been caught on CCTV entering the pub, but there was much relief at their reappearance and that they could resume their positions of influence. The Shine Foundation for the Advancement of Peculiars and Humdrums had done a marvellous job filling in the roles temporarily.

Good old Rob and Orpheus.

Gaia's vines cocooned the cottage still. I hacked at them with Death's sword to get to the door. The door jammed when I tried the key. Ezra was leading the seekers in a hunt for Phinnaeous—they were determined to see him be tried at court—so I had to be the muscle. I twisted the key again and tried to shoulder it open, letting the swear word die on my lips. On the third attempt, it worked.

I lifted my hands to let a breeze run through the cottage before turning around to smile at Mirabel. "Come on. There's some paperwork to get through, but Rayna reckons we can swing it so you can stay awhile. Or longer, if you want." I paused. "It's a bit dingy because of the vines, but you'll see, it's a lovely home."

Her blue eyes widened as she took in her new surroundings. The newly painted walls, the chocolate-box-shaped rooms, the tiny galley kitchen and the living room hearth. The small bedroom that would now be hers and the larger one that I shared with Ezra. Her gaze lingered on Echo's water bowl.

I set down her two duffel bags of belongings just inside the door. So much for a young mind to process. "What do you think, sweetheart? Will it do?"

Her bottom lip quivered. "What if you get fed up with me? You're not my mum. What if I annoy you or make you angry? You could pass me on like I'm an old coat to one of those charity shops we passed on the way. What if no one ever loves me like they did ever again?"

Her hands sparked with fire.

I rushed to hug her, my chest constricting. I kissed her fingertips instinctively.

The sparks died out.

I ignored the bubble of snot in her nostril. "I promise you can stay with me as long as you want." I squeezed her against me. "I'll tell you a secret, shall I? I've liked you from the moment I set eyes on a little fairy in the vaulted cabin at Wildwoods, holding her own against teenage wolves."

Mirabel gave a watery smile. "Yeah, that was pretty cool. I gave one of them a wedgie. Do you remember? Best spell I ever learned."

"Uh-huh. Don't you *ever* do that to me, okay?"

This time, she giggled, although it quickly fizzled out.

I handed her one of the duffel bags to start and pushed her in the direction of her bedroom. "Go get settled in, okay? Take a look around, and open any drawer you want to. I'll be right through to give you a hand."

"Okay." She bit her lip and headed off.

"Mirabel?"

She turned back, her face blotchy with tears she tried to hide. "Yes, Alisha?"

I didn't mention the tears. There'd been an adult with her every second since her parents had died, but now she was in a safe space. Maybe she needed a cry on her own. "Echo will be home from his hunt soon. He's going to love hanging out with you. He was brilliant company for me when I was your age. You'll see."

I gave her an encouraging smile and watched her wander down the corridor before sending Ezra a text message. *Come home as soon as you're free. I've got something to ask you.*

Then I slipped off Transcender from my back and found a loose floorboard in our bedroom to hide it under. I pulled a rug over it and then returned to the kitchen to check the fridge, wrinkling my nose at the contents. I had a child to feed now. Slabs of frozen meat for Echo and the odd probiotic yoghurt weren't going to cut it anymore. Neither would mouldy cheddar. How long did it even take for cheddar to grow mould? I'd have to get in fruit, vegetables, maybe some ice lollies. Did twelve-year-olds still eat ice lollies? I made a mental list. They definitely ate chocolate cereal. Oh, and milk. I'd need milk. Wine wouldn't cut it. Maybe some cheese sticks. Oh, and some cookies to dip in the milk. But what if she had a dairy allergy? I groaned. There was more to the motherhood malarkey than I'd realised.

I startled at a noise behind me. The hair on the back of my neck rose, and I swivelled, palms ready.

Ezra stood in the doorway, the perfect guy to soothe my frazzled heart. "Easy, tiger. Put those weapons away."

He usually lived in the same pair of jeans, but today, he wore an odd bootleg cut and a weird thick-knit jumper that wasn't his usual style. But the days were getting colder, and who was I to judge a man's fashion choices? He probably kept some random bits at the farmhouse now that most of his stuff was at the cottage after his beautiful tuxedo got ripped.

I dropped my hands and laughed. "Since when do you call me tiger? Can't wait to see what Echo says about that."

His brow furrowed. "Is the leopard here?"

"No, he's out hunting. Are you okay?"

He made a beeline for me, splayed his hands on my hips and pulled me towards him. The kiss was a shadow of the kisses we shared before. Weirdly probing but emotionless.

I gave myself a mental shake. We all needed a proper rest. "Did it go all right at the farmhouse? You didn't need to rush back."

"Not yet." He hesitated, his grey eyes cold. "Whose bag was that at the door?"

I took a deep breath. It meant so much to me that he was on board with this. Reaching out for his hand, I traced circles on his palm. The words rushed out. "It's Mirabel's. Ezra, last night, in the midst of it all, when Mirabel lost her parents, I was the only one who could calm her down. And then, when she asked me if I would look after her, I had this sense of meaning, unlike anything I'd ever felt before. She was one of the first people I met in the Otherworld, and my instincts told me to protect her, even then. Don't you remember? What if that was meant to be? Ezra..." I put my heart on the line. "I know I should have asked you first before bringing her home, but I couldn't bear the thought of her going home with strangers. She trusts me, and she's been through so much. I want her to move in with us. For us to look after her together. To be a part of our family."

Ezra's face hardened. "No."

Blood rushed to my head, making me lightheaded. But this was my dream. It all made sense. Why couldn't he see it? Why couldn't he see what he'd be missing out on? "No?"

He'd change his mind once he thought about it, once he got to know her like I did.

He'd fall in love with her, too.

He edged closer, his breath fanning my face. "You heard me. It's bad enough that the leopard has crowbarred his way into our relationship. I don't want the girl in our lives."

I wanted to vomit. I couldn't go back on my word. Not after all Mirabel had been through. "Can we sit down and think about it?"

Ezra's jaw clenched. "Make a choice, Alisha. Me or the girl."

He couldn't even bring himself to say her name.

A wave of nausea crashed over me. It was true. He hadn't ever wanted children. What a fool I had been.

I wanted the ground to open and swallow me up.

The answer was clear. My voice trembled, and I hated myself for it. But I held my chin high. "I choose her, Ezra. I'll pack up our things and leave the cottage by morning."

He gave a brisk nod and then turned on his heel, leaving me alone.

I followed him, despite my better instincts, my pride and heart in tatters. "Ezra? Aren't you even going to celebrate our win last night? We did it. We got the better of Phinnaeous Shine."

He paused and looked over his shoulder.

"Did we? He's free as a bird." He walked out the front door.

Mirabel shuffled down the corridor in thick socks. "I heard voices. I thought it was Ezra."

I pulled myself together and rearranged my expression. Today, I would pretend everything was okay. Mirabel deserved that. "Hi, sweetheart. He'll be back tomorrow." I opened a cupboard and spied a packet of pasta. My appetite was gone, but she needed to eat. "Tell you what, I'll whip us up a simple lunch, and we can eat in front of the telly."

Mirabel gave a tentative smile. "*Fresh Prince of Bel Air*? I'm halfway through series three."

I pulled out a saucepan. "You get a head start on the next episode. I'll be right out."

MIRABEL, eyes bleary from tears and exhaustion, curled up on her bed for a nap after lunch. I tucked her in, gently closed the door and then put an ear to it. Within minutes, light snores told me she had slipped into slumber, so I headed for the front garden, already speed-dialling Marina.

"I can't come to the phone right now. Leave a message after the tone, and I'll get back to you within three months," she sang on her voicemail.

That voicemail lost its charm when my need to speak to her was desperate.

I gave her a second before trying again. She was probably operating on a guinea pig or rat. Pet rats were all the rage among schoolchildren nowadays. After all, they weren't very expensive. You could just nab one off the streets. And they were very clever and could be housetrained if you could get over their unsightly teeth. What worried me was how it could lead to Lavinia's rats being planted all over the city. Like some sort of spy camera or speaker. Only alive, toothy and capable of movement. It was all very dystopian. I released a shuddering breath and tried Marina again, willing her to pick up.

No luck.

That was the thing about best friends. They had lives of their own.

She'd better not be swinging around a pole with Rob at this hour. With the Shadow Squad back in the game following our unpicking of Phinnaeous Shine's equality foundation and the return of the humdrum high-fliers to their positions, the detective had plenty on his plate.

I wracked my brain for another friendly voice to offload my love woes to. I could ring the foxes, but it seemed selfish after all they'd been through. Sahil was at the very bottom of the list for obvious reasons. Mum had always been a wonderful source of emotional support, but love advice from Dad was the pits. He'd probably tell me to go to temple to find a replacement. Worse still, he'd tell me to put it in the hands of the temple grannies. I cringed just thinking about it. Either that, or he'd tell me that Ezra was a good catch and I'd misunderstood something.

Had I misunderstood something?

Hadn't Ezra fumbled our conversation about children? Hadn't he made excuses for Rashida being a cow, even though the woman clearly wanted to stick ice-picks in my eyes? Hadn't he carried me through the universe in his arms, stood by my side during battles, and made me melt with longing, only to crush my heart to smithereens when I actually laid my dreams at his feet?

I'd call Orpheus. Orpheus was my friend.

Orpheus could fill the role of girlfriend. Sure, he didn't have Marina's listening ear or social skills, but he'd tell me what an arsehole Ezra was. He'd be a hundred per cent in my corner. Maybe he'd learned that in the boxing ring. Or maybe it was a vampire's black-and-white way of seeing things.

Either way, it didn't matter. The only thing that would make me feel better right now was unwavering support.

He picked up on the second ring. "Alisha, what can I do for you? I have a club full of ravenous vampires and an influx of scantily clad humdrum women with a death wish. Plus, I'm due at Wildwoods to sort out the mess Phinnaeous Shine left behind, but I can always make time for you."

The world spun. I sat heavily on the doorstep. When my words came out, I sounded alien to my own ears, as if I'd reverted to the old me. The divorced bereaved me. The one who didn't know she had magic. The one who felt she had no control.

"I wanted Mirabel to be part of our family, but Ezra said no," I said. "It's over between us, Orpheus."

A flurry of curses fell from his mouth. Then I heard the chink of a glass. "He left you because you wanted to take in Mirabel? The man's a fool. Are you at the cottage?"

My throat scratched with tears. "Yes."

"I'll be there in under an hour."

At that moment, I hated my vulnerability. "Orpheus..."

His gruff voice pulsed with emotion. "You gave me something to live for when life had lost its lustre. Let me return the favour."

The line went dead.

I sighed. For some reason, I didn't feel any better.

True to his word, Orpheus roared up to the cottage in his Lotus forty-five minutes later. He folded himself out of the car and slammed the door shut. He wore his usual dark trousers and dark shirt—ironically for a vampire—a sort of priest's garb without the clerical collar. But his demeanour was nothing like a priest's. He walked like a stalking horse, and his face held none of a priest's benign grace. His pale skin was tight across his cheekbones, his mouth in a thin line.

This was a man on a mission.

His dress shoes clipped up the garden path, and when he greeted me, my nostrils filled with the familiar scent of his dark chocolate and sweet cherry beard oil. He did not bother with a hello. "I didn't think Neuhoff, of all people, would be capable of this. Both of us know what it is like to care for strays. To be one ourselves."

I stood up. Usually, he was quick to put the boot in with Ezra. Something niggled about Ezra's reaction, but I pushed my logic into the back of my mind, overwhelmed by the pain instead.

Air particles oscillated beside me—I had more and more of a feel for air currents linked to my wind talents—that I recognised as the precursor to Ezra arriving. My heart leapt into my mouth.

He appeared between us, his chiselled face wrapped in a smile that made my heart melt.

That made me think maybe he'd changed his mind.

He'd changed out of the weird outfit. Breathing my name, he leaned in for a kiss, but before our lips touched, Orpheus's hand landed on his shoulder and wrenched him back.

Ezra's eyes widened in surprise.

"How dare you, Neuhoff? The eternal girl allows you into her bed, and you react like a knave. Why I'll..." The vampire spun Ezra to face him, circling his raised fists like a 1930s boxing champ, before landing a quick jab to Ezra's nose.

Ezra jolted backwards. "Are you out of your mind?"

My mouth opened like a fish before I found my voice. "Stop it. This isn't what I want."

"It doesn't matter what you want. It only matters I protect your honour." Orpheus opened the top two buttons of his shirt and then barrelled into Ezra with frightening speed.

Both men flew against the lawn, flattening blades of grass in their wake.

When Ezra clambered to his feet, his face was incandescent with rage.

"I have wanted to do this for a long time." He opened his palm, crouched to where Orpheus, a few centuries his senior, was heaving himself up, and slapped him clean across the face.

The vampire jerked in surprise and drew himself up to full height, his tone dismissive. "You fight like a girl."

I covered my eyes in embarrassment, praying they'd stop this foolishness before any neighbours—or worse, Mirabel —saw.

Ezra dropped any restraint. He set his jaw and flung a kick at Orpheus's knees, presumably hoping to target the vampire's brittle bones. But the kick came up short when the vampire sped backwards and bumped into a wheelie bin.

"Ha," said Orpheus. "I'm too quick for you."

Ezra teleported towards him, used two strong arms to cartwheel him headfirst into the bin—the one I'd emptied mouldy cheese and fruit into that morning—and shut the lid. Only the vampire's legs were too long for the lid to close fully. "How do you like your new coffin, minister?"

It was clear they didn't *really* want to hurt each other. Orpheus hadn't used his fangs. Ezra hadn't shifted.

I'd seen the blood and guts and broken bodies when peculiars really wanted to hurt each other.

"You are both ridiculous," I said from my place of relative safety by the front door. "I have a right mind to go inside and have a cup of tea."

Orpheus clambered out of the bin with a browning banana peel on his shoulder. He flung it at Ezra in disgust before bending his knees, driving off the earth and landing next to Ezra. They traded blows, legs, arms, and fists a blur, a hodgepodge of speed and teleportation, so fast my eyes couldn't follow.

What were they fighting for anyway? Bloody willy-waving men when we could just have a conversation. I had to put an end to it.

A warm, slinky body around my legs and a familiar, honking laughter filled my ears.

Echo purred. "I steal away for a few hours of hunting pleasure and find only a mangy rabbit and a particularly vicious terrier in a tartan jacket. But coming home to this spectacle is just the balm for my hungry heart."

I buried my head in his fur. This was the friend I needed. Like Marina, he'd always been there for me. "I should stop them."

He stood regally, his eyes following the fight. "Leave them to it. It will do them good to unleash their feelings. A good swipe does a world of good. Shall we take bets on the winner? My money is on the vampire. He has more of a killer instinct."

"You don't have any money, Echo."

The men had stopped for a breather, panting hard, but Ezra regained his composure sooner and pulled Orpheus into a headlock. The vampire struggled before raising a long leg to boot Ezra's backside to free his stranglehold.

Echo gurned in mirth. "What's this about anyway?"

"Ezra and I broke up," I said. "He didn't want Mirabel."

The leopard gave me a sharp look. "I see. Perhaps the vampire is right to give the wolf a hiding. Children are always a gift, however they come to us. Is the girl here?"

I bit my lip. "Sleeping in the back bedroom. I'm going to stop this nonsense and then take you to meet her."

Echo's tail flicked. "Spoilsport."

I called a pocketful of wind to each cupped hand. When the warring men pulled apart for a moment—seemingly to gather the room to kick each other in the jingle bells—I sent the wind slamming into their chests. "Enough."

They staggered up, straightening their clothes and muttering like schoolboys.

The stupid, loveable imbeciles.

"Leave," I said to Orpheus.

The vampire opened his mouth to protest.

I shook my head. "Now. I need to talk to Ezra."

Orpheus straightened his shirt and stormed off. "I was only defending your honour."

I sighed and waited for him to climb into his car. The door slammed, and the Lotus roared away from the pavement in the direction of the city.

"You too," I told Echo. "We need a moment."

The leopard gave Ezra a filthy look, inclined his head and pounced into the border hedge.

We watched his progression away from us through the rustling bush.

I turned to Ezra, trying not to cry. "I didn't want it to come to this."

He flushed. "What the hell was that about?"

I frowned. "Our run-in this morning."

He patted down his clothes. Grass stains covered his jeans. His dishevelled hair looked like he'd been through a hedge backwards, and his favourite Beatles T-shirt was ripped, showing his tanned pecs. "What run-in? I've been desperate to get back to you but have been at the farmhouse all day."

My stomach knotted. "You told me you didn't want Mirabel to be part of our family."

Ezra shook his head. "Alisha, I have no idea what you're talking about. I'm telling you. We haven't talked today. I've been chasing Phinnaeous's scent all day with the pack."

My thoughts ping-ponged. "You haven't found him yet?"

He raked a hand through his hair, scowling. "We're not going to stop until we do. He's not our average mark. He knows we're coming and keeps shifting, but we're closing in."

A horrible thought spilt into my head.

The kiss had felt so strange. The clothes. The cold, emotionless delivery of the rejection. Revulsion sent bile to my mouth. "It wasn't you here this afternoon. It was Phinnaeous. He shapeshifted. Phinnaeous pretended to be you."

He spoke slowly as understanding dawned. "Phinnaeous pretended to be me."

Horror snaked through me at how he'd played me. Jesus, I had kissed him. I resisted the urge to scrub my mouth. "He wanted to drive a wedge between us."

Anger stiffened Ezra's posture. "And you fell for it. You thought he was me. How could you?"

His anger was directed at me. We'd fallen out before, but this time felt different. It felt raw and dirty.

"I didn't mean to." My voice was small and pleading. My nails dug into my palms.

Though he didn't raise his voice, every syllable hit home. "Then why did you doubt me?"

I ignored the sense of doom that expanded in my belly. "His words were believable. I...I wasn't sure you wanted children."

His face crumpled, and he looked away for a second before spelling it out. "I was all in. Whatever you needed. Whatever you wanted. I was all in. Kids. No kids. Adopted. Surrogate. Fostering. Hell, I would have been the Waltons for you."

I trembled, realising how badly I'd messed up. Phinnaeous had masqueraded as Ezra before when he'd asked me to return from the Celestial Library. Of course, he'd do it again. "I'm sorry. My insecurities took over. It won't happen again."

He clenched his jaw. "How long was he here? How long

was Phinnaeous Shine here, in my parents' cottage, dammit?"

I laid a hand on his arm, but he didn't soften. "Five minutes. Maybe less."

Ezra shook his head. "You listened to his words, Alisha. Five minutes is all it took for his words to convince you. When I've spent months showing you with my actions and my words that your dreams could be mine. That as long as we had each other, everything else would work out."

I grasped for anything. Anything to make him understand. "You refused to turf Rashida out of the pack, even when she didn't lift a finger against Cardea at the farmhouse. I kind of felt like maybe you had her on a back burner in case things didn't work out between us."

"That's bollocks, hellfire. I accepted it when you didn't want her to be part of the Wildwoods team. I understood." His voice rasped. "I love you. There was never a competition between the two of you. All thoughts of her went out of my head—*stayed* out of my head—the minute I met you. I'd never seen a woman with such fire as you. And then I realised your potential, and all I've thought since is how lucky I am that you chose me. I'd never have jeopardised that."

"You're an exceptionally good man. I don't deserve you."

His mouth was pinched. "That's just it, Alisha. You *do* deserve me. When are you going to realise that and act like we're meant to be together forever? Because we are." He shook his head. "I can't go on like this."

My breath caught in my throat. "Don't leave me."

His shoulders slumped. "You hurt me. You believed me capable of turning away an orphaned girl. God, Alisha. I was an orphan myself." A pause. "Is she inside?"

I nodded. "I want more than anything for us to be a family."

A look of anguish crossed his face. "Do you know what happened the night my parents died?"

I frowned, not understanding where he was going with

this. "There was an ambush. They died protecting each other."

His face twisted. He dug in his jeans for a roll-up, lit it and took a deep drag. "Yeah, that's the gist of it, all right. Dad gave up a lot to be with Mum. He gave up being pack alpha. He gave up his position as Minister of Justice. And she gave up a lot for him. When he became a plain old seeker again, she sometimes joined him on his missions. But some witches frowned on that—same old story. *Stick to your own gene pool. You'll regret settling down with a wolf.*" He pulled absentmindedly at his ripped shirt. "The night they died, they were following a lead on the eternal girl."

I sucked in my breath. "You never wanted to go into any detail."

He puffed out a curl of smoke. "That's normal, isn't it? I don't like to relive it. It's opening up old wounds."

"They were looking for the eternal girl…"

He nodded. "Long before anyone knew it was you. It was a witch child, a dainty little thing who had been showing remarkable skill for her age, so the senate sent Dad. Mum was supposed to meet him there. But this supposed friend of Mum's fed her some story about Dad bedding another woman. And Mum, for a split second, believed her. She turned up late to the village where the mark was. Dad was already wounded. He'd knocked on that little girl's door, and all hell broke loose. But Mum, she couldn't leave him like that. So she ran in, wielding her umbrella. God, I wish I could have seen her in action. Lavinia said she was an excellent warrior in her own right, but I didn't see that side of her. I just saw the mother who tucked me into bed at night, taught me about witching herbs, and sang haunting songs from our ancestors. That night, they were outnumbered. They both died."

I reached out to him. "Ezra, I'm sorry. I'm so sorry."

"I know." He stubbed out his cigarette, cupped my chin

and kissed me. A feather-light kiss, tasting of smoke and mountains, that I wanted him to deepen.

When he pulled away, I was bereft.

"Do you know what gets me? If she had trusted him, they might both still be alive. They would have gone in together as planned and would have made it out of there because he would have teleported them out. But he was waiting for her, you see. He was waiting for her to turn up, and so he didn't leave. And now they are both in the soil."

I trembled. "Ezra, Gunnolf just died. I want to be there for you."

His face clouded with grief. "I wish it could be that way."

God, I had messed things up. "How can I make it up to you?"

He looked away, his neck corded. "Whatever's happened between us, I won't leave you in the lurch. You and Mirabel can use the cottage for as long as you need it. I'll be at the farmhouse. We're friends. If you need help, call me. I'll come running."

I lifted my chin, my heart in fragments. "My personal bodyguard and nothing else?"

The dancing copper flecks in his irises were swamped by the grey. "We'll always be friends."

"I wish you'd found him before he came here."

"Me too." Then he was gone.

The scent of earth, roll-up cigarettes and mountain air lingered in his absence.

21

T he leopard shook his handsome head. "Your separation from the wolf is a tragedy of farcical proportions, Alisha. I wouldn't have urinated on your ex-husband if he was on fire. However, to my surprise, I find I miss the smell of wet dog around the cottage. It is a pity I was distracted by the mangy rabbit. I feel sure I would have sniffed out the shapeshifting, succubus-humping Prime Sorcerer if I had been there."

I sighed as the Otherworld taxi raced up the motorway towards the ancient stones. "You're probably right. Let's hope a trip to Stonehenge with Rayna and Flinar can take our minds off it. Nice of Marina to look after her."

After much soul-searching, I'd decided to accept Ezra's offer of staying at the cottage. It didn't seem right to pull the ground out from under Mirabel's feet again, and the green swathes in Windsor would help heal her heart. Nature had a way of doing that.

Marina had pulled out of the trip and was in our front room giving herself a manicure, then planned to nap on the sofa. With any luck, Mirabel would be woken by a nightmare, but if she did, Marina had pledged to do her nails, too. In all truth, I would have stayed home to nurse Mirabel's heart and my own, but I couldn't bring myself to puncture Flinar's excitement at me joining the elf day out.

Rayna had also insisted it was essential for my druid education.

"I've only been to Stonehenge once, you know, as a teenager," I said. "It'll be a different experience at night with no tourists around."

The leopard stretched out on the mattress on the floor of the taxi. "As rejuvenating as a siesta in the Otherworld taxi is, it saved us a lot of time to have you sleeping with a teleporting werewolf-wizard. You didn't really think the breakup through."

I cuddled up next to him, luxuriating in the feel of his soft, rosetted fur against my cheek. "You really know how to make a girl feel better."

His salmon breath made me wrinkle my nose.

"Your grandmother had bumps in the road, Alisha, but she would be proud of you," purred Echo. "You won back Wildwoods, freed innocents and sent the red woman running into the night along with Phinnaeous. And after the wizard's move last night, Neuhoff's rage can only have increased. The wizard will soon have a wolfpack circling him and Neuhoff's teeth firmly in his derrière." A pause. "Do you know what would make us both feel better? Exacting our dues from the werepigeon. I'll just have to find a way to do it without failing my pledge to protect the Verma family line. Maybe we can get him to marry into another family or change his name by deed poll."

I shook my head. "We're staying with my gut, Echo. No hurting my brother."

He huffed. "You're the boss. Although someday, I would like to be a boss too. Then I will kill all the werepigeons my heart desires."

It was close to midnight when the taxi pulled into the car

park at Stonehenge. It was empty, apart from the coach that had brought Rayna and the elves. We paid our fare, and I grabbed my satchel and slipped on my baldric with Transcender. No more leaving my magical tools in my knicker drawer. They had become like a second skin for me. Then we trudged up to the stones, where the elves explored the monument beneath a sky of glittering stars, their joy palpable.

A light mist shrouded the prehistoric stone circle. Echo and I marvelled at the monument. The rock surfaces had weathered through time, but the stone circle continued to inspire myth and speculation. It consisted of an outer ring of vertical sandstones topped by connecting horizontal stones, an inner ring of smaller stones and freestanding ones scattered about. A memory hit me of my previous visit, and the same sense of tranquillity settled over me as we absorbed the quiet energy of the stones.

"It is a good place," said Echo. "But a place that has also known death. I can feel it in the soil beneath my paws before we even wander amongst the stones."

I nodded. I felt the power and terror of the place, too. "Come on. The elves are waiting."

Flinar gave me an excited wave as we approached, his sail-like ears billowing in the breeze. "Alisha, leopard, you made it. I thought with everything that is going on in the Otherworld, you'd drop out."

I bent down to kiss his downy cheeks. "Anything for my favourite elf."

His dull skin flushed a murky red, and he seized a passing elf. "Pass it on to the others; the eternal girl has arrived. And tell Rayna, too. We are ready for her talk."

Emerald eyes flashed in the dark. "I have arrived, too."

We greeted Rayna and the gathered elves, perhaps two dozen of them, dressed in aubergine-coloured sacks like a type of school uniform. I was pleased that, despite her reinstatement at Wildwoods, she had kept her promise to undertake this trip, and I hoped with fervour that her commitment to the elves continued. Then, we clustered around the headmistress as she delivered her talk a few hundred yards from the stone circle.

"Well, elves," she began, "it's wonderful to be here with you tonight in what is my favourite place. After all, Stonehenge is of great significance to druids, but I think it is also significant for all of us. It shows our potential. This monument was built in about 3000 BC, using simple tools. These huge stones were transported and installed without modern construction expertise. Archaeologists have estimated that the project took 1,500 years to complete. Can you imagine how clever you would be if you had even a fraction of that determination and focus?"

The elves tittered, milky eyes wide with wonder.

Rayna talked with animation, her potions and dagger clanking at her waist as she pointed to the site. It was easy to see why she was so good at her role. "We now know that the site was created based on a solar year of 365 days to help our ancestors keep track of the days, weeks and months. But it was also very much a domain of the dead, associated with burial from the very beginning of its existence." Her eyes twinkled. "So you see, it's very much a place of both the future and the past. Which is why every single one of us here has goosebumps."

Two dozen heads dropped to investigate their knobbly arms.

"How does she know?"

"She's not a witch, is she?"

"I love school."

Rayna beamed. "Of course, you may take all I have said with a pinch of salt if you believe in Arthurian legend. In that case, you'll know that the great wizard, Merlin, transported the stones you see from Ireland, where giants had erected them."

The elves absorbed every word, transfixed.

"So, my little learners—" The smile slid off her face as the ground beneath our feet juddered.

But there were no cars roaring past, no train that disturbed this sacred ground, no earthquake predicted or caused by the god Pan, busy as he was on the board of Battersea Dogs Home and rediscovering his faith.

The ground juddered, and the centuries-old stones of Stonehenge became portals through which the gods appeared —one, two, three, more and more.

Sweet Jesus. Gaia and my brother amongst them.

My heart thundered. I remembered the red woman's words. *Like squabbling siblings, we find a reason to come together eventually. I am the convener of spaces. The gods are gathering, and when they do, there is always a trail of human blood and guts.*

Echo's roar of indignation thankfully went unheard.

It galvanised me into action. "Into your black holes, elves. Now. Stay in small groups and spread out."

"You heard the woman. Be quick." Rayna put her hands to the earth, and even as the judders slowed, she fashioned a bush for us to hide behind. It grew thicker, faster and more luscious than the plants I had witnessed her coax to life before, and I understood all at once that her talents deepened because of where we stood.

The elves disappeared into their black holes with a pop, and only Flinar stayed behind to join Rayna, Echo and me behind the bush. I peered over the greenery, lightheaded with anxiety, and counted seven gods plus Sahil, each in a gateway of their own.

Cardea, in a red skater dress, conducted their arrival. As Gaia had predicted, her fingers had regenerated. They had grown back as diseased as before, a sign of the darkness in her heart.

There was Ra, a sphere of golden light around him, restored to health. There was no Pan, but as we had feared, the

Ravenmaster had returned, stitched together from the pieces the crows had carried away. Mami Wata, recovered from Kraglek's attack, in a pencil skirt and shell bikini. Two more I didn't recognise. A bearded man with a gaunt face wearing a poppy on his breast. My blood ran cold at the sight of a blue, multi-armed woman, almost feral in her beauty, with a naked torso and an ornate necklace of decapitated heads. And Gaia, her sari a dull brown, her face crumpled with worry, looking older than her centuries. My heart twisted to see her there.

But it was Sahil I couldn't take my eyes off. Sahil, beside the Ravenmaster, the Jericho necklace in his hands. The necklace Mum had wanted to protect me. That he had stolen and then fought to keep, wounding Fei Yen in the process.

And still, I loved him.

Still, I worried that the immortals would crush him and we would never be able to make amends, laugh together, weep together, get angry at each other and make up all over again.

Because he was my brother, my first friend, whatever he had done.

"What's the plan?" said Echo. "Do we tear them limb from limb?"

"We should hide. I have a black hole ready right here." Flinar peeled back a piece of hedge and showed us the endless dark beyond.

"The elf is right," said Rayna. "This is a death wish, and I'd rather we didn't add ourselves to the bodies that have been cremated here. Far better to live to fight another day."

I had Transcender, but the sword was useless against a whole host of gods. I had only just escaped with my life when I had challenged one at a time.

But still, I knew deep inside I couldn't leave Gaia and Sahil here. What if they needed me? What if I was their only chance to escape? I wiped my sweaty palms on my trousers and considered texting Ezra for help, my knight in shining armour, but it wasn't fair on him to be at my beck and call. He didn't owe it to me.

And I could save myself.

"You should take up Flinar's offer, but I'm going to stay here until I know what's going on and if the Earth goddess and my brother need me."

Rayna exchanged a grim look with Echo and Flinar. "What kind of peculiars would we be if we abandoned the eternal girl? The Four Musketeers it is."

Echo purred. "But Alisha must free me from my oath so I can chew up the werepigeon and spit him out now that he is a butler to rogue gods."

I sighed. It did look that way. "If anything happens, you hide. I couldn't bear more blood on my hands."

I sent a silent prayer to Gaia.

The Earth goddess's beloved voice—that had become a source of wonder, counsel and friendship to me— drifted to me on the winds, a wail of despair. *You should not be here, druid. Stay hidden. What happens now has been written. It cannot be changed.*

Anger filled me. How was I supposed to help if she was always so cryptic? How was I supposed to fulfil my fate as the eternal girl if she wouldn't tell me everything? Her half-truths were as toxic as lies.

I poked my head above the bush again, squinting into the dark, straining my eyes and risking discovery to figure out what the gods were up to.

"You failed to bring me the sword, Cardea," said the feral blue woman.

Cardea bowed her head. "Forgive me."

"All is not lost. We have one of the three artefacts." The blue woman, clearly their leader, indicated the Jericho necklace in Sahil's hands. "And what I once gifted, I can remake. Made from a heavenly cloud and blessed by me. I shall call it Surrender." She held a blade aloft.

A chill ran up my spine.

It was Transcender's twin. The same shimmering obsidian blade, the same slender, double-aged blade. Even the same mammoth tusk hilt. But the stone on the hilt differed from the one on my back. Whereas the stone in Transcender was small and blue, the one in the twin sword was large and orange, shaped like the elliptical pupil of a snake.

Gaia had told me the story once of the former lover who had made the blade.

The blue woman smiled, and I realised she was Death.

Ra leaned on one of the ancient stones, his amber eyes burning. "Pan should be here with us. It's insulting that he prefers sheep and deer for company."

"It is not Pan we have gathered to punish." Death's voice was shards of molten glass, hot and sharp and full of wrath.

All eyes turned on Gaia.

My stomach clenched.

Death's four hands held Surrender above her head. "Who will kill the Earth goddess, and who will crush the Jericho necklace?"

"I will kill the goddess," said Ra. "She dimmed my light for too long."

"And I will crush the necklace," Mami Wata's sultry tones filled the air. "A sad necessity to destroy such a piece."

"Very well." Death threw the sword. It arced through the air, landing like a spear at Ra's feet.

He picked it up, admiring it. A slow smile spread across his swarthy face as he swivelled to Gaia. "Kneel."

The Earth goddess did as she was told. She stumbled forward, her cherubic face benign.

"No," I whispered from our hiding space. "They can't. Why isn't she fighting? She should be in her best sari. She should be raging like the night, her hair flying out behind her,

her back ramrod straight, her energy a young girl's once more."

Echo rumbled in my ear. "This is part of her plan. She won't give up. It is not in the earth's nature to give up. Even after cataclysmic events, Earth rejuvenates itself. Comet impacts, volcanic eruptions, tectonic shifts, ice ages, and nuclear disasters. Gaia's not going to let a poke with a tiny sword stop her."

Ra lifted the sword and drove it deep into Gaia's heart before giving it a final twist.

She collapsed over it, and he kicked her back before wiping the bloody blade on the leg of his boiler suit.

I screamed, and Flinar clamped his four-fingered hand over my mouth. But it was too late. The gods in the prehistoric stone circle jerked their heads in our direction.

Too late, also, for Gaia, whose fallen body hardened like a statue before becoming porous and then breaking into ashes. The Earth goddess's ashes latched onto the breeze, looping and surging past us until there was nothing left of what she had been. Her dear, cherubic face, her worldly eyes with their hidden depths, her hands that worked the soil and made chapatis.

All was gone as if she had never existed in the first place.

But her voice, her voice had one last thing to say. It came to me in my air—a gift or maybe an echo.

Take heart, druid. This time, she didn't sound distraught. She sounded free. *I made an oath never to betray my siblings. But tonight, they have colluded to kill me on sacred ground, and their terrible sin has freed me from my oath. You must find Pan. He will know how to resurrect me. Find the book of names and keep a flask full of chai ready for me.*

"Alisha," said Rayna. "Alisha, we have to go with Flinar. They are coming. The gods are coming. Alisha, move!"

Something snapped in me.

I moved all right, propelled forward by burning rage—

leopard at my side, sword on my back, catalogue of creatures bumping against my thigh in my crossbody satchel. As I ran the yards towards that ancient circle of stones, my power swelled within me, where men had died, women had birthed, and priests had prayed. Where gods walked and goddesses fell. Where tranquillity met power, and anger met purpose.

Sahil's eyes widened in recognition, but there wasn't time to focus on him.

Not when vengeance and raw grief filled my heart. Not when the dam had burst, and I was tired of my friends and me being the punching bag. Not when I was determined to punch back.

Ra whipped a current of electricity in my direction, but suddenly, Rayna was there, a vine snaking around my hips to lift me clear. I called the winds and released a tornado, a vortex of twisting currents that swept up Ra and flung him into a vertical stone.

Next to me, Echo bounded across the green and launched himself at Mami Wata's ankles.

I gave thanks that the water goddess wasn't in her strongest element.

The gods approached en masse, glee written on their faces. Like they'd enjoy crushing me. Like it would be the perfect way to end their evening.

But fear didn't consume me. Instead, awareness chimed in me, a sure certainty that this place and this moment had changed something in me at a granular level, allowing me to push deeper and harder than I had ever done before.

The satchel with my catalogue of creatures butted against my leg, but intuition told me not to stop and flick through the pages in the heat of battle. Not to reach for the threads on the page. But instead, to pull the images from my head. The winged creatures Dad had drawn. The ones Rajiv had drawn. The ones on Mum's bookshelves and in the libraries of my youth. The ones in my dreams and on Marina's arms. The ones I had yet to meet.

I plucked the fiercest winged creatures from my brain, clear in the knowledge that the magic of this place had unlocked my deepest self, and set them into the world with the sole purpose of attacking the gods that remained.

My breath came in short bursts, adrenalin kicking in. Vampire finches. Slobbering gargoyles. Red-tailed hawks. Turkey vultures. And beady-eyed charging ostriches. Their shrieks filled the air, and I watched them do my bidding, lightheaded at what I had achieved.

Except the gods were strong and as furious as me.

Cardea came for me, her diseased fingers outstretched.

The Ravenmaster was there too, wearing his Yeoman Warder's tunic, swinging his staff.

A sudden rush of doubt filled me as I raised my hands. Echo fought his own battle against Mami. The snake from her chest had come to life, its tongue flicking and greedy as Echo pranced about, entwined in a death dance with it. Rayna and Flinar, too, tried to land blows, though less successfully.

Death smiled, waiting her turn, confident that the evening spelt my demise.

I blocked her out, kicked Cardea in the chest and pulled out my sword, slashing at the crows that came my way. A rush of whispers met my ears. The sword channelled voices from the spirit world, telling me to be careful.

The red woman reached to touch me with her blackened hands of doom, and the Ravenmaster closed from the other side, cornering me.

But at that moment, a werepigeon flew into my peripheral vision and looped the Jericho necklace around my neck with his pink-clawed toes. He tilted his green-tinged head and spoke with his nasal werepigeon voice. "Over here, Alisha." His fluorescent yellow shield was up, and he splatted the gods with rapid-fire pigeon poo. "This won't hold them off for long."

The skin on my left inner arm burned, and as I followed him, I wondered if Cardea had touched me after all and in the midst of it all, I hadn't realised.

"Echo!" I called.

The three of us converged on Rayna and Flinar under the twinkling night sky at Stonehenge. When Flinar pulled us into a black hole, my breath burned in my chest.

"Thank you, Flinar," I gasped.

Rayna beamed. "Such a talented elf. That was quite something. I feel positively wonderful about surviving a run-in with the gods at my age."

I put my head between my knees to calm myself, wincing at the recollection of Gaia's collapsing body and the ash wind that followed.

We'd just lost our most powerful ally—a friend.

I swallowed the lump in my throat, then straightened to look at my werepigeon brother, perplexed. He'd helped me despite the risks to his own neck, despite the lack of applause, despite the ill feeling between us. "Why did you do it? Why did you help me?"

He cocked his feathery head, and one fiery eye found mine because eye contact was difficult with a pigeon. "Was it selfish of me to team up with the Ravenmaster? Maybe. Did I get something out of it? Hell, yeah. I love my magical shield. I'm not so keen on the spider form, but I got to see some things I never would have imagined, being friends with him—"

Echo hissed, dangerously close to taking Sahil in his jaws. "Why did you help her, werepigeon?"

A nasal grunt. "Because she's my sister. And when it came down to it, I couldn't watch her die."

I bit my lip, drawing blood. Gaia had been right to encourage me to go softly. Sahil had come through for me because I had never closed the door. "Well, at long bloody last. You realise you have a target on our back now?"

"Yeah, I'm trying not to think about that," Sahil cooed. "I feel strangely zen, but that might just be my empty bowels."

"I told you this place was special. Let's add sibling reconciliations to its list of marvels." Rayna beamed at me. "And did my eyes deceive me, or did you just animate multiple creatures of different species without using your father's paintings?"

I nodded. "It was like the stone circle somehow managed to unlock my potential. Something that was always there but I couldn't access. I wonder what Dad will say."

Rayna frowned. "I'm more worried about the gargoyles and vampire finches flying over Wiltshire. I better get Helio to see to those. Or else the government will mistake them for another case of bird flu."

I raised my hand to caress Echo. He'd need to see Marina for the slashes and swollen nodules on his face.

"Alisha," growled Echo. "Your scar."

Flinar leaned forward, concern writ large on his triangular face. "What is that?"

My pulse raced as I looked down at the familiar circle of nine braille-like dots on the soft flesh of my left inner arm. Except they weren't dots anymore. A line weaved in and out of them. A line that made my decades-old scar seem more than an accident.

A line that made it look like a map.

22

No ripples drifted across the surface of the koi pond in my parents' garden. Echo's depression about Gaia's death left him listless, even though I promised him we'd find a way to resurrect her. He was uninterested in terrorising the koi, much to Dad's relief. Even the harem of local pussies we'd allowed into the living room with him hadn't cheered him up.

I felt the loss keenly, too. All three women, a trinity of women who had looked out for me in real life and from the grave—Rajika, Mum and Gaia—had now gone. But we had a plan for Gaia, and the ones we loved were never truly gone. Not when those who remembered them still lived.

A sigh escaped me as I traced the scar on my arm. The weaving of the lines made me feel like I hurtled towards the future. Like I had no control.

"Your aura just darkened," said Marina. "You're worried about something."

My words flooded out. I had no filters with Marina. "Isn't the eternal girl supposed to save the world? I didn't beat the gods. Cardea still roams this city. And there are more gods wreaking havoc than ever before."

Marina hugged me. "Alisha, you stayed alive to fight another day. We can't always succeed the first time. Isn't that what being in midlife is about? Realising things aren't rosy but still dusting yourself off and trying again? I'm so proud of you."

"I needed to hear that."

"I know."

Orpheus approached with a plate of peeled tangerines. "Here you go, Alisha."

"No, thanks," I said.

"But I peeled them myself. You're looking awfully pale for a druid." *Stonehenge took its toll on you. If I had been there, I could have helped you overcome our enemies.*

I'm lucky to have you in my corner, Orpheus.

"I'll have one," said Marina, next to me.

"They're for Alisha." Orpheus swatted her hand away before stalking back to the kitchen.

I frowned. "I wonder why he's behaving so oddly."

"I have a pretty good idea," she said.

We sat on weather-worn wooden chairs underneath Mum's favourite tree after Alma cooked us Sunday lunch. A chestnut tree—its boughs bare of foliage—which had once, long ago, held a rope swing for me and Sahil.

Wasn't it funny how, even though Mum had been dead nearly a year, I still thought of this house as hers? Despite Alma making doilies for every surface? Despite how the place was so often full of magical beings these days, which never would have happened when she was alive? Maybe I would always think of this house as hers. Even decades ahead, when my coarse smattering of grey hair had widened its reach, and my bones were too brittle to kickbox or take down gods. Because a house was only a home when the people you loved lived in it. And the spirit of those people imprinted themselves on the bricks and mortar. An echo of love once shared that could never be erased.

I felt Ezra's presence in the cottage, too.

Just like he felt his parents' imprint there.

I didn't know why he had let me and Mirabel live there, but I loved him for it. My heart was a raw wound that only he could heal, but I had to keep it together. A little girl's happiness depended on it.

I snapped back to the present. The mild early winter's day allowed us a moment to come out for some fresh air, wrapped up in scarves and bulky jackets against the English weather. The sky was a cloudless, pale blue expanse lined with aeroplane trails across our heads, but part of me wanted a bleak, leaden grey one instead, in mourning for the Earth goddess.

"Mirabel, are you okay?" I said.

"Uh-huh." She didn't look up. She sat on a bench next to Sahil, both engrossed in their phones. Her parents had taken good care of her financial needs in the event of their untimely death, but the emotional trauma was going to take a while to overcome.

"Want me to get you some juice?"

Her brow knitted in a frown. "Nope."

By the speed of her fingers, I suspected I was disturbing a game. Hopefully, it was the sort of game where you dressed up Barbies or looked after electronic pets rather than a game where predatory strangers lurked. I'd have to check that.

Dad hid in bushes just behind her, waiting for the right time to scare the bejesus out of her like some park weirdo. At least he wasn't doing drugs anymore. Alma had finally confiscated the pipe.

Marina clicked her tongue. "How sad the children don't play outside willingly anymore. In our day, we were outside, riding bikes into the path of oncoming cars, drinking vodka in the park, stealing car badges and throwing rocks at each other. Mirabel is missing out."

I pressed the healing blisters on the palms of my hands.

"She'll get there. Let her grieve. She's in awe of your hair, by the way."

Marina smiled. "Most people are. Wait until she sees my unicorn tattoo." She placed a hand on my arm, and the warmth seeped through to my cold skin. "It's not just about Mirabel, though, is it? Or your anxiety about the gods. I can sense the emotions swirling in you. Don't bottle up your feelings about Ezra."

Ezra should have been here with us, but he was with the pack.

Dad jumped out at Mirabel with a shout. "Boo!"

She lifted a hand, a bored look on her face, and fried the potted plant next to him. That would teach him to mess with a fire fairy. Twelve years old, with the attitude of a delinquent. Seemed pretty cathartic to me.

I decided to let her get away with it.

We laughed at poor Dad's disappointed expression.

"It's okay, Joshi. You'll get her next time," called Marina.

"Do you think we should break it to him that, at twelve, she's kind of over peekaboo games?"

Marina pursed her lips. "Nah. He'll figure it out. Don't think you're getting away without answering my question, Alisha."

I swallowed the lump in my throat and shrugged. "Sure, the break up was tough. That's life, isn't it? It's like you said. At our age, we know it's not all beach days and roses. We know that we fall on our faces or have to swallow our fair share of tragedy and keep wading on until the waters are calm again. It will be okay in the end."

"Yeah, but don't be like me. I've nursed myself back to emotional health after dozens of heartbreaks. After Sadie left me, I never thought I could be whole again."

I laughed. "You said that about Trey and Salima, too."

She frowned. "What I was trying to say is that I can come round to yours for takeaway and wine, you can lean on me, and we can relive every stupid thing you did when you should have held onto that man, clamped between your thighs if that's what it took—"

I winced. "For an empath, that's not very sensitive."

She held up her hands. "Or these healing hands of mine can take away your emotional pain. I'm better at it now, I think. You'll still have feelings for him, but I'll dull them slightly to take away the edge of your loss."

Dismay filled me. I shook my head. "The pain's mine. It shows how much he means to me. I'll deal with it the old-fashioned way and sob into your shoulder. Ezra was right to be angry with me, Marina. I'm not going to wash that away. I'm going to do better. I'm going to win him back."

Marina grinned. "That's my girl."

Orpheus popped up out of nowhere. He'd probably used his vampire speed. He whipped a Thermos out of the pocket of his satin-lined jacket. "Would you like some tea? It's very cold for a druid out here."

"And an empath," said Marina, hopefully.

I drew my eyebrows together, puzzled. *Are you all right? You're behaving strangely.* "I'm okay, thanks. We're just having some girl time."

Of course, I'm all right. Why wouldn't I be all right? He grunted and rushed off, clutching the Thermos between his pale piano player's fingers.

"What's wrong with him?" I said. "And why's he dressed like he's going to a dinner party when we're just all bumming around at my parents' house?"

Marina giggled. "I think it's safe to say that's vampire flirting. I reckon he thinks he stands a chance now Ezra's out of the picture."

I blanched. "Holy shit."

"Nope. There's nothing holy about vampires. Sweet, really. If he had a heart, it would be beating just for you."

I swatted her. "Stop it."

Dad and Alma ambled over with Sahil between them.

So much for girl time. We'd have to decrypt Orpheus's weirdness another time.

"All right, sis?" said Sahil.

Things weren't wonderful between us, but they were on the up, and I was grateful for it. Without him, I would have been toast. But it was more than that. I finally realised he loved me.

I gave him a warm smile. "Fei Yen and Faeza told me you'd been over to Shanghai Moon to apologise to them and that you'd offered to pay for takeaway for them for a month, plus some front-row K-pop tickets next time their favourites are in town."

His lips turned downwards. "It's the least I can do. And that's not the end of this. I'm going to make it up to them. I wish I could turn back the clock."

"I know." I believed him, but his penance would never be enough. He'd have to live with what he'd done.

He paused. "You've been wearing the necklace and sword everywhere."

Marina bristled next to me. She always had my back. "Why you..."

"Hey. Don't shoot the pigeon." Sahil rushed to correct the assumption that he was plotting something. "I only meant that things have been hard. I mean, I had this sexual encounter in my spider form when this beautiful, leggy female spider actually tried to eat me. Things got pretty hairy for a second. I thought I was a goner, but it's nothing compared to all you've been carrying. No wonder you feel you have to carry those things with you all the time. I gave the Otherworld a good go, but it's dog-eat-dog out there. I'd rather be drinking a beer and playing the stock market. But you, sis... You're badass." He tilted his head in that werepigeon way of his. "My new niece is pretty cool, by the way. We were bonding over there."

Confusion coloured Dad's face. "You didn't exchange a word while I was hiding in the bush." He brightened. "But I'm so happy you kids are getting along again. I'm so proud of you both. And now you've brought Mirabel into our lives. Your mother would have loved to have met her."

"I'm going to teach Mirabel to make doilies," said Alma.

I grinned. "I'm sure she'll love that."

"It's all the rage with pre-teens," Sahil deadpanned. "Up there with embroidery and playing croquet."

"Oh, wonderful." Alma gave a delighted smile. "Come, Alisha. All of you. I have something to show you."

Marina and I followed the three of them to a dark corner of the garden, where overhanging branches and a swell of ivy meant that usually nothing would grow. A heart-shaped stone burrowed into the ground, and around it, a riot of blooms had grown, splashes of colour and life despite the cold snap and nearing winter. They reminded me of Gaia's garden on her estate.

"What is this?" I said in awe.

"Gaia's shrine, of course. I've been preparing it for a while. I found just the right space and just the right stone from the garden centre down the road. I erected it here. It took some puffing and heaving, and your dad was working on a portrait, so he wasn't at all interested in helping."

"A portrait of Gaia, because Alma did her flour seer thing and thought it might be good to have one. You know, for the eventuality that the goddess popped off," said Dad. "I didn't get her nose right, though. Or her eyes. She had very difficult eyes to get right. The chin, though. I got that. And maybe the forehead."

Alma continued. "Anyway, when I came back this morning, all these flowers were here. Isn't *she* clever?"

"She?" I said.

"Gaia, of course," said Alma.

Grief expanded like a nebula in my stomach. "She was right. The key to winning was friendship."

"The Earth goddess is good at friendship. She has the weight of the world on her shoulders, and she still made time to give us a sign." Alma looked around shiftily as if Gaia might appear from behind a nearby tree, dressed in a glittery sari for extra pizzazz. Then she bent down to gently touch an orange tulip petal. "My job is to remind you not to lose faith. And to keep an eye on her flat so no one defecates in it for fun while she's away. She's very attached to it and said that would make her very cross."

Dad sighed. "It's a very important job."

Alma rubbed her stomach. She clearly had indigestion after the big lunch. "We wanted to share some news with you."

I froze. I bloody well hoped they weren't pregnant. "What is it?"

Dad cleared his throat. "You kids are independent. You don't need me anymore. You don't even need me to draw for you anymore, Alisha. Your mind can conjure up anything it needs to. You've outgrown your old dad."

I hugged him. "Oh, Dad, I'll always need you."

"That's good of you to say, even though it's not true." He paused. "I would much rather you had a husband to look after you, and I wish Ezra were still hanging about in that devilishly handsome, laidback way of his. But even with him gone, I know you'll be okay. You can look after yourself."

I blinked back tears. I *could* look after myself, but life was better with Ezra's love in it.

"What about me?" said Sahil. "You're kind of focussing on Alisha."

"Well, son, you've got all that paid help you like to use. I don't mean just the hookers. I mean the cleaners, the secretaries, that odd little fellow whose job is to press the collars of your Saville row suits and flush the toilet when you forget."

Mirabel crept over to my side like a stealth operative, ears primed for secrets.

Alma gave Dad a prod. "Tell them, Joshi."

He took a deep breath. "We're going on holiday. Just a little mental reset. We thought we'd start with visiting the dragon in Bulgaria and see where life takes us. And when we come back, I thought I could start a little art class at Wildwoods; now it's under new leadership. And Alma is thinking about helping Rayna with the Wildwoods greenhouse."

I hugged him. "That sounds like a wonderful idea, Dad."

It was a relief having Wildwoods back to normal. It belonged to all of us, not one man. I wasn't sure who was going to end up Prime Sorcerer, but it looked like a tossup between Orpheus and Lavinia. Lavinia had already engaged the coven to shore up Wildwoods' defences against intruders, and Rayna was going to resume her position as headmistress.

Mirabel bounded up behind me, for a moment forgetting her grief. "Can we put up a rope swing on the chestnut tree again? Joshi said you used to have one when you were little."

"Why don't we see if we can find it in the shed?" said Sahil.

I mouthed thank you to him as he followed her.

A flock of birds passed overhead, and a feeling of peace settled over me as if somehow, somewhere, Gaia was willing me to succeed. I traced the raised dots of my scar and the lines weaving out of it, marvelling at my sense of purpose.

My friends and I might have taken some knocks, but there was a path forward. Somewhere in the stars, the book of names waited for me. The book my grandmother had hidden for me in the Celestial Library on the night she died. A journey so long in the making that a goddess had bridged the gap between generations.

Fate had to be on my side. I was convinced of it.

We had lost Gaia, but I had reconciled with my brother. We had the Jericho necklace. We had Transcender and the map gifted to me at Stonehenge. That had to mean something.

For all our sacrifices, pain, and striving, the dark could never win when good people stood against it.

ACKNOWLEDGMENTS

My first thanks, as ever, goes to my readers. I'm so grateful for each and every one of you, for every review and every question asking when the next book will be ready. Writing in series is new for me, and it's been such a joy to see these characters grow. I have so much more in store for them, and I can't wait to see what you think.

To my editor Jeni, thanks for your skill with my manuscript, your flexibility when life has thrown me curveballs and encouraging me to push my creativity in a sustainable way. Thanks, Toni, for your eagle-eyed proofreading magic. Thank you to my cover artist Maria, whose art for this project influenced the scene in which Faeza's fox coat changes colour. I am so lucky to be able to work with you.

To my beta readers Debbie and Sherry, who I trust to tell me the truth and who always do it with love and encouragement, and sometimes a whip, I appreciate you.

For our children, who have watched me build this story world brick by brick. I hope you see persistence. Dreams are fragile. We can't wait to see where your dreams take you. A special thanks to my Hana, who, along with Jan, is my first reader, even though she cringes and skips the sex scenes.

To my husband Jan, my favourite person and story consultant, who is convinced that Ezra is based on him (I'm not telling). Thank you for the room you give me to grow, shouldering more than your fair share as I inched towards the

finish line and holding my hand. We've had a wild few
months. I can't wait for a quiet moment in the sun together,
just you and me.

FREE SHORT STORY

If you enjoyed this book, please leave a review online to help other readers find this story.

The Druid Heir novels are written in Alisha's perspective, a 40-year-old teacher living in London. The short stories explore the world from an alternate character's viewpoint.

You can get the Druid Heir short stories for free by signing up for my fantasy newsletter at www.nillunasser.com.

MIDLIFE ECLIPSE: DRUID HEIR BOOK 6

So the Father of the Gods is alive, and Gaia kept it a secret from me. Not only that, but the Earth goddess is now ashes in the wind, and it's up to me to figure out how to resurrect her. As the solar eclipse nears, the trees at Wildwoods curl unnaturally, but the senate is too busy clashing over its next leader to notice.

Like all women in midlife, I juggle balls like a circus act. There's my broken heart to nurse, a lusty vampire to fend off and a grieving fire fairy to parent. Not in my wildest dreams did I think I'd be a mother. The world might need the eternal girl, but Mirabel needs plain old me. Her grief threatens to ignite an inferno, and part-time mothering just isn't going to cut it. Especially when the dream god and his djinn target her.

I yearn to win back Ezra and give Mirabel the home she deserves, but I have to live up to my gran's legacy and stop the gods. My gran, who put magic above everything. With my personal life and magical destiny colliding more than ever before, will I be forced to walk away from the daughter I've always wanted?

If you're a fan of Paranormal Women's Fiction and magic-wielding heroines over forty, continue this journey with Druid Heir Book 6.

ALSO BY N. Z. NASSER

DRUID HEIR

Midlife Dawn, Book 1

Midlife Tremors, Book 2

Midlife News, Book 3

Midlife Drift, Book 4

Midlife Portals, Book 5

Midlife Eclipse, Book 6

Midlife Battle, Book 7

Druid Heir Collections

MAJESTIC MIDLIFE WITCH

To Save a Sister, Book 1

To Curse a Rival, Book 2

To Trick a Raja, Book 3

To Hunt a Foe, Book 4

NEWSLETTER EXCLUSIVES

The Magical Grandmother, Druid Heir Short Story 0.5

A First Date in Paris, Druid Heir Short Story 1.5

Midlife Battle, Druid Heir 7 Bonus Epilogue

To Become a Witch, Majestic Midlife Short Story 0.5

Biryani Junction, a Majestic Midlife Witch Cookbook

ABOUT THE AUTHOR

N. Z. Nasser is a writer of paranormal women's fiction. Her stories are about women who change the world, filled with magic and rooted in friendship.

A lover of barefoot walks along the beach, she is glad to have left behind her career in the civil service and to never wear heels again. Whether she is writing in her garden office or wrangling laundry, she is happiest with a cup of tea at her side.

She lives in London with her husband, three children, two cats and a fox-mad dog.

For new release alerts, you can follow her at Bookbub or Goodreads. For a more personal touch, join her Facebook reader group Nasser's Book Nymphs, say hi on social media, or visit her online store at www.nillunasser.com.

facebook.com/nillunasser

instagram.com/nillunasser